Praise for Dan's Jack Turner Suspense Novels

When Night Comes (Book 1)

"Though Walsh steps into a different genre, fans will not be disappointed. He continues to infuse historical facts into his books, bringing history to life in this character-driven tale. The pace quickens as events unfold, making it challenging for the reader to predict the twists and turns."

—*RT Book Reviews*, 4.5 Stars

"Dan Walsh surprises with his new novel, *When Night Comes*. This engrossing mystery/thriller is a break from his normal superb Christian fiction and proves Walsh is more than one-dimensional."

—*New York Journal of Books*

Remembering Dresden (Book 2)

"Few authors can straddle multiple genres successfully but Dan Walsh is proving he is in that elite group as he releases his second suspense novel…*Remembering Dresden* gripped me from start to finish. Once again, Walsh weaves together historical and contemporary events, resulting in a compelling tale…He fills the book with believable personalities well-suited to the story, as well as a plethora of heart-wrenching and heart-pounding moments, making it impossible to set aside."

—*Mocha with Linda Blog*

"Walsh has another suspense-filled hit, proving that his flair for an engaging tome spans genres. History buffs will love his latest, which could be read as a standalone, though it is second in the series. The past and present scenes seamlessly blend together to create a fast-paced, intriguing story which will leave readers anticipating the third book."

—*RT Book Reviews Magazine*, 4.5 Stars/Top Pick!

For these and more of Dan Walsh's books, go to danwalshbooks.com/books

Unintended Consequences

Unintended Consequences

A Jack Turner Suspense Novel
Book 3

By Dan Walsh

Unintended Consequences
Copyright © 2017 Dan Walsh
ISBN: 978-0-9979837-1-5

All rights reserved
Published by Bainbridge Press

Cover Design by DanWalshBooks
Cover Photos –
    Licensed through Adobe Stock
        #122554769
        #12445744
Author photo by Cindi Walsh

1

JACK GOT IN the car and handed Rachel an ice cream cone. "I wonder when I'll get used to it."

"Get used to what? And what's this? I didn't ask for an ice cream cone."

He closed the door. They were driving through the charming little seaside town of Chatham on Cape Cod, Massachusetts. "I know you didn't ask for one, but you're getting one anyway. I couldn't believe it. The owner of the little shop still remembers me." Jack had come here so many times over the years visiting his grandparents. Unless it was the dead of winter, he'd always stop in to get an ice cream cone. "The man looked out the window then asked why I wasn't getting one for my girlfriend. I told him, that's not my girlfriend. That's my wife. When he heard that, he insisted on giving you one for free. If you don't want it, I'll eat it when I'm done with mine. You just need to—"

"Oh, I want it." She took a big lick around the edges. "I just didn't want to say it."

He smiled. "You were gonna eat half of mine. That was the plan."

She smiled, took another lick. "Is this coconut?"

He nodded. "As soon as I saw it in the case, I knew I was bringing one out to you. When do we ever see coconut ice cream?" He turned the car on, took a big lick of his own double-scoop raspberry.

"What can't you get used to?"

"What? Oh, calling you my wife. I love whenever I get to say it. Afterwards I think, I can't believe it. Rachel's my wife." They were married two months ago, but Jack hadn't been able to break away from his duties at the university for a honeymoon trip until this past week.

As he turned his blue, BMW sedan left onto Main Street, she leaned over and kissed him. "How much further till we reach your grandmother's? I don't want to still be eating this when she first sees me."

"Turns out, this ice cream shop is exactly one ice cream cone away from my grandmother's place. Over the years, I've lost count of the times I had to finish one to avoid getting a lecture about spoiling my dinner. But I can't drive by that place without stopping whenever I come here."

"When was the last time you visited her?"

"Almost two years ago. But I can't wait that long anymore."

"Didn't you say she was ninety-four?"

"Almost."

"And she lives alone?"

He nodded, took another lick of his cone. "That's how she wants it. My folks and I have tried over the years to get her to move someplace else. They even bought their last house because it had a mother-in-law apartment, but she says she doesn't want to leave. All her memories with my grandfather are there."

"I can see that," Rachel said. "If you're married to someone that long."

"Sixty-one years," Jack said. "Grandpa has been gone now since 2001."

"That's a long time to live alone."

"It is." He turned right at Cross Street, drove past the town hall.

Rachel's eyes were looking all around. "I get why she wouldn't want to leave here, besides all the memories. I already love this place. What a beautiful little town. Really, this whole drive through Cape Cod has been amazing." They drove past a string of homes. "Look at these. They're so adorable. Every one of them. I get now why they call this style of house *Cape Cod*."

"You're going to love her place. It's not far. It's just like these but on water."

"She lives in a beach house?"

"Not quite. It's a big pond. That's what they call it anyway, but it really connects to the ocean if you trace it out far enough. My grandfather bought the house a long time ago, after he retired from the military. It was pretty affordable then. Now it's worth over a million, and it's not even that big a house."

"What's she like?"

"She's…pretty frail, but she's always been petite. Her mind, though, is as sharp as ever. You're gonna love her. And she'll love you right off the bat. I've told her all about you." His grandmother wasn't physically able to make it to the wedding, which was why Jack made this little detour during their honeymoon drive through New England, so the two of them could meet.

"What's her name?"

"Renée."

"Sounds French."

"It is, and she really is from France. Still has a slight accent, even after living here so long. They met in England during World War II a short time after she left France, right after the Nazis took over."

"You grandfather was a fighter pilot, right?"

"He was, for several years. But he did a whole lot more things in his military career. I can't wait for you to hear their story. That's the other reason I wanted to come here. So she could tell you my grandfather's story. I only heard bits and pieces of it while he was alive. Two years after he died, I came up to visit her for a week, and she told me the whole thing. How they met, how they fell in love. How he even came to be in England in the first place. When he took that boat ride across the Atlantic, America wasn't even in the war yet. It was more than a year before Pearl Harbor. What he did was actually illegal. If he got caught, he could've been sent to prison. Maybe even lose his US citizenship."

"You're kidding."

"I'm not. You're not gonna believe their story. It's the wildest thing I've ever heard."

"Weren't you were named after him?"

Jack nodded. "I am. Flying Officer Jack Turner. That's who he was when she first met him. He was an American pilot flying for the RAF. He even fought in the Battle of Britain, and he's the reason I majored in military history and focused mainly on World War II. It all started after my grandmother told me his story. Well, their story."

"How come you've never told me their story before?"

He made a quick left turn, then a quick right. "Because…why hear a great story retold from a third-party when you can hear it told in person by a living eyewitness?"

"Won't talking about these things stir up a bunch of painful memories for her?"

"It might. No…it probably will. But not all the memories are painful. I think she'd say most of them aren't. The way she tells it, it's not really a war story at all. Although there's a ton of action and suspense in it. But hearing her tell it, it sounds more like a love story."

"I like love stories."

"I know you do."

"You sure she won't mind?"

"I know she won't. I called her yesterday before we left our hotel in Newport and asked her."

"What did she say?"

"At first, there was a long pause. I was about to say not to worry about it. But then she said—with that sweet French accent—that she'd be willing to tell their story one last time. Just for you."

2

Jack turned right onto a private road that led to his grandmother's property, as well as a few other homes that bordered the pond. They drove past an open area filled with flowers, bordered by bright yellow bushes.

"I keep seeing these beautiful yellow flowers and bushes," Rachel said. "What are they?"

"The flowers are daffodils, and the flowering bushes are forsythia. You're also seeing some dandelions, which God throws in for free. My grandmother said everything started blooming last week. She's got plenty of all three on her property. It's just up ahead on the left. You can see the water straight down the road."

"I could get used to this," Rachel said. "At least, in the spring."

"Summer and Fall are both really nice here, too. Really, just the winters are tough. And they can be brutal. Sometimes they go pretty long, too, swallowing up the first part of the spring. But I knew we'd be coming at a great time." He slowed the car down and turned left into a driveway. "Here we are."

"Oh my gosh, Jack. It's adorable. I love those little dormers sticking out of the second story."

Jack looked it over, trying to imagine seeing the house for the first time. "It looks a little small at first, but wait till you see inside. Those dormers are the front windows for the bedrooms. There are some really cool angled ceilings up there. And you're gonna love the furniture. Pretty much all antiques, except for the family room. She made everything comfortable in there." Jack drove past the house and stopped in front of a freestanding garage.

"I thought you said the property was on the water."

"It is. When you get out, walk past the big tree. You'll see it." He pointed to the covered porch that ran along the back of the house. "You can see the water plainly sitting there, by those tables and chairs."

She came behind the car, walked past him onto the grass and continued past the oak. A big smile came over her face. She turned around and looked at the back porch. "I'd love to drink my morning coffee sitting right there."

"You can, but you'll need to wear a sweater. Still pretty nippy here in the morning."

One of the French patio doors opened. Jack instantly recognized the smiling face of his grandmother as she stepped outside. She looked almost the same, though, if possible, even more frail than before. This would be the last time he'd wait this long to see her. "Hey Grandma." He waved and walked toward her.

"Jack," she said, reaching out her arms. "You're here."

He got to her before she made it to the steps. Tears filled her eyes. He gave her as tight of a hug as he dared.

"I'm so glad you came."

"Me, too." She released the hug, but he clung to her a moment more. When he let go, she took one step to the side to welcome Rachel.

"Look at you," she said to Rachel. "Even prettier than the pictures." She reached out to hug her and Rachel quickly responded.

"Thanks," she said, "and thanks so much for having us. I'm so glad to finally meet you."

Jack's grandmother continued to hold one of Rachel's hands as they walked. "No, thank you for taking time out of your honeymoon to see me. I can't believe you did that."

"There was just no way we were going to get this close and not stop by," Jack said. "When I mentioned it to Rachel, she didn't even hesitate a moment before saying yes."

"Well, I'm so glad it worked out. I was sad I couldn't make your wedding. I'm just not able to travel long distances anymore. The last time I flew, my ribs cracked with just a little bit of turbulence."

"Ouch," Rachel said. "I've had cracked ribs before. It's very painful."

"It is. And at my age it takes forever to heal." She turned back toward the patio door. "Why don't you two come in and we'll show Rachel around. Then you can get your things from the car and get situated in your room. While you do that, I'll make us a fresh pot of coffee. We can chat out here on the porch and get caught up."

"I would love that," Rachel said.

"Great. Then that's what we'll do."

RACHEL THOROUGHLY ENJOYED the tour of the downstairs. Jack was right: she loved every stick of furniture in his grandmother's home, and every choice she had made decorating it. Even her choices in wallpaper, which Rachel didn't use on her walls anymore, but it seemed totally appropriate here. And she loved listening to her talk: a sweet, almost lyrical voice with a trace of French still present, especially with certain words and phrases.

After showing them the first floor, she hesitated at the stairs. Jack interjected. "Grandma, I noticed you're using the guest room down here as your bedroom. Is that because you're letting us use the master bedroom upstairs?"

"No, I moved myself down here permanently. The stairs are just too hard for me to navigate anymore. They make me dizzy."

"That's what I thought. How about I show Rachel the upstairs, and you go make the coffee?"

"That might be a good idea. Don't forget to show her the balcony."

"I won't."

Jack took Rachel by the hand and led her up the stairs. There were three more bedrooms. The master bedroom to the right of the stairs had its own bath. Another fairly big bedroom was down the hall at the other end of the house. In between was a smaller bedroom and a family bathroom. Rachel loved the hardwood floors, and the nice collection of Oriental rugs centered in each room.

"Oh, almost forgot," Jack said. He brought her back to the master bedroom. "The balcony."

She could already see it through two French doors, beyond the four-post queen-size bed against the left wall. Jack led her past the bed and opened one of the doors. Crisp, cool air blew in. They walked out together. "Okay, I changed my mind. This is where I want to have my morning coffee."

"Isn't this perfect?"

The balcony didn't stick out from the house but was set inside with walls on each side. Thick limbs from nearby oak trees arched over the left side but did nothing to hinder the view of the water. Two well-worn wicker chairs were angled in each corner, each with a small circular table. Rachel sat in one and put her feet up on the balcony. "Can we just move in? Can we just live here from now on?"

Jack laughed. "I know, right?" He leaned over and kissed her. "But we better head back down."

She sighed. "I know. But I claim this corner." She stood, put her arms around him and kissed him. Then kissed him a little longer.

"This is not a good idea," Jack said, smiling. "I mean, it's a great idea, but maybe a few hours from now." He pulled away gently but continued to hold her hand. "Let's head back downstairs. I'll get our stuff from the car and bring it back up here. Would you feel comfortable visiting with my grandmother?"

"Sure."

"And maybe...fix our coffee?"

"I can do that." They walked past the bed, out into the hall and started down the stairs. Halfway down, Rachel whispered, "What should I call her?"

"I'm not sure. I think I know, but why don't you ask her what she'd like you to call her?"

"Okay."

When they got downstairs, Jack's grandmother was just pouring the coffee and setting the mugs on a tray. "Let me get that for you," Rachel said, "...uh, Mrs. Turner? Or...I'm not sure what I should call you."

The old woman smiled. "Well, my name is Renée. That's what my friends call me. But since we're family now, you can call me what Jack does, if that doesn't feel too strange?"

"I think I would like that."

"Then just call me Grandma."

Rachel pointed to the tray with the coffee mugs. "Then, may I get that for you, Grandma?"

"Thank you, that would be lovely."

Just then, Jack's phone rang. It startled them a little. He hadn't gotten any calls since they'd started their honeymoon several days ago. Before they'd left, he had given strict instructions to his personal secretary and the rest of the staff he interacted with at the University. Under no circumstances were they to contact him on his honeymoon, unless it was an absolute emergency.

He pulled his phone out of his pocket and looked at the screen. A stern look instantly appeared on his face.

"Who is it, Jack?" Rachel asked.

"My secretary." He sighed, conflicted about what to do.

"You better get it," she said. "It's the first time they've called. It must be important, right?"

He sighed again. "It better be." He touched the screen and held the phone to his ear. "Hey Aileen, this is Jack...."

3

"Hi, Dr. Turner. I'm so sorry interrupting your honeymoon like this. I wouldn't do it unless I was absolutely forced to. It really is an emergency. Not the life or death kind, but it's pretty serious. Dr. Mendelson called a few minutes ago and insisted I contact you about it."

Dr. Mendelson was, essentially, Jack's boss at Culpepper University. If he had insisted Aileen call, she really didn't have a choice. The other slightly irritating thing was hearing Aileen refer to him as "Dr. Turner." Jack had received his doctorate a few months ago but didn't enjoy everyone on staff addressing him so formally. But Dr. Mendelson had insisted on it, insisting it was a show of respect.

Jack put his hand over the phone. "I'm going to take this outside." As he opened the patio door, he said, "Okay, Aileen. What's going on?" He closed the door and leaned up against the wood railing, facing the water.

"Dr. Watson has been in a car accident."

"Oh no," Jack said. "Is he all right? How serious was it?"

"I don't have all the details," Aileen said. "Just what his personal assistant told me when she called about thirty minutes ago. It didn't happen here. It happened back in Cincinnati, on his way to the airport. The taxi he was riding in got T-boned at an intersection. The driver's in critical condition. Dr. Watson's condition is listed as serious. He has some broken bones and a concussion, but his assistant said he's expected to make a full recovery."

"I understand," Jack said. He was responsible for a huge annual fundraising gala this weekend back in Culpepper. Hundreds of alumni, many of them big donors to the school, planned to attend. The only way Jack could get Dr. Mendelson to agree to let him schedule his honeymoon this week was to bring in a guest speaker that Dr. Mendelson would see as talented as Jack, if not more. When Jack told Mendelson that Dr. Watson had agreed to come, a big smile came over his face. "Okay, now you can go."

Jack was sure, with this news, that smile was no longer present on Dr. Mendelson's face.

"As you know, Dr. Turner," Aileen said, "Dr. Watson was scheduled to speak at both the luncheon tomorrow at twelve thirty, and then again at the big gala tomorrow—"

"I know, Aileen. I'm the one who set up the schedule, remember?"

"I'm so sorry, Dr. Turner. I know how much you and Mrs. Turner were looking forward to this New England trip. I asked Dr. Mendelson what instructions he wanted me to give you. You know, to gauge his expectations. It seems he's really just concerned about the two big events. I don't think you'd have to cancel your whole trip. I looked up some flight information. You're in Chatham now, right?"

"Yep."

"I did some checking. It's about a forty-five minute drive to

Hyannis. There's a nice municipal airport there. If you leave within the hour, you can make a flight to Boston's Logan Airport and easily catch one of several flights from Logan back to Atlanta this evening. Dr. Mendelson said to spare no expense, so you'd be flying first class all the way. Both of you. He agreed to pay for Mrs. Turner's flights here and back. I can get you guys on the same setup flying back to Cape Cod on Sunday morning. You could be back on track enjoying the rest of your honeymoon by Sunday afternoon."

Jack sighed. Until this moment, their honeymoon had been perfect. Not a single thing had gone wrong. He and Rachel had joked about it on the drive here. Trips never go this smoothly. He was expecting something more like a flat tire, a couple of rainy days, maybe one of them catching a cold.

Not something like this.

"Dr. Turner? What do you think? Should I book the flights?"

Jack really had no choice. There was no one at the school he could delegate this assignment to, no other guest speaker he could grab on such short notice. He was just about to say yes, when he got an idea. It wasn't a perfect solution, but at least it was a way to make the next forty-eight hours a little more pleasant for his new bride. "Go ahead and book the flights, Aileen. But just for me."

"You'll be traveling alone? It's really okay if you bring Rachel. Dr. Mendelson said it was the least he could do, since he was interrupting your—"

"No, I'll be traveling alone. We just got here. She's really enjoying this place. And most of the reason for including the stop here in Chatham was for her to get some time with my grandmother. There's no reason that part of the trip has to end. So go ahead and book the flights, but just for me. Could you also set me up with an Uber driver for the drive from here to Hyannis? That way I can leave our car here for Rachel, in case she needs it."

"You sure you don't want a taxi? I could probably even get a limo, since we're not paying for Mrs. Turner's tickets."

"An Uber driver's fine. Thanks. And thanks for setting this all up."

"I really am so sorry."

"I know. It's not your fault." He said goodbye and hung up.

When he turned around, Rachel was still inside, standing behind the French door sipping her coffee mug. A concerned expression on her face. He motioned for her to come outside. He knew this news would disappoint her, but she wouldn't freak out or say anything to make him feel guilty. She'd worked at the university, too. She knew how things went.

"Is everything alright?" she asked.

"Not really."

Jack's grandmother came out behind Rachel then stepped around her toward the outdoor table. "Then why don't you two have a seat over here by me and, Jack, you can tell us all about it. No sense letting this perfectly good cup of coffee go to waste."

"I don't know if I have time, Grandma. I need to get my things together. An Uber driver will be on his way here shortly to get me."

"An Uber driver?" Rachel repeated. "That doesn't sound good."

"No, it doesn't."

"You said, *get you*. Are you going somewhere, and I'm staying here?"

"That's what I was thinking. Let me explain what happened."

"That's a good idea," Grandma said. "But why don't you sit here and explain it to us over coffee? You don't have to get your things all together. You didn't unpack yet, did you?"

"No, we didn't."

"Then you can take a minute, catch your breath and explain what's going on."

Jack laughed. She may be old and frail and weigh less than ninety pounds, but she was most definitely in charge. He and Rachel joined her at the table. Over the next five minutes, Jack explained the situation, including his plan to leave Rachel here until he got back.

RACHEL'S HEART SANK as the realization of Jack's news sunk in. Her immediate reaction was to insist that she be allowed to join him on this detour back to the university. But Jack began to explain how crazy-busy he would be over the next two days and how little real quality time they would have together.

"Contrary to that," Jack continued, "you could have the most wonderful, refreshing time in this beautiful setting, with this magnificent view and all these lovely yellow flowers and blooming bushes all around...*and* spend some undistracted, quality time getting to know one of the most remarkable women I've ever met, who also just happens to be my grandmother."

Rachel reached for his hand and squeezed it gently. "As usual, you make a most convincing argument Dr. Turner."

"That's right, Jack. I forgot you received your PhD a few months ago," his grandmother said. "I forgot to congratulate you…Dr. Turner."

Jack smiled. "Thanks, Grandma. But there's no way in the world you're going to start calling me that."

"But I do like the sound of it," she said. "You're the first Turner to be given that honor. I always knew you were smart. Just like your grandfather. He was a brilliant man, too. In his own way."

Rachel noticed her looking away, as if she was seeing him now.

"That's one of the reasons why I love talking to you so much," Grandma said. "You sound just like he did when he was your age. And you resemble him so much."

"I may look a little like him, and sound like him, but that's where the comparisons end I'm afraid. Grandpa was such a man of action. Like Rachel's dad. Did I tell you he was an Air Force general, too? Those men made history. All I do is teach it."

"I beg to differ, sir," Rachel said. "All you do is teach it? You don't think you're a man of action, as you put it?" She looked at Grandma. "Did he tell you that last year he rescued me from a kidnapper and stopped a murderer who was just about to kill a police sergeant back home? He made the local TV news and the whole city honored him with a big award. The mayor gave it to Jack himself."

"No, he didn't tell me any of this." She looked at Jack. "But I can't say I'm surprised to hear it. I guess the legacy of the first Jack Turner lives on in you, Jack. A lot more than you know."

"I don't know about that," Jack said, "but that's another

great reason for you to stay here, Rachel, until I get back. Grandma, are you still willing to tell Rachel Grandpa's story even if I'm not here? I don't mean the short version, either. I mean the long one. As I recall, it took almost two days to hear all the different parts. I want her to hear it all. Like you said, she's family now."

Grandma thought a moment, smiled and said. "Of course." She reached for Rachel's hand. "She may not look very much like me, or sound very much like me, but I can tell she loves you every bit as much as I loved your grandfather."

Jack stood. "Thanks, Grandma. I better get my stuff down from upstairs. I don't know when that driver will be here, but it could be soon." He leaned down and kissed Rachel.

"See, even the way you kiss her, reminds me of your grandfather." Grandma smiled at Rachel. "But you know, Jack's grandfather wasn't the first man in my life, or even the first man I thought I was going to marry."

"This is such a great story," Jack said.

"Then who was?" Rachel asked.

"It was Elliot, his twin brother. And Elliot wasn't even an American."

4

THE FOLLOWING MORNING, Rachel awoke and rolled over in bed, her eyes still half-closed. She reached for Jack and was startled by the empty space beside her. Then she remembered. He'd left yesterday afternoon. They'd only been sleeping together two months, and she was already completely used to him being there when she awoke.

She already missed him.

The clock on the dresser informed her it was 7:49AM. Back home in Culpepper, Jack was probably already up, either having his quiet time or doing his Muay Thai routines. She had decided to take Grandma's advice last night. *"Don't you go setting your alarm tomorrow. You're on vacation."* She then said no matter what time Rachel got up, she'd find some fresh coffee waiting for her downstairs in a carafe and homemade blueberry muffins in the breadbox.

Rachel sat up and immediately glanced out the window, past the trees and lawn at the water. In the distance, a bright yellow sailboat drifted by. "Jack would have loved this." As she stood, she reached for her bathrobe hanging on a post by the foot of the bed. She was glad to feel a slight nip in the air.

She walked to the French doors with the thought of enjoying the view more fully on the balcony. But as soon as she opened the door, the chilly air rushing in changed her mind. *Maybe I won't be having my morning coffee out here after all.*

She walked back toward the master bath, deciding to wash her face and take stock of things. Should she take a shower now or wait until after breakfast? Coffee had already begun to whisper her name. After fiddling with her hair in front of the mirror, and considering how gracious Grandma was, Rachel was convinced she could afford to go downstairs, as is.

She became aware of a fresh, almost fragrant scent in the room and wondered where it came from. There weren't any air fresheners plugged into the outlets. It seemed stronger by the shower. She pulled back the curtain and was greeted by a brass vase full of bright yellow daffodils sitting atop a stool. A note taped to the front said:

> *So very sorry to leave you on our honeymoon, my love. Even for two days. Enjoy these and your time with Grandma. Will be thinking of you constantly.*
> *Love, Jack.*

How had he managed to sneak these up here? She carefully lifted the vase of flowers and walked them to the dresser so she could see them better. She smelled them up close. They were pleasant but it wasn't a strong, flowery smell.

She put on her slippers and headed downstairs. As promised, Grandma was already up and sitting with a coffee mug at a dinette table in front of the window.

"Good morning. I just put a fresh pot on when I heard your footsteps. Should be ready any minute."

"You didn't have to do that. It couldn't have been that old."

"I've been up for almost two hours. I don't sleep during the night as much anymore. Of course, I take naps most afternoons like a toddler. This is my third cup of coffee. I know, I shouldn't drink so much caffeine. But I love the taste of it so much, and it warms me up in the morning. And apparently, it's not the thing that's going to kill me."

Rachel laughed. "You drink as much coffee as you want. You won't get any looks from me. My father used to say, 'Anyone makes it past eighty, gets to do whatever they want.'" The coffee pot stopped dripping, so Rachel filled her mug.

"Sounds like I would like your dad."

"You definitely would. And he would love to meet you. He's going to be so jealous when he hears I got to be with you, *and* I got to hear about your experiences in World War II. He served in the Vietnam era but, like Jack, he loves the World War II time period the best." She walked her mug to the dinette table and sat across from Grandma. It dawned on her that Grandma had sat with her back facing the French doors, so Rachel could get the seat with a view of the water.

"Jack told me you have a really good relationship with your dad, and that you even took some military history classes just so you could have more in common with him. That's remarkable to me. Seems like young people today are more likely to pull away from their parents than work that hard to connect with them."

Rachel took a sip. It was so good. "I don't know. Guess I never really thought about it that deeply. Growing up, I always loved my dad, but he was gone a lot. When he retired, I noticed how much he loved to read about military history. I found out I could use military history classes as electives for my political science degree. It seemed like a way to give us something to talk about. And it worked. It became so easy for us to talk together that now we can talk about all kinds of things." She took another sip. "The best part about taking those courses was, I got to meet Jack."

"I'm so glad you did. I've never seen him so happy."

Rachel liked hearing that, coming from someone who would know.

"Are you hungry? There are those blueberry muffins, or I can make you some scrambled eggs and bacon."

"I'll get a muffin in a little while. My stomach hasn't woken up yet."

"I'm the same way," Grandma said. "You eat whenever you're ready."

Neither spoke for a few moments. Then Grandma said, "When would you like me to begin telling you the story about how I met Jack's grandfather?"

"Whenever you're ready," Rachel said. "I'm ready whenever you want to start. You could start now, if you'd like. But I want to say something first. Yesterday, I asked Jack if he was sure you really wanted to do this. He said you did. But I want to give you an opportunity to back out if you want. I'm sure there are all kinds of other things we could talk about."

"You don't want to hear how we met?"

"No, I really *would* like to hear it. It's just…I know talking about traumatic times can be emotionally difficult. And war is certainly a traumatic thing. Even though my dad and I can talk about military history and other military things, he never really gets into the specifics of what he went through, especially in

Vietnam. My mom said he doesn't really talk about those things very much with her, either. But whenever he gets around his Vietnam vet friends, they talk openly and freely about everything. She said that's because they can relate to everything he went through. It isn't the same talking with someone who'd never experienced the horrors of battle firsthand."

Grandma didn't reply at once. She seemed to be thinking. "I understand what you're saying. There certainly is some truth to that. But I think that's something men struggle with more than we do. A man can be friends with someone for several years, even call him his best friend, but still never share the things he hides in his heart. His hurts, wounds and fears…maybe for years. If a woman meets another woman on a park bench, and she senses that woman can understand her, she might start pouring her heart out in the next ten minutes. We're just different that way."

"Did Jack's grandfather open up to you before he died?"

Grandma smiled. "He didn't have to wait so long. Child, we went through most of the suffering together. We experienced equally horrible things during the war when we were apart. Our love was fused through the moments we experienced together and the times we poured our hearts out about what happened when we were apart. He was my comfort, and I was his."

"So," Rachel said, "he talked to you the way my father talks to his Vietnam war friends?" Grandma nodded. "And it doesn't bother you to share these things with me, even though I've never…I've never gone through anything like that?"

Grandma shook her head no. "It won't cause me any pain. I haven't felt pain over these things for many years. If anything, it might be just the opposite. I love to remember anything that takes me back to those times when Jack and I first met. It was the most exciting time of my life. It set the stage for everything else that followed."

Rachel smiled. Grandma had convinced her. She really wanted to hear the story, and now she could listen guilt-free. "Okay, I'm ready. Well, wait. I don't want to interrupt you once you begin. I'm starting to get a little hungry. Maybe I should grab that blueberry muffin."

Grandma stood with her mug. "You do that, and join me over on the sofa. We might as well be comfortable while we talk. This is going to take a little while."

Rachel joined Jack's grandmother in the living room. "Can I sit over here?" She pointed to a comfy looking upholstered chair. "So, I can see your face better while you talk?"

"Sure." Grandma took a sip from her mug. "Okay, where should I begin?" It wasn't really a question. "I don't think I've told this story to anyone since that time years ago when I told it to Jack. And I guess the story really doesn't begin with me, but with Jack. I mean, my Jack, not yours. I'm going to tell you his part of the story too, the way he told it to me."

5

Somewhere in the North Atlantic
May 19th, 1940

JACK KNEW IMMEDIATELY SOMETHING was wrong.

The Canadian sailors on their merchant ship suddenly stopped laughing and joking and began running in different directions, panicked looks on every face. An alarm had just sounded all over the ship. It looked to Jack like they were going to assigned stations. But this was a freighter, not a warship. So, these were not battle stations.

These sailors had no way of defending themselves.

"Look," Joe Bassett said. He and Jack had been friends since high school. "They all got binoculars, and they're all looking in the same direction. Think it's U-boats?"

God, he hoped not. "I don't know what else would spook them like this." Jack, Joe and the four other Americans onboard ran to the railing nearest the side where everyone was looking. It was a windy, cloudy, overcast afternoon. Not a great deal of contrast between the color of the sky and ocean. It would be hard to spot a lone periscope sticking out of the water in conditions like these.

"Anyone see anything?" Joe said. "With all these whitecaps

how can you tell if you're seeing a periscope?"

"You can't," said Ozzie Holmes, one of the young pilots in their group. Ozzie was from California. "The first thing any of us'll see is a long, straight-line about ten feet underwater, heading right for us."

"A torpedo?" Joe said.

Ozzie nodded. "Read an interview with a survivor in the papers. No one ever saw the sub that sunk 'em. Speaking of surviving, if we do get hit we got no chance if we don't put on a life vest. See the Canadians? They're wearing 'em." He headed for the cabin below.

Joe was just about to follow, looked at Jack. "Want me to grab yours when I'm down there?"

"Yeah, thanks." Jack wasn't sure how much good it would do. If they were hit by a torpedo, he gave them maybe a 50-50 chance of surviving the first few minutes. If they lived past the initial explosion, they'd be thrown in the sea. In that freezing water, with no other ships for miles around, they'd all die of hypothermia in less than an hour.

The guys returned a few minutes later wearing yellow life vests. Jack put his on. For the next thirty minutes, everyone's eyes stayed focused on the water, scanning every section between the ship and the horizon.

Then, with little to no fanfare, the tension broke. All the sailors began putting down their binoculars and stepped away from the railings. Jack observed a blonde-haired guy named Harold coming down a set of stairs in his direction. "Everything okay now?"

"Captain gave the all clear. Looks like another false alarm." A look of relief on his face.

"Don't you guys feel like sitting ducks out here?" Jack said.

"We guys? In case you haven't noticed, you guys are stuck on this tub with us."

Jack laughed. "No, I get that. What I mean is, this ship doesn't have any means of defending itself. Canada is officially in the war now, right? Why don't you have any deck guns? If we did see a U-boat, you'd at least have a chance of fighting back?"

Harold walked up to the rail and stood next to Jack. "I agree with you," he whispered. "But the captain thinks if the Germans see any deck guns, it might provoke them to attack. For now, at least some of the time, they just board ships and inspect them, make sure we're not carrying any weapons for the Brits. They're not sinking all of them. But I think that's gonna change soon. Could be any day. Things are really heating up over there. Heard on the radio the Dutch surrendered to the Nazis five days ago."

"You're kidding?" Jack said. "Already? The Germans just launched their attack, what, nine days ago?"

"They've already broken through Belgium's front lines. The day after the Dutch surrendered, German tanks crossed the River Meuse into France. More tank divisions have broken through the Ardennes. The reports are, the French army's in retreat all up and down the line."

Jack couldn't believe it. The Ardennes was considered an impenetrable forest. Joe and Ozzie came over. Jack shared the news. They were as stunned as he was. When they all had talked back in Nova Scotia about what to expect on this trip, most worried whether they'd see any action at all. In the first war (called The Great War), things had pretty much reached a stalemate after the first few months. That stalemate lasted four years.

Up until now, this war seemed to be following the same crawling pace. England and France had declared war on Germany when they invaded Poland in September of last year. That was eight months ago and very little actual fighting had taken place. People in the press had nicknamed this "The Phoney War."

Clearly now, things had changed.

"I guess it makes sense, though," Ozzie said. "Colonel Sweeney must've seen this coming. Why he told us, all of a sudden, to board this boat back in Nova Scotia, instead of the one heading to France."

"But the French and British are gonna stop the Nazis, right?" Joe said, looking at Jack then Ozzie. "This is just some kind of temporary thing, don't you think?"

Ozzie didn't look so sure.

Jack wasn't, either. "I don't know," he said. There were some major differences between the weapons used in the Great War and now. Jack had been keeping up with all the developments in Germany over the last several years, especially since Hitler had started showing up in the news more and more. Hitler had created a new *illegal* air force, called the Luftwaffe, which sported some extremely fine looking fighter planes and bombers. Jack had read all kinds of stories about their exploits a few years ago during the Spanish civil war. And the new Nazi tanks seemed far superior to anything the French or British had built since the first war.

Jack had read everything he could about how quickly the Nazis had defeated Poland eight months ago. Everyone in the press kept saying, well yes, of course they did. The Poles were no match for the Germans. Some of their cavalry troops still rode on horseback. But the French and British forces were far superior to Poland. It would be a very different matter once this "Phoney War" ended and the real fighting began. And yet, here the news seemed to be saying…the Germans were doing the same thing now with Holland, Belgium and France that they had done with Poland.

No one spoke a few moments.

Jack couldn't stop thinking about the news. The Nazis had already accomplished more in a week then they had in several years during the Great War.

For at least a few minutes, the magnitude of all this war news had pushed aside the dark thoughts that had preoccupied Jack's mind ever since he'd come aboard this ship.

Really, even two weeks before that.

AN HOUR LATER, the atmosphere on the ship had mostly returned to normal. The sense of danger from U-boats, even the anxiety stirred up by the news in Belgium and France, had subsided. Five of the six young Americans were standing along the rail enjoying the light breeze, watching the sun begin to set.

The sixth man, Seth Norman, sat on the steel deck about fifteen feet away, his knees folded up by his chest. His chin rested on his forearms. Jack couldn't tell by the look on his face if he was angry, worried or afraid.

Whatever it was, it wasn't good.

Joe noticed Jack looking at Seth. "What's up with him?"

"I don't know," Jack said quietly. "Something."

"Hey Seth," Joe yelled. "What are you doing sitting over

there by yourself? C'mon. You're missing it. Nice breeze is blowing. The ocean's calming down. A nice sunset is shaping up. Not a U-boat in sight."

Seth didn't answer. He just stared down at the deck.

"Seth?" Joe repeated.

"Leave me alone. I don't want to be here anymore. I want off this boat."

"What? It's a little late for that now, don't you think? You're pretty much stuck here with us for the duration. At least till we reach England. But even then, it's gonna be pretty hard to get back to the US with a phony passport."

"Joe," Jack said. "You're not helping." The man was just afraid. Jack walked over and slid down the steel wall beside him.

"What's bugging you, Seth?"

"This isn't what I signed up for."

"What did you think it was gonna be like? You're a pilot, right? How long you been flying?"

"Four years."

"What kind of planes?"

"Jennie's mostly. The occasional Stearman."

"Okay then, like the rest of us, you faced death every time you hopped in the cockpit, right?"

Seth didn't immediately answer. Finally, "Yeah, I suppose so. But that was different."

"How?"

"In the cockpit, I got the controls in my hands. Out here? Some invisible ship can just blow us out of the water. At any time. We won't even see it coming. It can happen when we're asleep. Colonel Sweeney didn't say anything about U-boats when I signed on."

"He didn't mention them to me, either," Jack said. "But it was all over the newspapers."

"I wasn't reading the news."

"He told you about what we're doing being illegal, though, right? That if we got caught, we could go to jail? Lose our citizenship?"

Seth looked at him, nodded.

"That didn't bother you? Going to prison?"

"I figured we could dodge the law easily enough. And the passports he gave us looked pretty official. I figure they'd pass muster. If not, going to prison a few years isn't the same thing as sitting out here for weeks on a boat waiting to get blown to pieces. Or else slowly freezing to death in ice water."

Jack didn't know what to say. "You got me on that one, Seth."

They sat a few moments in silence.

"If it helps any," Jack said, "that guy Harold—you know, the blonde-haired fellow? He told me this morning, he thought we'd be in England in two days. That's not that much further, right? We made it this far, we'll make it the rest of the way. And you got to figure…the Nazi subs aren't going to want to get that close to England, so we might be in the clear already."

Seth looked up at him. "You think so? Think we won't have any more…false alarms?"

"Maybe."

Joe walked up. He'd caught the last few moments of their conversation. "Another way to look at this, Seth. If you do blow up from a torpedo, it'll happen in the blink of an eye, so there's no pain. You'd be dead before you screamed ouch. And if you don't blow up but get tossed in the drink, if you want, I got a Colt 45 on me. I can shoot you in the head right off the bat, so you won't freeze to death. It'll be over before you know it."

Jack looked up at Joe. "Was that supposed to help?"

6

AN HOUR LATER, the sun had completely set. The ship moved along at a nice clip. Were they moving faster, or did it just feel that way because the water was so calm now? The dinner bell was supposed to ring any minute. Jack hoped so. He wasn't hungry, but the activity would give his mind something else to dwell on besides the singular theme that kept plaguing his thoughts every spare moment.

He felt betrayed. By his own father.

Jack shook his head in disgust, picked a different point on the horizon. He tried focusing on the droning sound of the ship's twin-propellers, see if that could shut down this barrage of disturbing thoughts.

It did. For about twenty seconds.

What made this thing even harder to understand was how close he and his father had always been. At least he thought they were. Growing up, it had been just the two of them. His father had been stuck in a wheelchair since before Jack was born, put there by injuries he received as a pilot during the Great War. It meant he grew up poor, but Jack didn't care. All his friends were poor. Besides, they always got by. And because his father was disabled, Jack got to spend more time with him than most kids did with their dads.

"Say Jack, what's that city in England we're docking in? It's Southampton, right?"

Jack looked toward the noise. "What?"

"C'mon, you said it yesterday, the place where we're getting off this crate. It's Southampton, the place where the Titanic was built, right? That's what you said." Joe whispered the next part. "I'm about to make an easy five bucks. This big farm boy is saying we're heading to Liverpool."

Joe had been Jack's best friend for almost a decade. But Joe didn't seem even remotely aware how upset he was. Jack looked right at him. Nope. Joe didn't have a clue. Had that same *ain't-life-great* look on his face he wore most of the time. "It's Southampton, Joe. Bet the guy fifty bucks if you want. I heard the captain tell one of the crew members myself, the day we boarded."

"I knew it." Joe headed about fifteen feet down the deck toward this broad-shouldered, red-headed kid, all set to make his deal.

Jack knew he shouldn't get mad at Joe. Some guys are just born dull. Joe thought he was just fine the way he was, said if there was a problem in their friendship, it was Jack. He was wound too tight. "*Your job is to get me to think some,*" he'd say. "*My job is get you to lighten up.*"

Jack didn't think he'd ever lighten up about this thing. How could he? His whole life had been a lie. He hadn't told Joe anything about it yet. Wasn't even sure if he wanted anyone else to know. He wished he didn't know.

"Pay up, pal."

"I'm not paying you a thing."

Jack turned to find Joe leaning into the face of the farm boy.

"It *is* Southampton, so you owe me five bucks," Joe said.

"What, 'cause he said so?" Farm guy pointed at Jack.

"If Jack said it, it's a fact."

"Not in my book."

"Slow down," Jack said. "I'll tell you what…why don't you make it double-or-nothing, payable when we dock? It's not like it's a matter of opinion. When we reach the port, you'll see whether I was right, or you were. Actually, you'll know before then. When we get close. If the ship turns north up St. George's Channel, you'll know it's Liverpool. If we keep heading east in the English Channel, it's Southampton."

Both men seemed okay with that. They shook on it then Joe came back and stood next to Jack. "Nice goin' Jack. Now I get ten bucks."

"Glad you're happy."

"You're sure about it being Southampton, right?"

Jack nodded. "You'll win that bet. And here's another tidbit. Southampton wasn't just the place the Titanic was built. They also designed the Spitfire there."

"Really?"

"Said so in that article you showed me the other day."

"Guess I didn't catch that when I read it," Joe said. "Can you believe we get to fly those birds? I can't wait."

Jack smiled. "Don't get your heart set on flying Spitfires yet. The RAF's got Hurricanes, too. Remember? We could end up flying them."

"Either way, they're both like hot rods compared to those rickety Jenny's we been flying back home."

Joe was right about that. And Jack had to admit…that part

of this adventure did excite him. Until a month ago, he and Joe had made their living wowing crowds at air shows doing stunt routines, mostly in rural areas where folks had never seen an airplane up close. Jack couldn't imagine being at the controls of a Spitfire and having so much power in his hands.

They'd seen pictures of them in an aviation magazine Joe bought the day before they boarded. The main article was all about the new British fighter. Jack had never seen a sleeker, faster-looking plane. All the guys were talking about it. Every one of them had read that article. Like Joe, they didn't care too much about the political aspects of this new war.

They just wanted a chance to fly that plane.

Jack wanted that, too, but he had a totally different reason for getting to England.

He sighed as he thought about the book tucked away in the duffel bag under his bunk down below. Wedged inside its pages was a black-and-white photograph, now yellow with age. Next to it, a telegram. It was still so hard to fathom. But he knew it was true. His Dad admitted it. But then he'd said, that was *all* he could say. He couldn't tell Jack anything more. If Jack wanted to know the rest of the story, he'd have to pursue the answers himself.

So that's what he was doing. That's why Jack was on this boat.

He still loved his Dad but felt so betrayed. In the last few days, it felt like every sure thing in Jack's life had suddenly given way. It wasn't just his relationship with his Dad; Jack's faith in God had been shaken, too. His Dad had raised him going to church. Had Jack memorize and, as best he could, live by the Ten Commandments growing up.

And here his dad was…lying all that time.

Sitting there by the rail, looking out over the water, Jack thought about the photograph again. As long as he could remember, it had sat inside a small mahogany frame on his Dad's dresser. It showed a little boy, eyes squinting in the sun, wearing a little gray suit and knickers, standing in front of an ornamental iron gate. He'd never asked his father about it before. No reason to. Jack had always assumed it was just the earliest picture his Dad had of him.

Now he knew the truth. It wasn't him. Had never been him. And the picture was no longer safely hidden behind the confines of a frame. Jack had read the handwriting on the back. He recalled the words again, for the hundredth time since he'd first read it.

Elliot – 1921 – 3 yrs old.

It was a picture of Jack's brother, his twin brother. Until two weeks ago, a brother Jack never knew he had.

7

TWO DAYS LATER, as the captain had predicted, they arrived at the bustling seaport of Southampton, shortly before noon. Jack had never seen a more active harbor. Ships of all sizes and shapes; some tied up, others being eased into their slot by tugboats. And just as many still out in the water, coming or going. Military and merchant vessels in equal number.

Like the rest of the Americans, Jack was totally ready to get off the ship. It was so nice to finally walk on solid ground, although every time he stopped suddenly or moved his head too fast, it felt like the ground was still moving.

"Okay everybody," Ozzie said. "Stay close together as we walk. With this crowd, if we lose you, you'll stay lost."

As things typically go when a group of guys hangs out together, one of them starts to function as the leader. Ozzie had assumed that spot. No one seemed to mind, least of all Jack. When this started becoming evident back on the ship, Joe had taken Jack aside, thought he should speak up more, maybe vie for the role. Jack had other, bigger things in mind for his time here in England. Ozzie could take the lead.

Jack still hadn't told Joe why he had really come here to England.

"It'll be so nice not to have to eat that crap food on the ship anymore," Joe said. "I wasn't sure I could swallow another bite. As soon as we get off this dock, what say we find a nice English pub and grab some lunch?"

Most of the guys agreed with Joe. Jack didn't answer, just kept moving along with the group.

"Don't get your heart set on anything fancy," Ozzie said. "England's known for a lot of things. Great food isn't one of them. And that's in the best of times. Now they're on war rations."

"I heard they put everything in a pie," one of the guys said.

"Pie sounds good," Joe said.

"This ain't your grandma's apple pie."

"I know. More like chicken pot pie, right? I'm okay with that."

"You'll be lucky to find any with chicken in it. More like meat pies. And who knows what kind of meat you're getting?"

"Whatever it is," Joe said, "it's gotta be better than what we've been getting since we left the U.S."

Jack wasn't hungry. He'd been fighting a head cold since he woke up this morning. But he probably should eat, since he'd skipped breakfast. He was more interested in finding someplace warm, maybe a pub with a fireplace or at least a decent heater.

"How come there wasn't anyone there to meet us as we got off the ship?" Seth said. "Aren't they're expecting us? We're here helping them out."

"What'd you expect?"

"I don't know. Thought there might be at least someone standing there by the gangway holding a sign."

"They're expecting us in a general way," Ozzie said. "They know we're coming. But it's not like we're getting some red carpet treatment. We're not celebrities. We came here to fight Nazi's."

"And fly Spitfires," Joe said.

"Then how are we supposed to connect with Colonel Sweeney?" Seth said.

"One of his aides gave me a phone number," Ozzie said. "I'm supposed to find a phone booth and call it when we arrive. I think he's supposed to be in London. I figured I'd call after we get something to eat."

They continued their trek for several minutes, turning right at one point on Canute Road. Ozzie stopped to ask directions to the closest pub from a British sailor with a friendly face. He was friendly enough, but no one understood a word he said. They walked in the direction he pointed until they reached a three-story building on a street corner, called the Canute Castle Hotel. The front door was around the corner on the cross street. Once inside, it was apparent they'd finally found a pub with enough room to accommodate them all.

After all that walking, Jack was actually starting to feel a little hungry.

FORTY-FIVE MINUTES LATER, everyone had eaten until their bellies were full. At least they had plenty of cash to hold them over. Colonel Sweeney had taken care of that, at least. Jack just hoped everything he ate would stay down long enough to digest. The sense of motion had begun to calm some, but he still felt a little queasy.

One thing all the men acknowledged, something very different from what they'd expected on their first visit to a British pub—the overall atmosphere. It was anything but festive and lighthearted. A radio on a shelf behind the counter had been left on to catch any BBC news updates. Most of the news the patrons had been hearing wasn't good.

Not just today but for the last several weeks.

Seth had heard a middle-aged British man in the booth behind them talking. He'd gotten up to use the restroom—what the Brits called *the loo*—and on the way back, stopped briefly and stood next to the man. "Excuse me, sir. My friends and I are Americans. We actually just got off a boat a little while ago. We're all pilots. We came here to fly for the RAF, to help you guys fight the Nazis."

The man turned in his seat to face Seth. "I thought you fellows might be Yanks. I was telling my friend that not two seconds ago. Does your presence 'ere mean the U.S. is finally getting into this bloody war? Roosevelt change his mind?"

"No, I'm afraid not. We're here on our own. In fact, we had to sneak over by way of Canada. If we got caught, we'd all be sent to prison."

"How terrible." He sighed. "What is wrong with Roosevelt? What's it going to take for him to come in on our side?"

"I don't know, sir. But I was just wondering. We haven't had too much news this past week, being out on the ship the whole time. Could you share with us what's been going on? Here and over in France? We've been hearing things are pretty bad." Seth sat back on the last seat facing the aisle.

"Bad is not the word," the man said. "But sure, I'll fill you in." He picked up his pint, half-empty, then slid an empty chair from a nearby table and turned it around so he faced the group.

His friend came over and did the same.

Ozzie noticed their glasses and got the bartender's attention. When he came over, Ozzie said, "Could you bring another round for everyone, including our two friends here?"

"I can," the bartender said. "I'm assuming you have enough money with you to cover all this?"

Ozzie motioned for the man to come close and showed him a big wad of British pounds from his inside coat pocket.

The bartender got a big smile. "I'll be right back with your drinks."

"Well, that's very kind of you," the first British man said.

"The least I could do," Ozzie said. "So please, tell us what's been going on?"

The man's smile disappeared. He leaned forward. "The Germans have Holland, Luxembourg and Belgium now. They're all under Nazi control. Everyone is saying, France will fall any day. It's a foregone conclusion. All our troops are retreating to the coast near the English Channel. Near Dunkirk and Calais. I fought in the first War. I know the region quite well. From everything I can gather, our boys are surrounded."

"What about the RAF?" Joe asked. "Aren't they over there taking out the Luftwaffe?"

"Apparently not," the first man said. "I'm not sure what's 'appening there. From what we hear, it seems like the Luftwaffe is overwhelmin' the situation in the air. Most of our fighter planes aren't even over there. They've been kept 'ere to defend the 'omeland."

Jack knew that meant France was finished. If the Brits were keeping their best planes in England, and no longer using them to save France, then they had already decided France cannot be saved.

"I don't understand something," Ozzie said. "You said all the British troops were retreating to the coast and the Germans have them surrounded. And there aren't any RAF planes to support them. What's to keep them from being totally wiped out?"

Both British men looked at each other, grave expressions on their face. "We're not totally sure," the first man said. He leaned even further forward and lowered his voice to a whisper. "Nothin' official has been announced. But I think something big is being planned. Word 'round the docks is, Churchill's asking for every privately owned boat of any size—long as it can cross the Channel—to be ready on a moment's notice to leave."

"They're going to evacuate the troops?" Seth said. "All of them? There must be several hundred thousand men, at least?"

"Not to mention all the equipment," Ozzie added. "The tanks, trucks and jeeps. And all the artillery?"

"I dunno," the man said. "I'm just tellin' you what I've 'eard."

No one said anything more for a few moments. The weight of the news settled on everyone's soul like a blanket of fog.

Jack's mood had already been in this condition for weeks, ever since finding out the news about his brother. Now, he'd sunk even further. What had he gotten himself into by coming here? How would he ever locate his brother and get answers to all the questions racking his brain…in a country that was on the verge of falling completely apart?

8

Dainville, a village near Arras, France
1pm, May 21st, 1940

RENÉE SAT HUDDLED next to her mother in the cellar of their home, terrified. The far off explosions she had begun to hear earlier that morning were now just south of town. So close, many of them caused the windows to rattle. Several times, bits of plaster had fallen from the ceiling.

"Where is Philippe?" Mother cried. "He should be here with us." Her shawl was wrapped tightly around her head and shoulders.

Philippe was Renée's brother. She was nineteen; he had just turned seventeen. "I'm sure he's fine. He's with his friends in Arras." But Renée wasn't sure at all. Ever since war had been declared eight months ago, Philippe had begged their mother to let him join the fight. She had refused. Since their father had died last year, Philippe was the man of the house. With her being so unwell, she needed his help here at home more than ever. Besides, he was still a boy, too young to be a soldier.

"Which is it?" Philippe had replied angrily. "*I cannot be both—the man of the house and still just a boy.*"

It didn't matter what Philippe had said or how often. Mother would never agree to let him join the military. The thought of losing him was more than she could bear. Renée wondered where he was right now. She hoped he had enough sense to run away from the danger rather than toward it.

"You're shivering, Mother. Are you cold?" Renée had been able to grab a blanket from the closet before they'd fled downstairs. They were sharing it.

"I don't know. Maybe it's just fear."

Renée took off her half of the blanket. "Take this."

"No, keep it on."

"But you need it more than me."

"I'm fine the way it is."

Just then another explosion, the loudest one yet. The entire basement rumbled. A loud crash. A wall shelf collapsed, sending pots and kitchen utensils to the floor. They screamed.

Renée scrunched closer to her mom. "We're okay. It didn't hit the house." She wondered if these bombs were Germans or British. British forces had occupied the area around Arras for the last several months. That's how she had met Elliot, a young officer she had started to date. She hoped he was alright. He was stationed on a makeshift air base just north of Arras. The opposite side of town from the explosions. He wasn't a pilot, but an intelligence officer. That's what he'd said, why she didn't have to worry. His job rarely brought him to the front lines in the heat of battle.

For months, until now, the battle had stayed far away.

Elliot was supposed to join them for lunch today. Renée knew that wouldn't happen once she saw the flurry of activity around town a few hours ago. Dozens of British tanks and lorries filled with soldiers had driven by outside their house, heading south. Townspeople were told to take cover in their homes and stay off the streets. The Germans were on their way here.

Just then they both heard a low, sputtering, mechanical sound outside. Very close. She got up to check, tucking her part of the blanket under Mother's legs.

"Where are you going?"

"I want to see what that is. I'll be right back." God, she prayed, whatever it is let it be British. She walked across the cellar toward the only window with a view out front. It was about two feet wide and a foot tall. She had to step on an overturned metal tub to see clearly.

More explosions. She grabbed the wall to steady herself.

"Renée, come back. You need to get away from the window."

"Those were further away, Mother. See? The window barely rattled." She looked out the window again, in time to see the back end of a British tank driving by, away from the direction of the fighting. Black smoke trailed behind it.

"What do you see?" Mother asked.

"No Germans yet," Renée said. "I wish I could talk to Elliot. He could tell us what's going on." The phone lines had stopped working just after breakfast.

"He's been telling us to expect this for several days," Mother said. "I was hoping he was just being cautious."

Renée knew that he wasn't. He had told her much more when they were alone than what he shared in Mother's presence. He knew her heart couldn't take the strain if he had told her the truth. At dinner two nights ago, Elliot talked about how much ground Hitler's forces had gained so far. Mother had said although the Germans seemed to be winning now, it wouldn't be long before Elliot's troops and the French army stopped their advance. Then things would quiet down for a while, like they did in the last war. She just hoped that when that happened, the front lines would be set much further away from Arras than they had been last time.

Elliot had responded to this carefully and respectfully, saying he couldn't go into the details but, he assured her, this wasn't going to be like last time. He insisted they should keep some bags packed and be prepared to evacuate their home on short notice. He wasn't sure when, but he didn't think it would be much longer.

Renée realized, that day was already here.

THIRTY MINUTES LATER, Renée heard someone pounding on the front door. At first, she wasn't sure if it was just rumbling from an explosion. But it continued. "I better go see who it is." She stood and walked to the cellar stairs.

"What if it's the Germans?" Mother said.

What if it was, what would she do?

"Maybe you should ignore it. See if they'll go away."

Someone was yelling, calling her name. "It's Elliot, Mother. Elliot," she shouted, "I'm coming."

She ran up the cellar stairs, through the winding hallway and past the stairway that led to the second floor. The foyer and front door were just ahead.

He pounded on the door again. "Renée, it's me, Elliot. Please open the door."

He must not have heard her calling from the stairs. "I'm coming." She fumbled with the lock and finally got it open.

When the door open, he rushed inside and they embraced.

"When you didn't answer, I was afraid the Germans had already come."

"Are they that close?"

"I'm not sure. I didn't think they were, but it won't be long now." He took a deep breath. "I'm so glad you're all right. Are your mother and Philippe here? Are your bags packed? We have to leave very soon. We really should leave now."

She took him by the hand and walked him into the parlor. They sat on the edge of the sofa. "Mother is here. She's downstairs. But Philippe is not. He went into Arras this morning to see one of his friends. I hope he's okay."

"He should be fine, for now. I just came through it. None of the bombs have reached there yet."

"Yet? Do you think they will?"

"Renée, it's happening. Right now. Just like I told you. The Germans have broken through all our defenses. The French army is in full retreat. Our troops are making a stand south of town. That's all the explosions you're hearing. A major battle is about to happen."

"It's about to get worse?"

"Much worse. That's why we have to leave. Now. This battle south of town is just buying us time. Nothing will come of it. France is lost. Our own forces are in danger of annihilation. The Germans have already swept through and taken everything south of here, all the way to the Channel. We've been urging General Gort to order all our remaining troops to the coast. To Dunkirk and Calais."

"The British are leaving France?" Renée could not believe what Elliot was saying.

"We have to, Renée. We're surrounded. Even if we manage somehow to get everyone to the coast, there's no way to get them all across the Channel. I've been ordered to return to London. My plane leaves in two hours."

Renée felt a panic coming over her.

"I want all of you on that plane with me. It's a small one, but I've secured three seats…for you, your mother and Philippe. Each of you can carry one small bag. But we have to leave now."

"Hello, Elliot."

They looked up and saw Mother standing in the hallway. She looked so frail and weak. But Renée saw a different look in her eyes.

"I heard much of what you said, Elliot. I'm grateful for all you've done to try and help us. But I can't leave with you. I'm afraid I would not survive such a trip. And besides, Philippe isn't here. I couldn't possibly leave him here alone. But I would be very grateful if you would take my daughter away from here. If the Germans are really coming…I don't want her anywhere near this place."

9

RENÉE LEFT THE COUCH and hurried to her mother's side and helped her walk into the living room. "Mother, I can't leave you here. Who will take care of you?"

Slowly, they walked across the wood floor. Elliot stood. "I can send a Jeep for you, Mrs. Bouchard. You won't have to walk very far. Really, at any time during the trip. The plane ride across the channel will be a little bumpy, but once in London, I will personally drive you to our house. It's a big beautiful place several hours north of London. Nice and quiet. You'll have your own room and even servants to wait on you. I'm sure our family doctor will take you on."

Mother smiled. "That's very kind of you, Elliot. And I'm sure your home is lovely. But I can assure you, I will not be leaving this one. I can tell how I feel inside. I would not survive the trip." She looked at Renée. "You asked who will take care of me? God will take care of me, Renée. And Philippe will help, too, once he realizes you're gone. And we still have friends in the village. Some have already fled, but many are still here. And like me, they will stay here."

Renée hugged her. Tears welled up at the thought of them parting. It wasn't right. Her mother had always been there for her, had always taken care of her. How could she leave her now, especially at a time like this?

She looked at Elliot. They had been seeing each other for several months. Even though their lives and their backgrounds were so different, she genuinely cared for him. But did she love him? She wasn't sure. She thought he loved her. "You get on that plane, Elliot. I want to go with you, but I can't leave Mother here. There is no way that Philippe will look after her properly."

"You *will* go with him!"

Her mother's voice and tone startled her. She held Renée in front of her, staring into her eyes with a fierceness Renée could not comprehend.

"You cannot stay here with me. Not if the Germans are coming."

"But Mother—"

"You don't understand what these men are like, Renée." She sat in a nearby upholstered chair. "I've never told you this, but I had two girlfriends who lived in Cambrai. We didn't see each other for several years during the last war, because Cambrai had been taken over by the Germans. When I did see them after the war, I almost didn't recognize them. The horrible stories they told…"

She was staring at the floor, her eyes wide. Her hand started to tremble. She looked up at Renée. "You must go. You *will* go with Elliot."

Elliot looked at his watch. "Did you pack a bag like I asked you?"

Renée nodded. "It's in my room."

"Then we should go. We don't have much time."

"But Elliot, I cannot go without at least saying goodbye to Philippe. Who knows if I will ever see him—" She started to cry.

Elliot rushed over and held her.

"I will tell him goodbye for you, Renée," Mother said. "He will understand."

"It's not just that." She looked up at Elliot. "Can I speak with you down the hall?" She led him by the hand, until she was sure they would not be overheard. "Elliot, I *have* to speak with Philippe. Not just to say goodbye but to make sure he understands…he must take care of Mother while I'm gone. I've always done everything for her. He never even helps. Mother doesn't have any real friends left in the village. Not the kind who will take the time to come out and check on her every day. The closest ones have either died or left town. I have to know that Philippe understands this, that it will be up to him and only him once I'm gone."

"Okay, I understand. But we really don't have much time. Can I drive you into Arras? I can wait there while you talk with him?"

"I'm not even sure where he is. There's at least two or three places. I'll get my bag and you can drive me into town and drop me off. Then you take my bag back to your base. As soon as I find Philippe, I will come join you."

Elliot glanced at his watch again and sighed. "Renée, we have less than two hours. I have to be on that plane, or I could be court-martialed. Please promise me, you'll keep an eye on the time. If it even gets close, and you haven't found your brother yet, you will leave that instant and meet me at the base."

"I will, Elliot. I promise." She kissed him on the cheek. "Now go. I'll go upstairs and get my bag and meet you by the jeep."

He walked toward the door but stopped a moment and looked at Renée's mother. "I wish you could come with us, Ma'am. But I understand why you cannot. I will take very good care of your daughter and bring her back to you just as soon as we defeat the Nazis."

"I know you will, Elliot. You both will be in my prayers."

He offered a feeble smile, nodded and left.

Without looking at Mother, Renée quickly hurried up the stairs and grabbed her bag, which she'd left on a chair by the door. She rushed back down and set the bag by the front door.

Then, slowly, she turned around to face the most difficult decision she had ever made in her life.

10

RENÉE CRIED ALL the way down the Avenue Levoisier. She was still crying as they made the turn down Rue d'Amienes, now less than ten minutes till they reached the place Elliot would drop her off in Arras. He was being so patient with her. She'd been so afraid he'd be lecturing her now, telling her how it was all for the best, and to keep a stiff upper lip, and other such phrases proper British actors said in the movies.

But he just drove along with one hand on the wheel, the other resting gently on the back of her seat. Occasionally, he rubbed her shoulder.

It wasn't just leaving her mother at a time like this. It was everything else, besides. Leaving the only home, the only town she'd ever lived in. Leaving the country she loved, knowing that everything it ever was or had ever been, was about to be mercilessly destroyed. It was leaving her brother this way. They weren't that close, at least they hadn't been since he'd become a teen. But still, he was her brother. And when she thought of him, she didn't just see the tall, half-man, half-boy with all the attitude; she also instantly remembered him as a toddler, as a cute little boy with dark, curly hair; as a handsome but awkward pre-teen trying to hide his first crush on one of her girlfriends.

Now she was on a mission to find him, to say goodbye. Maybe for the last time.

Oddly enough, what helped her to finally regain her composure were all the people she began seeing along the other side of the road. All leaving town in the same direction. Some riding bicycles, some sitting on horse carts, some without horses pulling wagons, mothers pushing baby strollers. Their belongings, all they could carry or tie down, traveling with them. A lifetime of treasured possessions left behind, now plunder for the Nazis. Their faces, a mixture of fear, dread and total exhaustion. None of them knew where their next meal would come from, the next place where they would sleep at night.

Her loss suddenly seemed so much smaller.

They turned right down Rue Saint-Aubert, drove a few blocks toward the center of town. The streets were deserted, as far as she could tell. Everyone had either left or were hiding. Up ahead she saw a caravan of military vehicles heading in their same direction, toward the southern end of town.

"You want me to drop you off along this street somewhere, right?" Elliot said.

"Yes. It's right up here. See on the left? Where the big intersection opens up? You can pull over right there. One of Philippe's friends lives close to here. I'm going to check there first."

Three explosions in quick succession sounded off in the distance, forcing their gaze toward the south. Beyond the edge of town, dark clouds of smoke rose high in the sky.

"Those seem closer," she said.

"They are."

"Were those our troops? Our cannons firing off?"

He shook his head. "No, we'd be firing away from town. I think that's the Germans firing back at us."

"So the battle's getting closer?"

"Could be. You sure you have to do this? I'm sure your brother's taking cover like everyone else." They had reached the big intersection, so he pulled the Jeep over to the curb.

"I won't be long. Please try to understand."

"I'm trying." He looked at his watch. "Thirty minutes, Renée. It's at least a ten-minute walk from here to the base. You must leave here in thirty minutes, no matter what."

"I will. I promise." She leaned over and kissed his cheek, then hopped out. Quickly, she turned to walk away before he tried to talk her out of it again.

RENÉE WAS NEARLY frantic. Twenty minutes had passed, and still no trace of Philippe. She had tried his two best friends' homes. Not only were they not there; there was no one at either place who could even give her a clue as to where they might have gone.

She was about to give up hope when she remembered one of his favorite hiding places as a child. A wooded area on a hillside just outside of town. Once when he'd gotten mad at a punishment received from their father, he ran away. Children often do this and usually nothing comes of it. But this time, Philippe did not return. He stayed out all night and wasn't found until noon the following day.

He'd hid at a place hollowed out in the woods, where Renée was headed now. *Please God, let him be there.*

Fortunately, it was in the right direction and only a few

minutes' walk to the RAF base. If he was there, she could at least take some comfort that it was on the opposite edge of town from the fighting.

As she walked past the final two blocks of paved streets, she didn't see another soul. It felt so strange. What would become of her town after today? Would it be in ruins? Would it remain intact but totally occupied by Nazis? As she walked further down the road toward the woods, she looked back at Arras. Would she ever be coming back to this place? And if so, when?

She reached the edge of the woods. It began at the road and ascended a hillside. The brush was thick and dense, which was why Philippe and his friends liked it so much. Twenty meters in, a person literally disappeared. She tried to remember how to get in. There was a path somewhere.

After a few minutes, she found it. She'd walked past it twice and missed it because it had been deliberately covered over with fresh-cut branches. She hurried up the path, ignoring the painful slaps from overgrown branches. Glancing down at her wristwatch brought a fresh sense of panic. She only had eight minutes before her thirty minutes were up.

The area they had carved out for their hideout was just up ahead, beyond this small hill and behind a large boulder.

Reaching the top, brought instant relief. She heard Philippe's voice. But that relief turned to dread when she heard what he said.

"I don't think we have enough ammo for these guns. If we get into an actual fight with the Germans, this won't last twenty minutes."

"It's all the ammo my father had. He would kill me if he knew we'd taken it."

She recognized the other voice. Louis, one of his two best friends. She started coming down the other side of the hill and saw the makeshift entrance to their hideout. It was something of an archway cut through thick branches and vines. Since they were armed and probably nervous, she decided to call from a safe distance. "Philippe."

Silence. Several seconds ticked by.

"Who is that?" Louis' voice in a whisper.

"It's me, Louis. Renée, Philippe's sister."

"Renée!" Philippe yelled back. "What are you doing here?"

"The question is, what are you doing here? And why do you have guns?"

Philippe stepped out into the opening, holding a shotgun. "We have to protect ourselves, and our families. You've heard all the fighting south of town. Everyone's talking about it, those who are still here. The Germans are coming this way."

"And what do you and Louis think you're going to do about it? If the British can't stop them, do you think you will?"

"We may not be able to stop them, but we're not going to give up without a fight. Not like so many of our generals have done. Have you heard the radio? Our leaders are giving up. Our troops are fleeing the fight."

"Oh, Philippe. Please put down that gun. I need to talk with you. It's urgent, and I only have a few minutes left."

His expression totally changed. He was her little brother again.

"Why? What's the matter?" He set the gun on the ground, rested it against the branches of a bush.

"Please come here. I need to speak with you alone." She turned and headed to the top of the hill. She heard his footsteps behind her. When she was certain they were far enough away from being overheard, she turned around. "Philippe, I'm leaving. As soon as we're finished this conversation."

"Leaving? Where? Leaving town?"

"No, leaving France."

"What?" Shock all over his face. "Why? How? Is it Elliot? Is he taking you away?"

Philippe liked Elliot, for the most part. He would have liked him better had he been a French officer. "Yes, I'm leaving with him. He's been ordered back to London. His entire base is leaving."

"Then we *are* lost. If the British leave, we have no hope."

Renée started to cry. "I'm so sorry. I didn't want to leave."

"But what about Mother? Does she know?"

"She's the one making me leave with Elliot. I told her I wanted to stay, but she wouldn't hear of it."

"But why?"

"Because of the Germans." She could see by the look in his eye, he instantly understood. The part of him that had grown up.

"But if you leave, who will take care of her?"

"That's why I've come looking for you. To say goodbye and to plead with you to take care of her for me. For us. You see the things that I do for her. They are not hard, and they don't take very much time. They only require someone who will accept the responsibility. Please Philippe, promise me you'll do this. If I could stay, I would. You do believe me, don't you?" Tears streamed down her cheeks.

They embraced.

"Of course, I will," he said, still in her arms. "I will do my best."

"Then that means, you can't go off with Louis or any of your other friends to fight the Germans. You understand that?"

He nodded.

"I talked with Elliot about this a few days ago. He's certain the Germans will be occupying this area, maybe in just a few days. But he said we don't have anything to worry about. You and Mother won't. We're not Jews or gypsies, or any of the kinds of people they go after when they take over. All you have to do is stay out of trouble and do what they ask. I know it will be hard to go along with them. I know how much you hate the Nazis. But can you do that for me? For Mother?"

"I'll try."

"No, Philippe. Promise me you will, or else I cannot go. I will go find Elliot at his base and tell him I cannot—"

"I promise, Renée. I will take care of Mother. I won't let you down. And I agree with her. You do have to go." His expression was stern, but his eyes were filled with tears. He wiped them on his sleeve. "Will I ever see you again? Will you ever come back?"

"Of course, I will." She drew him close. "I will come back the moment it is safe to return. I promise I will."

11

ELLIOT STOOD ANXIOUSLY by the entrance to the base, glanced again at his watch. Ten minutes late. It was obvious in the dozen or so dates they'd had, she took a far more casual approach to time than he did. But it never mattered before.

He looked again down the tree-lined road. Still no sign of her. He hurried past the gate to the guardhouse. The soldier inside saluted. Elliot returned the salute. "Listen, my good man, I need to ask a favor of you."

"Anything, Major."

"I have to run back and have a chat with a pilot. I won't be gone five minutes. If you see a young lady hurrying down that road, and she gets here before I get back…"

"The brunette I've seen you with before, sir?"

"Yes, the very one. If you see her, tell her to wait right here. I'll be back to get her in a jiff."

"Very good, sir."

"Right. Well…" Elliot turned and headed toward the grass runway. Walking fast then, after another glance at his watch, he took off running.

This was not a time for decorum.

He rounded the last tent and saw the plane, an Avro Anson,

and the pilot standing by the small open hatch at the base of the wing. The pilot's expression instantly changed from frustration to confusion. Elliot slowed to a fast walk. The young Flight Lieutenant pointed to his watch and gestured clearly that they had to leave…*now*. Elliot outranked him. The man would never say what he was really thinking. "I'm sorry, Lieutenant. I don't know what's keeping her."

"But, sir. We have to leave. We're almost fifteen minutes late."

"Can you give me just five more minutes, Lieutenant?"

"I want to, sir. But if we don't leave, we're in danger of missing the rendezvous point with our Hurricane escorts. With all the enemy action in the area, we don't want to risk meeting the Luftwaffe in the air on the way home. Not in this thing."

"I understand, Lieutenant. Just five more minutes. If I'm not back by then, you take off without me."

"Sir? My orders are to get you back to London."

"I know. You let me worry about that. If I'm not back, you take off. I'll make sure you don't get in any trouble for it." Of course, Elliot had no idea of the trouble he'd be making for himself, should that happen.

"If you say so, sir."

"Five minutes, Lieutenant. You can go ahead and start the engines." He turned and ran back toward the gate.

When it came into view, he was so relieved to see Renée standing there chatting with the guard. The guard saw him first and interrupted their conversation. He pointed with his eyes in Elliot's direction. Renée saw him. He wanted to be angry at her for all the trouble she'd caused, but the look on her face melted his heart. She was so sad, and it was obvious she had been crying a good deal.

As he got close, she ran toward him, wrapped her arms around him and buried her face into his shoulder. The guard, sensing the moment, looked away. Elliot returned her embrace and whispered, "It'll be all right. You'll see."

"I'm so scared, Elliot. Are you sure I'm doing the right thing?"

"Very sure, Renée. I wish the choices weren't so clear. But we have to leave, now. The pilot is on a very tight schedule, and we're already late." He released her, took her by the hand and began walking fast back toward the airfield.

"I'm so sorry I'm late. When I didn't see you at the gate, I thought I had missed you. The guard told me—"

"I would never leave without you, Renée. Are you able to run with me, even a little?"

"Yes. I'm actually a fast runner. I can still beat my little brother in a foot race."

Elliot laughed. "Well, I don't think we have to run that fast. But really, we must hurry."

RENÉE WAS EASILY able to keep up with Elliot. She saw the plane up ahead. It wasn't big but so very loud. Two engines were making all that noise. A row of windows extended from the front to behind the wing. At the wing's edge a small door hung open. The pilot stood beside it, looking relieved to see them. With little effort, he swung his legs through the opening and made his way toward the front of the plane.

As they got closer, Renée realized how far off the ground the opening was, and she didn't see any ladder. She also noticed how tiny the plane looked inside. She'd expected several rows of seats, like she'd seen in the magazines. But there were only three very flimsy seats, one toward the back that faced forward and two behind the cockpit facing the rear of the plane.

"Your bag's already stowed inside," Elliot said. "Here, I'll help you get inside."

"What should I do?"

Elliot surveyed the situation and realized he'd have to lift her up like a child. "Give me your purse." She did, and he set it inside. "I'm sorry, I don't see any other way to get you in. We need to take off."

"That's okay." She raised her arms slightly and he picked her up, high enough for her feet to clear the opening. She ducked her head as he gave her a slight push. "I'm in." The noise was almost as bad inside. She backed up to make room and fell into one of the seats. Elliot lifted himself up like the pilot did and swung his body through the opening, feet first.

"We're in, Lieutenant." Elliot closed the door and latched it.

"Hold on," the pilot said.

Elliot quickly moved to the seat beside her. They grabbed hold of anything they could as the plane lurched forward. Renée had to dig in her heels to keep from sliding forward, since the plane tilted downward as it taxied across the grass.

"It'll get much smoother once we're in the air," Elliot yelled.

"That will be nice. Will it get any quieter?" The look on his face said he didn't hear her, so she said it again louder.

"A little, but not much," he yelled back. "They don't make military planes for comfort. How many times have you flown?"

"This is my first."

"I'm so sorry. I'll have to take you flying on one of the new airliners sometime. Maybe after the war. They're a little quieter than this, but way more comfortable." Elliot looked out the window just as the back of the plane swung all the way around. "Hold on tight. We're about to go very fast."

He wasn't kidding. The engines grew much louder and the scenes outside began zipping by. It was still bumpy, but less so. The back end lifted off the ground. They were sitting level for the first time. Now the front-end lifted, and all the bumpiness disappeared. "Are we flying?"

"We are. Look." He pointed out the window.

She saw the ground getting further away. Now she could see the edge of the line of tents closest to the runway. Soon she could see the entire base; what was left of it. Soldiers were breaking down an entire row of tents. "When will the rest of the soldiers' leave?"

A grave look came over his face. "Not all of them will. Only certain ones have been ordered to return home. We don't have near enough airplanes to transport them all."

"What will the rest do?"

"Join the remainder of our units, as soon as the fighting here around Arras is through. They'll head back to the coast, around Calais and Dunkirk. We're going to try and get them out on ships."

She couldn't imagine it. Tens of thousands of soldiers cramming onto hundreds of ships, crossing the English Channel while German planes attacked. Once again, her challenges seemed to shrink further still. She was flying high above it all. In a few hours, they'd be landing in London or somewhere nearby. Elliot would probably treat her to a nice dinner.

She glanced out the window. The city of Arras and Elliot's

base were no longer in sight. They continued to climb toward the clouds. A patchwork of farms and winding roads spread out below in every direction.

There was a crackling sound over the radio. She heard the pilot talking but couldn't make out the words. Elliot could see him, so she watched his face. The more the pilot said, the more concerned he became. Finally the static stopped.

The pilot turned his head and yelled loudly so they could both here. "Bad news. That was the wing commander for the flight of Hurricanes supposed to escort us over the Channel. While they were waiting for us at the rendezvous point, they got pounced by a flight of ME-110's. They got in a terrific scrap and had to fight their way out of it. They didn't lose anyone but used up too much fuel to wait for us and had to return to base."

"What's that mean?" Renée asked.

"It means we're on our own," Elliot said. He looked back at the pilot. "What are you going to do?"

"Only thing I can, sir. I'm heading for the clouds now. We'll fly in them as far as we can and hope for the best."

12

May 22nd, 1940
Air Ministry Building, Whitehall, London

AFTER SPENDING HIS first comfortable night of sleep in weeks at the hotel in Southampton, Jack, Joe and the four other American pilots woke up with instructions obtained by Ozzie to take the first train they could to London.

It was a crowded but fairly smooth train ride with many stops along the way. It took just over three hours. Jack sensed the mood of the people on the train to be the same as in the pub in Southampton yesterday. *Tense.* People were very concerned about the events taking place in France.

He'd overheard numerous conversations. Almost all of them discussing their fears and worries of what might happen next. Stunned disbelief abounded that Hitler and the Nazi forces had so quickly overwhelmed the French and British defenses. They were certain France would fall at any moment and wondered, when that happened, how could Britain possibly stop them from coming here?

Jack and the others had left the train at Victoria Station where they met an associate of Colonel Sweeney, named Franklin. He'd found them as they waited at a specific rendezvous point. Thankfully, Franklin was also American, so they had no trouble understanding each other.

He'd been living in London for several months. Enough time to figure out the maze of buses, trollies and underground subways that made up London's mass transit system. Over hot cups of coffee at a café, he'd explained how to get around in London, as well as their basic plan for the day. They were to take a certain bus to Whitehall and make their way to the Air Ministry on Horse Guards Avenue. There they should ask to see a Group Captain West with the RAF and present the papers Franklin had just given each of them.

Captain West would help them get situated, Franklin had said.

At that, Joe had blurted out, "Situated? We don't want to get situated. We want to fly Spitfires."

Forty-five minutes later, they were waiting in a lobby for Group Captain West to appear. They had met briefly with a young woman at a reception desk dressed in military attire. Apparently, Franklin had called ahead to say they were coming. She seemed to be expecting them and said Captain West would be there momentarily.

"So," Joe said mostly toward Jack, "the RAF is like their Air Force, right?"

"It's not like their Air Force. It *is* their Air Force. The Royal Air Force. The *R* stands for Royal."

Three officers wearing blue uniforms walked by and headed up some steps. "Think those are the uniforms they'll give us?" Joe said.

"Probably," Jack said. "Of course, we won't fly in those."

"And we'll be starting at the lowest rung," Ozzie added.

"Whatever that is."

"So, what's that? Second lieutenant?

"I looked it up," Jack said. "They use totally different names here. We'll probably start off as Pilot Officers, or PO's."

"Pilot Officer," Joe repeated. "It's got a nice ring to it."

A moment later, Jack noticed a smartly dressed officer in his early thirties talking to the woman at the reception desk. She pointed to their group. He started walking this way.

Ozzie saw him, too. "Hey guys, here comes that captain. Right this way." He stood up, so they all did too. For some reason, they tried to form a straight line, as if standing for inspection.

"Should we salute?" Seth whispered.

"I don't think so," Joe said quietly. "We're not even in the club yet."

"Gentlemen, welcome to the RAF," the officer announced. "I'm told you are the six Americans Colonel Sweeney called me about?"

"We are, sir," Ozzie said. "We're here to help you folks fight the Nazis."

"That's good to hear. But we have a few important matters to settle first."

Ozzie held out the folder received from Franklin earlier. "We were told to give these to you."

"Right," Captain West said. "I'll take them in a few moments. But not here. Follow me to the elevator. We'll go up to my office on the third floor." He turned and walked down a wide, crowded hallway.

The men followed closely behind. Soon, they were standing before a pair of elevators. Captain West pressed the up button.

"I trust your journey across the pond wasn't too eventful?"

"Thankfully, no," Jack said. "Had a few close calls with some U-boats, but nothing serious."

"I'm glad. I'm afraid the U-boat situation will start escalating dramatically," Captain West said. "Very soon. We've already begun to see a significant increase in the number of attacks, in just the last few weeks." The elevator door opened. They stepped aside to allow the people to exit, then everyone went inside.

Jack looked over at Seth's face. White as a sheet. Hearing this didn't do him any good. A moment later the door opened on the third floor.

"Follow me." Captain West turned right and headed down the hallway.

"Do you guys have any way of stopping them?" Seth asked. "The U-boats, I mean."

"We're working on something promising," West said, still facing forward.

Jack was really beginning to wonder whether Seth had made the right decision, him coming here. As RAF fighter pilots, they weren't likely going to deal with U-boats anymore. But he was pretty sure the danger they'd soon be facing in the air was at least as great, if not more so, than the ride over in the boat.

Captain West reached a door on the left and walked through. The six Americans came in right behind him. They stood in a smaller office area. A young male officer sat at a reception desk just in front of them. Along the wall that extended from the doorway were a row of straight-backed chairs.

"Why don't you gents, have a seat? Well, four of you anyway. I need to speak with each of you for a few minutes. Go over some important things, get you to sign some papers. For the sake of time, I'll meet with two of you at a time. Who wants to go first?"

Joe raised his hand. "How about me and my friend Jack here?"

"Fine. If no one has any objections?" It seemed no one did. He walked around the reception desk and opened the door on the left that led into his office. "Bring those folders with you."

The other men sat in one of the chairs. "Sir, do you know where we'll be staying tonight?" Ozzie said. "Do we need to get a room at a hotel somewhere in town?"

Captain West turned and faced the men. "Not unless something goes wrong during our interview. What I'm saying is, if none of the information you've provided—about your health and flying experience—turns out to be false, you will all be getting on a lorry after you leave here. Heading to a flight training base in Middle Wallop, about three hours west of here."

"Middle what?" Joe said. "You Brits got the craziest names for places."

The captain looked at Joe. Jack couldn't read the expression on his face, but whatever he was thinking, he decided not to say. He simply closed the door. "Have a seat, gentlemen."

Jack and Joe sat in the straight-backed chairs positioned in front of Captain West's gun-metal gray desk. He came around and sat in a much more comfortable cushioned chair.

"Do you want these, sir?" Jack held up the file folder he had been given by Franklin earlier.

"Yes, you can set them right there on my blotter. Although, I probably already have the same information. All the information we have on you was provided by Colonel Sweeney, presumably from interviews you've had with him. However, our conversation today is the one that counts."

Joe leaned forward. "Well, we've got nothing to hide, Captain. Ask anything you want."

He picked up the file folders, spun them around and opened them up. "I understand the two of you are longtime friends. You both put down roughly the same number of flight hours."

"We have been friends for many years, sir," Jack said. "We learned to fly at the same time and, pretty much, been flying in the same air shows for the same number of years back home."

"Although you more than meet the minimum requirement for flight hours, it doesn't seem like you have much experience flying anything other than the Jenny."

"That's true," Jack said. "But sir, we've both learned every dogfighting maneuver in the book. Done all of them a hundred times. The Jenny may not have anywhere near the power of a Spitfire, or even a Hurricane but, the way I see it, pulling off all those moves in a Jenny requires even more skill. Put us in one of your new fighters, and you'll see what we can do."

Captain West allowed himself the briefest smile. Then it was back to the stern face. "Well, you can be sure we'll be putting all of your flying skills to the test. But you won't start off in a Hurricane or a Spit. Something way more powerful than a Jenny, though. And I must warn you, the officer who will be evaluating you in Middle Wallop will not suffer fools. If either of you, or any of your friends in the other room, have exaggerated your skills, he will send you packing. You'll wash out the same day."

"Where will we be sent?" Joe said. "Not saying that's going to happen, just curious."

"To one of our training bases in the north. They'll put you through our elementary flight training course. Takes at least seven weeks. That is, if we don't put you on a ship sailing back to the States. Middle Wallop is part of Number 10 Group Fighter Command, right on the front lines of the coming air war. We can't afford to have a single pilot there who can't hold his own in a dogfight."

Jack wondered why Joe was even asking the question. "That's not going to be a problem, sir. Joe and I will not be washing out."

"Good. That's what I want to hear. I'm just saying, it had better be true for all of you." He opened his middle desk drawer and pulled out two sheets of paper. "I presume Colonel Sweeney briefed you both about this." He set a sheet of paper in front of both of them.

"What is it?" Joe said.

Jack picked his up.

"It's a statement that says you are willing to swear your allegiance to King Edward VI and the royal British crown for the duration of hostilities."

Jack knew this was coming. Hearing it out loud brought home the seriousness of what he was about to do. By signing this document, he was essentially forfeiting his American citizenship.

Possibly for good.

13

AN HOUR LATER, all six Americans were riding in the back of a British Army truck, which the Brits called a lorry. They had just reached the outskirts of London and were starting to see signs of the British countryside out the back. Apparently, none of the other guys seemed too bothered by the fact that they were no longer American citizens. It didn't really bother Jack all that much. Just one more thing in a growing list of things necessary to accomplish his greater mission.

Finding his twin brother.

That, and unraveling the mystery of his family tree. Topping the list was the answer to this question: *Why all the secrecy?* Why had his father raised him with a fictitious, made-up story about how Jack had come into the world, how his mother had died in childbirth (which she had not), why he had no siblings and, for that matter, no cousins and no aunts or uncles, either.

That portion of the story was at least partly true. His father had admitted he was an only child and that his own parents had both died of influenza when he was in his early teens. But Jack's father had also admitted he couldn't shed any light on the status of Jack's mother's side of the family, since he had been completely cut off from them when Jack was three years old.

Why? Jack asked after his father dropped this bombshell. *Why did they cut you off?* In doing so, they had also cut Jack off, too.

"I can't tell you," his father had replied, then broke into heaving sobs. "I wanted to, all along. But I was sworn to keep quiet. I wish I could tell you the whole story, but I can't." He lifted his head, wiped the tears from his eyes and banged on his paralyzed legs. "It's because of these! All because of these!"

But that made no sense to Jack. His father was a war hero. He'd lost the use of his legs after crashing his fighter plane during World War I. Jack knew that part of the story was true. He'd seen old pictures of his father, dressed in full fighter pilot's gear, standing in front of his plane, a *Sopwith Camel*. He'd seen the medals, including the Purple Heart and read the commendations from the War Department.

How could a war injury be at the root of all these lies? And who had imprisoned his father's soul this way, had bound him up to a lifetime of deception and betrayal? Was it Jack's mother? His father insisted it was not. Although he did admit that, though she had not died during childbirth, he had solid reasons to believe she had died at some point during Jack's childhood. Did he think this revelation would help?

Now all Jack could think about was how many wasted years had passed, years he could have been with his mother before she did pass away. And how could his father imagine that anything would ever justify denying a young boy the opportunity to know and experience his mother's love?

And what of his twin? Did he even know Jack was alive,

that he had a twin brother living in the United States? How could his father deny his brother the chance to get to know him…his own father? Except for this glaring, horrific betrayal, Jack had always enjoyed his father's company. Through all the innocence and ignorance of Jack's childhood years, even throughout the awkward teen years, his father had been a constant source of encouragement and support to Jack. And yet, his twin brother had been denied the chance to ever share a single one of these moments.

It just didn't make any sense.

A sudden jolt, down then up, jarred Jack out of his thoughts.

"Whoa," Joe said. "My butt felt that one." They were sitting across from each other in the last spot toward the back. "A shame these things don't have windows. Here we are riding through the English countryside for the first time, and I can't see a thing. Except for where we've been." He pointed toward the roadway behind them.

The truck could easily hold ten to fifteen soldiers but today, it was just carrying the six of them. They had spread out across the wooden bench. Seth was sound asleep, stretched out on the floor. Well, he was until they'd hit that pothole a moment ago.

"Say Jack, you haven't said a word since we got in this truck," Joe said. "What are you chewing on in that old noggin of yours? We're living the dream, Pal, right? We talked about doing this a few weeks ago and, look, we're doing it. We're in England. Probably a few days away from hopping in the cockpit of one of the fastest fighter planes known to man. And you got a look on your face like you just been given a pink slip."

Jack looked up into Joe's bright, smiling face. How could he not smile back, at least a little?

"C'mon, Bud. Live in the moment. Not in the head." He pointed to his own head as he said this.

"Okay, you got me," Jack said. "I'll try and snap out of it."

"Snap out of what? You been kinda off this whole trip. On the boat, I figured you were just feeling a bit seasick like the rest of us. But we're on land now and everything's going our way, and you're still all…I don't know, moody. Something eating you? Something you haven't told your oldest and dearest Pal?"

Jack didn't know how to respond. This was the first time Joe had actually inquired about Jack's well-being. And apparently, he had begun to detect something was up even when they were on the ship. This was progress. He wanted to encourage this kind of effort, but did he really want to let Joe in on all this? "To be honest, Joe, something is going on. Something kind of big actually."

"Yeah? Big, eh? How big? What kind of big?"

See, now Jack just wanted to drop the whole thing. How could he possibly come up with a short version of this story? A short version was most definitely all Joe could absorb. "I learned a pretty big family secret a couple of weeks ago. From my dad. And to be honest, what he told me is the real reason I brought up the idea of the two of us taking this trip to England in the first place."

Joe's expression might have been just the same had Jack just hit his friend in the head with a bat.

"No kiddin'?" Joe said. "We're not here to fly Spitfires?"

Jack actually laughed. Being with Joe was good medicine sometimes.

OVER THE NEXT thirty minutes—broken up by Joe occasionally pointing out interesting sites from the back of the truck—Jack shared as much of his family secrets as he dared. He wasn't concerned about Joe's inability to comprehend the situation. Joe had a nasty habit of forgetting that things shared in confidence should not be blurted out after a few beers with friends.

In reality, Joe had done a passable job listening to Jack unburden his soul. He'd even asked a few decent follow-up questions. One in particular, helped Jack uncover one missing piece of information that might help him in his search for his brother. Joe had helped Jack see that his British side of the family was probably wealthy and possibly—as Joe put it—*a bit on the hoity-toity side.*

Meaning, they were upper class. Maybe even part of the British aristocracy. Joe had pointed out that *"people don't make big secrets unless they got big things to hide, unless they got a lot to lose if their big secret ever got found out. Who has the most to lose over here in England if big secrets get found out, if not the hoity-toity types?"*

14

FOR TWO HOURS or so, the truck continued rolling along on what seemed like the same country road they had been driving on since they'd left London. They'd ridden through or had seen signs pointing to a number of villages, but no big towns. Places like Camberley, Basingstoke and Andover. Nothing that Jack had ever heard of before.

The further they drove out into the country, the more nervous the other guys became. Most of them slid down the bench seat toward the back opening.

"Where is this place they're taking us?" Seth said. "We are way out in the boonies."

"I was thinking we'd be trained right outside London," Ozzie said. "At least we'd have some kind of decent nightlife for our time off. I haven't seen anything that even remotely looks like a modern town for the last hour. Am I wrong?" He was asking Jack and Joe who had been sitting in the back all along.

Jack shook his head no. Of course, he hadn't been paying that much attention, nor did he care much about his nightlife.

"Nope," Joe said. "Seth said it right. We're heading deeper and deeper into the boonies. I've only seen one or two pubs so far. And they looked half the size of that one we went to in

Southampton."

"Anyone know how much further we gotta go to get to our place?" Seth said. "What's it called? Middle Gallup?"

"Middle Wallop," Jack said. "Like, *that guy packs a wallop.*"

"What kind of a name is that? Is it a place known for fighting?"

"I have no idea," Jack said. "But I don't think so. Maybe when we get situated, we can ask one of the locals."

"Anyway," Seth said. "How much further till we get there?"

Jack looked at his watch. "Based on what Group Captain West said back in London, I'm thinking we could be there in the next ten, fifteen minutes."

"Hope so," Ozzie said. "I've got almost no butt left."

No one said too much of anything for the next fifteen minutes. The truck came to a sudden stop, causing everyone to bang into each other and tossing Seth on the floor. It made a slow turn to the left and that's when everyone heard, for the first time, a fairly familiar sound.

Airplane engines revving up. And they weren't far away.

"I think this is it, Gents," Ozzie said. "I think we're at Middle Wallop, or whatever this thing is called."

Joe held on to the tailgate with one hand and the canvas top with the other. "Jack, grab hold of my belt." He leaned far enough out to swing around and catch a glimpse of the view ahead. "Yep, definitely an airbase. Can't see the hangers from here, but there's the guardhouse and gate right up ahead. And beyond that a bunch of ugly buildings. Probably barracks. I also see some planes taking off, way off to the south. Not sure what they are. Definitely not Spitfires or Hurricanes."

"Well, we gotta be flying either Hurricanes or Spitfires,"

Seth said. "Those are their two best fighters, right?"

"Yeah," Ozzie said. "But they're not gonna let us train on their top-of-the-line planes. What are you guys, idiots? That Captain West even said as much in our interview." He slid back on the bench, away from the opening. "Just sit tight. Once they check us out, I'm sure we'll be flying the good stuff."

Jack listened to the back-and-forth banter and, it dawned on him—he wasn't having any of these kinds of thoughts. All his idle concentration went to things related to his mission. Like trying to figure out exactly how far this base was from London and what modes of transportation he'd be able to use to get back and forth. It was already a foregone conclusion. That's where he'd be spending all his leave time. In London, searching out leads that might lead to the true identity and whereabouts of his brother.

A few moments later, the truck stopped at the guardhouse. They heard the guard and driver chatting in equally strong British accents. The guard seemed to know and expect the truck's arrival. He asked for some paperwork. They talked some more, and he waved them through, after giving the driver directions about which building he should go to drop off the Americans.

As they passed through the gate, they all looked at the guard. He stood there looking at them like they were zoo animals. Joe gave him a wave. The guard did not respond. They drove for another minute then the truck pulled off to the left and stopped. The front door opened. As the driver walked toward the back he yelled, "Okay, Yanks. End of the line," and banged on the side of the truck. "Everybody out." He lowered the tailgate and everyone jumped out.

"Well, there they are." Seth pointed toward the south at two huge airplane hangars, now in view. A mid-sized, two-engine plane flew overhead. "Wonder what that is."

"That, Gentlemen, is one of our Airspeed Oxfords," came a booming British voice with a more refined accent. "And if you are very good, we might let you fly one of those someday."

Everyone turned to see a British officer walking in their direction, accompanied by a shorter, stockier soldier, dressed slightly different. It appears the truck had dropped them off at some kind of headquarters building.

"Why would I want to fly that crate?" Joe whispered to Jack.

"Okay," the officer said. "Everyone line up, just there along the edge of the road. Let me get a look at you."

The guys obeyed. Jack realized, he'd better start getting used to being told what to do from now on. That's what he'd signed up for, the cost of getting the British to fund his personal agenda.

"Well then," the officer said. "We'll have to teach you boys a thing or two about posture. I am Group Captain Reginald Gibson. This is Flight Sergeant Willie Peters. I know you've all been sworn in, so you're officially subjects of the British Empire. And apparently, others who outrank me have decided to let you become a part of the RAF. I've had a look at your paperwork. I understand you all are pilots and, supposedly, you've had a sufficient amount of flying experience to be allowed to jump in at this stage of the game, and skip our Elementary Flight Training. We'll see about that tomorrow. For now, Flight Sergeant Peters is going to find out whether you pass muster on an equally important matter. Physical Fitness."

A collective groan released from the Americans.

"I'm sure you've heard on the radio or read in the papers," Captain Gibson continued, "things are going pretty badly for us across the Channel. That may be. And it may also be likely that a major air war will soon be raging above our skies, especially here in southern England." He walked slowly back and forth in front of them. "We'll need every skilled pilot we can get. Emphasis on the word *skill*. But it is also essential that these pilots be in tip-top physical condition. Once the air war starts, you can expect to be sent out on missions possibly two or three times a day. Sergeant Peters here is going to help me decide whether or not I should even allow any of you Yanks to be checked out in one of our planes. I have ordered the lorry driver to remain here a little while longer before returning to London. Over the next hour, Sergeant Peters will be putting you through a barrage of physical training exercises. If you pass, we'll get you set up here at this base, give you the proper uniforms and assign you a place in the officer's quarters. If you fail, you'll be getting right back on that lorry and be driven back to London."

"What'll happen then?" Joe asked.

Jack had no idea why Joe asked these kinds of questions. He was in phenomenal shape.

"You'll be reassigned to another base whose training regimen will be centered more on physical conditioning. I think you Yanks call this kind of training boot camp."

"After that," Joe said, "do we get to come back here?"

Joe, what are you doing?

"Perhaps," Captain Gibson said. "What's your name, young man?"

"Joe, Joe Bassett."

"Well, Mr. Bassett. Sounds like you've already determined you're not up for these physical exercises. Perhaps you want to hop back into the lorry right now?"

Everyone laughed, except Joe. And Jack.

"No," Joe said. "I'm just asking. I'm the curious type."

"I'm the curious type, SIR!" the Flight Sergeant yelled, right in Joe's face.

"Sorry. I'm the curious type, *sir*."

"Well, we'll soon see if that's your only problem," Captain Gibson said. "Flight Sergeant Peters? They're all yours. Do with them whatever you want."

"Yes, sir." Peters saluted. The captain returned the salute and headed back toward the headquarters building.

"Right Yanks," Peters yelled. He backed several paces into the grassy area. "Line up in front of me. Give yourself plenty of room. Let's see what you're made of."

15

May 22nd, 6PM
London, England

WHAT A BIZARRE new world Renée had stepped into.
She stood alone in what could only be described as a luxury suite in downtown London, in front of a bay window that looked out across the river Thames. A beautiful view. This day was ending so radically different compared to how it had begun.

Even compared to how things had been just a short while ago.

SHE HAD SPENT half an hour flying through the clouds across the English Channel on a noisy plane, praying all the while that no Luftwaffe plane would find them. She'd breathed an audible sigh of relief when they'd finally dropped out of the clouds and saw the white cliffs of Dover up ahead.

Once over land, the bumpiness and turbulence had mercifully subsided. Elliot had said they still had a way to go. They were aiming for an airfield just north of London, called Hendon. For reasons he didn't explain, the pilot had flown around the western rim of town. She had hoped to be able to see London from the air.

Elliot had said not to worry. She would soon get her fill of London. He had picked The Savoy, a hotel in the very heart of town, because of its proximity to where he would be reporting for duty each day. She still didn't know what Elliot did in the military. Only that he was a major and that it had something to do with intelligence. But she had no idea what that meant.

Shortly after they'd landed at Hendon, they were met by a junior officer who seemed to be expecting them. Well, he'd been expecting Elliot. He seemed surprised when Elliot said she'd be coming with him. The officer had carried their things across the field and led them to a small office building. Once there, Elliot asked her to wait outside for a moment while he went in to secure an auto.

Ten minutes later, they were driving down the road toward London. The traffic wasn't bad until they got into town. She was fascinated by everything out the window. London was so different from Paris. So many things she wanted to see. But Elliot seemed distracted and drove like a man in a hurry.

He'd finally admitted why. At the airfield, he'd spoken on the phone with his commanding officer who, for some reason, had expected Elliot to arrive several hours ago. Now he had just enough time to get her checked in at the hotel and drive to wherever he and his CO were supposed to meet.

He'd apologized profusely. This wasn't the way he'd intended their first evening in London to unfold. After tipping the steward at The Savoy with instructions to take very good care of her, he'd left her standing there in this magnificent lobby promising to return and take her to dinner two hours from now.

The moment Elliot left her standing there in this majestic, high-class hotel, Renée felt terribly self-conscious. Her family was not wealthy, not anymore. They had been once, years ago when she was a little girl. Something had happened, something she didn't understand, and their fortunes had been dramatically and instantly reduced. The changes that followed didn't matter much to her, but they ruined her father. His health had immediately begun to deteriorate.

A few years later, he was dead.

"Madam?"

Renée looked up.

"Please, follow me." The hotel steward led her toward the elevator, carrying her one small bag. "Are these…all your things, Madam?"

"Yes."

She did own a few dresses that might make the grade in a place such as this, garments that used to belong to her mother. The two of them had made several alterations, attempting to modernize them and make them fit on Renée's smaller frame. But those dresses now hung in her wardrobe back in France.

After ascending the elevator to the sixth floor, they walked about halfway down a long hallway. When the steward had unlocked the door to her room, she stepped into this amazing suite. Once again, she felt so entirely out of place. He carried her lone bag into the separate bedroom, set the bag on the bed and opened the doors to a huge wardrobe. "Would you like me to hang up your things, Madam?"

"No, thank you." She'd be horrified to have him even open her bag.

She followed him back out into the main room and

watched him pull back the curtains, revealing this majestic view of the city. He walked back toward the front door and stood, as if at attention. A horrifying realization sunk in…he was expecting a tip.

She had no money. Not even a cent.

An awkward moment passed between them. She didn't know what to say. Finally, "Thank you so much for your help." Said more like a question. He seemed to get the message and promptly left, looking only slightly annoyed.

She walked back into the bedroom and opened her bag. It took all of three minutes to put away every stitch of clothing she had left in the world. Besides the handful of things in one drawer, hanging in the cavernous wardrobe were two blouses and a skirt. Combined with what she wore, she could patch together three outfits in total.

None of them up to par with the clothes likely worn by the staff of this hotel.

ELLIOT SAT AT his desk in a nondescript building on the fourth floor of 64 Baker Street, nervously rearranging some paperwork and file folders. He'd rushed over here after hurriedly dropping Renée off at The Savoy, thinking his commanding officer, or CO, had been waiting to see him for hours.

He'd arrived to find his CO's door closed. His adjutant said the Lieutenant Colonel was in a meeting and could not be disturbed. But he did want to see Elliot and left instructions for him to wait in his office. He didn't think it'd be much longer.

That was over an hour ago.

Elliot leaned back on his uncomfortable wooden chair and glanced around at his office space. Really, it was a waste that he even kept a desk in this building. This was the first time he'd been to it in several months. Before that, he'd barely spent a few hours a week in here.

His phone buzzed. He picked it up.

"Lieutenant Colonel Browning is ready to see you, Sir."

"I'll be right up."

Elliot made his way down the hall and up the stairs, preferring not to wait for the much-too-slow elevator. He walked down a longer hallway, back into the Lieutenant Colonel's office and was directed by the adjutant to go right in.

Lieutenant Colonel Browning looked up from his desk when Elliot approached. Elliot stood at attention and saluted. Browning returned the salute and said, "At ease, Major. Please, have a seat." His expression was serious, but not angry or annoyed.

Perhaps whatever business that had bumped Elliot out of the way had sufficiently distracted Browning, so that he'd forgotten about Elliot getting back to London late. At some point, Elliot would have to inform his CO about Renée, but certainly didn't want to have to talk about her now.

Browning made a few notes on a paper sitting in front of him, then set it aside and gave Elliot his undivided attention. "Well Major, it would appear that everything is falling apart in France. Would you concur?"

"I'm afraid so, Sir. Nothing there is going according to plan."

"Then I guess it's fair to say you weren't able to make the kind of connections in your assigned area that might benefit us later on?"

"No, sir. It's fair to say my mission was a complete failure.

Virtually every French leader I had identified and began to develop in my zone fled for southern France in the past few days. I lost touch with every single one. In their defense, sir, these men didn't have any decent weapons to defend themselves. They were up against Panzer tanks and Stuka dive bombers. A few said they would try to come back if the situation ever stabilized."

Browning sighed.

That had been the bulk of Elliot's mission. British intelligence had anticipated the possibility the northeastern area of France might fall into German hands someday. Elliot was sent there to develop relationships with potential leaders who could serve as a future resistance movement. Of course, no one had imagined the Nazis would steamroll over the Allied defenses in a matter of weeks. Elliot assumed he had months to accomplish this task, at the very least.

"Well, needless to say, your time there has come to an end. I've learned we're not just pulling out of northern France, but everywhere. All our planes will be returning home in the next day or two."

Elliot was relieved to hear this. "And what about the troops? The infantry and equipment?"

"The equipment, as you can imagine, will be lost. All of it. But plans have been approved and are underway to try and evacuate the men. It's a monumental effort."

"Where? At Dunkirk, Calais?"

"Dunkirk. But enough of this. I called you back now to get you started on your next assignment."

"Where will that be?" Please let it be here, he thought.

"For the next few months, Major, you will be staying here.

Not always in London but various locations in southern England. Just before you came, I was informed by Colonel Masterson that our operation is about to be dramatically expanded, in anticipation of a Nazi invasion."

Even though Elliot suspected this, hearing it said aloud by his CO made him shudder.

"Over the next month or so, assuming we have that much time, we will be combining with other intelligence agencies to form one unified branch. I'm not sure what it will be called, or who will be leading yet. But our outfit will definitely be involved."

"How can I be of service, Sir?"

"I don't have any of the details worked out yet. But the general idea is to have you doing the same kind of work you were attempting to do in France. But to do it here, working with selected, elite individuals in the Home Guard."

"Excuse me, sir. The Home Guard?"

"That's what we'll shortly be calling this massive mob of volunteers you see parading all about in uniforms. The old men and young boys? You'll hear Churchill make the name change on the radio soon."

"But sir, if I'm doing the same kind of work I was doing in France—organizing a resistance movement—do I take it to mean we're anticipating not merely a Nazi invasion, but that they will succeed? That England will be conquered?"

The Lieutenant Colonel looked straight at Elliot but did not immediately reply. Finally, he said, "You know how it is, Major. The job of this outfit is to prepare for every contingency."

16

THIRTY MORE MINUTES passed, when Renée was startled by the telephone ringing in her room. She hadn't even noticed it before, nor had she ever been in a hotel that offered one in your room. She hurried over to answer it, assuming it must be Elliot. "Hello?"

"Is that you, Renée?"

"Yes, Elliot. It's me."

"I'm finished with my business. I was just getting ready to drive over and pick you up for dinner. Thought I'd give you a little warning, to give you time to get ready."

Renée sighed. Get ready? She had done everything she could to be ready for his return. She'd finally given up.

"What's the matter?"

She felt a wave of emotion rising and tried to suppress it. "Oh Elliot, I can't go out to dinner with you."

"Are you tired? I should have asked. Of course, you are. That's okay. There are some wonderful restaurants right there at the hotel. We could just—"

"I can't go there, either."

"Why? What's the matter?"

"You always look so nice in your uniform. But, I have nothing to wear. You saw, I only brought the one bag. You said we must pack light. I have no dresses. Nothing I could wear in a place like this, or in any restaurant nearby. The people who work here have finer clothes than me. Maybe if you took me down to the docks or the warehouses. We could find some place to eat there." She heard him laugh on the other end. But she was only half-joking.

"I'm so sorry, Renée. I didn't even think about any of this. I was only trying to make your first days here in London comfortable. And here I have put you in a hotel that makes you feel just the opposite." He paused a moment. "I have an idea. The Savoy offers room service. You can order it right there using the phone. How about I start driving over, and you order us some food. Hopefully, it will be arriving there at the same time as me, and we can eat right there in your room? Just for this evening, so you don't have to go out? Then I will leave you, so that you can get some rest. And tomorrow morning, we'll see about getting you some new clothes. How does that sound?"

"That sounds very nice. But I don't want you to go to any trouble or expense. I don't have to stay in a place like this. You know I'd—"

"It's no trouble at all. A woman needs more than the clothes she can squeeze into one suitcase. And The Savoy is perfect for now. Very close to where I'll be working."

Renée suddenly remembered an important detail. "Elliot, there is another problem. A smaller one."

"What is it?"

"I'm sure it's customary here to tip the people who serve you, isn't it?"

"Yes."

"I have no money. None at all. I felt awful after the steward escorted me to my room. I had nothing to give him."

"And you'll have nothing to give whoever delivers the food? I understand. Then you just sit there and relax for about twenty minutes. When I get to the hotel lobby, I will order the food myself. That way I'm sure to be there when it arrives."

"That would be very nice. Thank you."

"Is there anything you'd especially like to eat? I haven't seen the hotel menu, but I'm sure—"

"Would they have fish and chips? I've always wanted to try that."

"Hmmm. They might. If they don't, we'll be sure to get some tomorrow when we're out shopping."

THERE WAS A KNOCK at her hotel door. She walked over and looked through the little hole just to make sure. It was Elliot. "I was hoping it was you." She noticed he carried two brown paper bags and smelled food as he walked by.

He walked straight over to a coffee table in front of the couch and set the bags down. "I learned that the restaurant doesn't serve fish and chips, but the concierge told me about a little place that did just a block away. He called and they were still open. So, you get your wish. Fish and chips."

"That was nice of you. I hope I like it after you've gone to so much trouble."

"Very little trouble, really." He sat on the edge of the sofa. "Come sit next to me. You have to eat this a certain way, because of how it's packaged."

As she came over to join him, he pulled some of the food

out of the bag. It looked like a big piece of newspaper wrapped in the shape of a cone. Pieces of fried fish and chips stuck out the top. "Why is it wrapped in newspaper?" He handed the cone to her and took his out of the other bag.

"I'm not exactly sure. But I know, because it is, I was never allowed to eat it as a child. My nanny always said it was too dirty."

It didn't look like the most sanitary way to handle food, but it smelled wonderful. So, he had a nanny. That was something. Was she the one who'd raised him? Did his mother? He had never mentioned either one before this.

"But whenever I was away from home and got the chance, I would buy it. Hope you like it." He was just about to take a bite of fish.

"I hope you don't mind, Elliot. But in my family we always say a quick prayer of thanks before eating."

"Oh, that's fine. Go right ahead."

"I can pray quietly."

"Whatever you prefer."

It seemed clear that this wasn't his custom, so she just said a quick, silent prayer of thanks. "While I'm thanking God, I want to thank you, too. This is such a special treat."

"You're very welcome."

Neither of them spoke for the next several minutes. Renée was the first, after finishing off her first full piece of fish. "This is so good. I can hardly taste the newspaper ink at all."

"Can you taste it, even a little?"

She laughed. "I'm kidding. It's delicious."

"Try the chips. I think you're supposed eat them together."

They both continued eating with very little conversation.

Renée ate quite a few chips and another piece of fish but then got full. "Feel free to eat the rest of mine. I'm totally full."

"Are you sure?"

She nodded.

"I might just do that. I don't know why I'm so hungry."

She thought back to their day and realized something. "We never ate any lunch."

"That's right," he said. "What a time that was. I'm so glad we didn't see any German planes on our way home."

She thought it funny, hearing him say the word *home*. She was in a totally strange place but, here, everything felt familiar and comfortable to him. Even this meal. She wiped her lips with the cloth napkin. "You mentioned earlier that your nanny never let you eat this kind of food before. Was she the woman who raised you? We've never talked much about your family."

Elliot finished chewing a piece of fish. "There's not very much to tell I'm afraid. As a young child, I was raised by my mother. I had a nanny, but my mother preferred to do most of the motherly tasks. The nanny would just look after me when my mother had things to do. But she died when I was nine. After that, another nanny took over and looked after me until I went off to boarding school."

"I'm so sorry to hear about your mother. That must've been a terrible time for you."

"It was the worst."

"And what about your father?"

"My father? Unfortunately, I never knew him. He was a pilot in the Great War and died when his plane was shot down. My mother said he was an ace. That means he shot down more than five enemy planes." The expression on his face changed, like he was suddenly deep in thought.

"What is it?"

"Nothing," he said. "I was just thinking about how differently my life would have gone had my father lived. You see, he was an American. A commoner, my grandfather would say. Not a proper gentleman, not part of British aristocracy."

"I take it your grandfather did not approve of him?"

"That would be putting it mildly." He wiped his mouth then his hands with the napkin. "My grandfather never speaks of him and never allowed me to speak about him after my mother died. But I do remember the way she spoke of him, never in Grandfather's presence, mind you. But it was very clear to me they had loved each other very much." He looked into Renée's eyes. "I've wondered sometimes…had my father not died, if he might have taken us away to America, away from my grandfather. I've wondered if that might be a second reason Grandfather resented him."

It sounded like Elliot was mistaken. There was much to say about his family. Compared to her own, it sounded very complex. And painful. "Are you and your grandfather close? Or has all this put something of a wall between you?"

Elliot sighed. "Close? I don't think my grandfather has ever been close to anyone. I'm not sure there's a wall between us, but we don't see eye to eye on a great many things."

17

EVERY ONE OF the six American pilots had made it through the entire hour of physical testing without a hitch. Including Joe. After, Joe had said to the flight sergeant, "We can go longer if you'd like."

"That'll be enough, Yank," the sergeant replied.

Then they were brought to a building to get their uniforms and other necessary items, like toiletries. The guys talked about how new everything seemed: the buildings, the furniture, even the streets seemed freshly paved. They learned it wasn't only how things seemed; everything *was* new. The entire base had just recently been constructed and turned over to the military less than two months ago.

Next, they were brought to their barracks building, a two-story affair that, although brand new, had been built devoid of any creativity or design. One of the guys said it looked like a bunch of shoeboxes stuck together. "And what's with the paint job?" Joe asked the sergeant. "Looks like big jigsaw puzzle pieces painted on the walls."

The flight sergeant said it was somebody's idea of camouflage.

"Camouflage?" Joe said. "You're kidding, right? Do they

really think this paint job is gonna make these buildings invisible from up there?" He pointed to the sky.

Jack could tell by the look on the sergeant's face, he didn't think much of it, either.

"You don't 'ave to like it," he'd said. "You just gotta live in it. I'll show you your rooms. You can get cleaned up. Change into your uniforms and 'ead across the way to that building." He pointed to a smaller building across a large paved area, painted the same way. "That's the officers' mess. Dinner's in an hour. You miss it, you don't eat the rest of the night."

"When are we going to get to see the planes?" Seth said. "After dinner?"

"After you eat, I'll take you over to the hangars," the flight sergeant said. "But you won't be doing any flying tonight. They'll be testing your flying skills first thing in the morning. That's my understanding. Follow me."

He led them through the front door of the barracks. Jack didn't see any other people in the building. The flight sergeant confirmed, for now, they had the barracks building to themselves. A lot more people were scheduled to arrive over the next few weeks. Most of them foreigners, from all over Europe: Poland, Czechoslovakia, Belgium, Holland and France. Men who had gotten out before the Nazi's took over.

"So, this is going to be a base full of mutts," Joe said. "I wonder if any of these guys even speak English."

Their quarters were not assigned, so Jack and Joe were able to bunk together. The rooms were very basic. A bunk on each side. Small desk in the middle beneath a tall window. A plain chest of drawers for each man near the foot of the bed. Joe quickly laid on his bunk, put his hands under his head. "Yep, this'll do just fine."

Jack didn't dare lie down, or he'd fall fast asleep. "I'm going to find the showers."

After getting cleaned up and putting on their new blue uniforms for the first time, the men walked together toward the mess hall. There were a handful of other officers already eating. They took note of the Americans' arrival but pretty much kept to themselves.

As promised, the flight sergeant arrived just as they finished up their meal. Outside, a lorry waited on the curb, similar to the one that had brought them from London except it was uncovered. He drove them around and showed them a few of the other buildings on this side of the base, explained their purpose, then spun the truck around and headed for the airplane hangars at the other end.

There were five of them, each of a similar massive size. Parked inside and outside they saw a variety of planes all painted in typical RAF colors. Mostly Airspeed Oxfords and Blenheims, both mid-sized two-engine planes. And only one type of single-engine plane that resembled a Spitfire, but wasn't nearly as sleek and attractive.

"What is that?" Ozzie asked.

"Looks kind of like a Spit," Joe said. "Like maybe it's ugly stepsister."

"That, gentlemen, is called the Miles Master," the flight sergeant said. "It's a two-seater trainer. Something to get you ready to fly the 'urricane and the Spitfire. She ain't pretty, but you'll be surprised by 'er power. That's what you'll be flying in the morning."

After it was obvious the tour was over and the truck was

heading back toward the barracks, Seth said, "We didn't even see a single Hurricane or Spitfire. What's the deal?"

"That's because there aren't any 'ere. Not yet anyway. As you can see by the size of those 'angars, this was supposed to be a bomber base. Because of what's happening in France, all that's changed. That's why they sent you blokes 'ere. We need to fly fighters out of 'ere, and that right quick. We're supposed to be getting a couple squadrons of 'urricanes any day. Thought they might show up today. Maybe tomorrow then. They'll put you through your paces in the Miles. Used to be, they'd train you in those for several weeks. You prove yourselves worthy, and you'll be flying those 'urricanes in a few days, I expect."

"What about the Spitfires?" Joe said.

"I'm sure we'll be getting some of them too. Exactly when I can't say." When he got to their barracks building, he stopped at the curb to let them out. "That's it for now, Yanks. Guess you have the rest of the evening to yourselves."

"Is there anything to do in…Middle Wallop?" Seth asked.

"That's right," the flight sergeant said, "you folks came in from London. You haven't driven through town yet. Well, it's not exactly a town then, is it? More like a village. You can see about checking out a staff car, if any are left. There's a nice pub not far in Monxton, called The Black Swan. Just head back the way you came in, take the first left heading north. Maybe ten, fifteen minutes and you're there."

"Is that it?" Ozzie said. "One pub fifteen minutes away?"

"Afraid so," said the flight sergeant. "But what'd you expect? They didn't send you out here to 'ave fun. Your 'ere to fly them planes, shoot down the bloody Nazis."

The men all piled out of the back of the lorry. All of them, except Jack, were eager to explore the area around the base, then head up to Monxton and find this pub. Jack said he was too tired and wanted to turn in early.

Which was true. But it was also true that he wanted to spend at least some time alone at the desk in his new quarters making a list of possible things he could do to narrow down the search to find his brother. So, he sent them on and headed inside the barracks.

He had just gotten himself situated at the desk with a pen and pad of paper when he heard a knock at the door. Who could it be? "Come in." It was Joe. "You don't need to knock, Joe. It's your room, too."

"I know. But I could tell, you weren't just tired. Thought I might find you doing something like this."

"Something like what? I'm just jotting down a few thoughts to get them out of my head."

"So they don't show up in your dreams?"

"Something like that."

"Well, a couple of the guys had to take a leak, so I thought I'd make one last pitch for you to join us."

"I'm okay. You go on, have some fun."

"Jack…"

"What?"

"It's this thing you told me about earlier, isn't it? The family secret, about this brother you never met. It's eatin' at you. I can tell. But you need to find a way to let it go. At least lighten your grip on it a little. Something that big can find a way of taking over. And that won't be good. It's not safe." Joe stepped all the way inside.

Jack turned around to face him. "It's not taking over. That's why I wanna write these things down. I told you, to get 'em out of my head. And what do you mean it's not safe? What does safety have to do with it?"

"Uh…tomorrow? Flying this new plane? You heard the sergeant. They're gonna put us through the paces. That means see what we've got, what we can do in the air. They'll probably have us doing all kinds of maneuvers, the kind that requires two-hundred percent concentration. You know what can happen, you get distracted. You're in the middle of a tricky move, all it takes is losing focus a few seconds, and—BAM—that's all she wrote."

"That's not gonna—"

"Don't tell me it's not gonna happen. You forget who you're talkin' to. Remember that air show in Iowa? What was that, just over a year ago? You got all hung up on that girl, and then she dumped you, and you got all bent out of shape over it? The next day we're coming at each other full speed doing those barrel rolls, and you missed your cue. I had to dive straight down to avoid smacking right into you. Barely had any time to pull up before I hit the ground." He was yelling now. "Don't tell me you don't get distracted."

Jack sighed. He had a point. And if for no other reason than to reward Joe for making all this effort on his behalf, Jack set the pen down on the pad and stood. "All right. You win. Let's go."

18

THE NEXT MORNING, the Americans were awakened at 6AM, told to get dressed, have breakfast, and the lorry would be waiting for them outside the mess hall to take them to Hangar three.

Once there, they observed three of these single-engine planes, called the Miles Master, lined up wingtip to wingtip just outside. A new officer they hadn't seen before was there to greet them. He introduced himself as Flight Lieutenant Benjamin Henderson. He was there to both familiarize them all with the Miles Master then would serve as their chief flight instructor, the one who would qualify them to graduate to the Hurricane or Spitfire.

"I read all the information you provided about your flying experience up until this point," Henderson said. "If any of you have exaggerated or embellished your abilities, now would be the time to speak up. As you've all heard, we expect a major air war to take place over the southern skies of England very soon. It is only this that forces us to allow you gentlemen to skip the two to three months of training we'd normally put you through. Once you step inside the cockpit of this plane, we will assume you are capable of doing everything you've said on these forms. If that is not the case, please see me before we go any further."

He paused and looked at each man separately. No one spoke up or even moved. Jack involuntarily glanced at Seth, who seemed unfazed by what was said.

"All right then, let's proceed." From there, the lieutenant explained the various procedures involved in starting, taxiing and flying this particular plane, as well as some of the customary terms and phrases pilots in the RAF used to communicate with each other and the control tower during flight.

Ozzie noticed there were gun barrels on the edges of the wings and asked about them.

"They are there strictly for target practice," Officer Henderson said. "There is no live ammo loaded on the planes today, but that will be part of your training soon." He walked toward the planes. "Right, follow me. We only have three planes ready this morning and there are six of you. I and the other two flight instructors will sit in the back of each plane. Three of you will go first, the other three in the second round. Each check-flight will last approximately twenty minutes. Split up into teams of two and choose among yourselves who will go first. It doesn't matter to me. You will all be tested exactly the same."

The group had already gotten used to Jack and Joe's friendship, so no one was surprised when they paired up. Joe said he'd be happy to go first and Jack let him. Seth and Ozzie joined Joe to make up the first three. Soon the American pilots had donned their fighter gear, including a helmet and goggles and a parachute that hung down past their rear ends. It served as a seat cushion during the flight. Henderson showed them all how to mount up and, minutes later, they were strapped in. He sat in the back of Joe's cockpit. Jack and the other two men backed up toward the hangar.

One by one, the plane engines turned on and revved up. Jack was shocked by how loud they were, easily twice the volume of a Jenny. His adrenaline instantly kicked in. All his anxieties and preoccupations disappeared. He was now officially excited and couldn't wait for his turn to fly this plane. The flight instructors yelled instructions to the pilots, but he couldn't hear what they said. Soon the planes taxied away from the hangar and moved in single file onto the grass runway.

They stood on the edge of the paved area watching as the planes traveled to the far end. One of the Americans walked back into the hangar and found a stack of wooden deck chairs. "Hey guys, grab one of these."

For the next twenty-five minutes, Jack and the two other Americans sat back in the chairs and took in the show. It all seemed pretty basic to him, other than the obvious difference in the airplanes' speed and power. It was almost shocking to see how much speed the planes gained when they dived and then, coming out of it, how quickly and how high they could climb. They zoomed way past the point his old Jenny would have stalled, and just kept rising.

The instructors were definitely taking them "through the paces." But again, all of them basic maneuvers. In addition to the dive and climb, they did flat and rolling scissors, loops and barrel roles, breaking turns in both directions around a specific point on the ground. Then they rose high into a forced stall then down in a controlled spin and came out of the spin with plenty of altitude to spare. With a few variations, all the guys handled everything reasonably well.

Apparently, no one had exaggerated their abilities.

A few minutes later, the planes lined up behind each other in the air and circled the airfield once in a rectangular pattern. As they came around again, Jack saw the landing gear released and the flaps let down. Each plane descended onto the center of the grassy field, bounced a few times then slowed to a crawl. When they reached the end of the field, they taxied back toward the hangar.

"Guess it's our turn, Boys," Jack said and stood.

DURING AN EXHILARATING thirty minutes, Jack repeated the same aerial maneuvers he'd seen Joe, Ozzie and Seth do, then led the trio of planes back down to the airfield. Before his flight, when Joe and Jack had exchanged gear, Joe was all smiles and said Jack was about to have the time of his life. Jack did. Flight Lieutenant Henderson sat behind Jack the entire time and said little, other than calling out tasks from his checklist for Jack to execute.

As Jack taxied through the final turn, taking the plane from the grassy field onto the tarmac, he headed for the hangar where Joe, Ozzie and Seth now stood. He was pretty sure he'd passed the lieutenant's exam and was just about to ask how he did when Henderson said curtly, "That was quite impressive, Pilot Officer Turner."

"Thank you, Sir. Want me to return the plane to the same spot we began?"

"Please."

Jack did as ordered. The other two Americans followed right behind him. After the three men and instructors were all standing on the tarmac, Joe, Ozzie and Seth joined them. Jack wondered what came next.

Flight Lieutenant Henderson motioned for the other two flight instructors to join him several yards away. He said several things to them, the others nodded in agreement. They walked back to the group and asked the Americans to form a semicircle around him. "Gentlemen, I'm happy to report that every single one of you passed the exam. My colleagues and I have conferred and we feel confident enough to proceed to the second level of testing, which is allowing each of you to fly the same plane and do the exact same maneuvers, but as a solo flight."

The Americans cheered. Clearly, no one was afraid to do this.

"I'm glad you are all so eager, but this is no time for bravado, gentlemen. If any one of you has any hesitation to do this, please speak up now. It will not be looked down upon or be cast as a strike against you. We will simply ask you to wait until the others have done their solo flights, and allow you to go up once more with an instructor. There is no shame in this. The stakes are too high, both in terms of your safety and the value of our airplane, to let your pride get in the way." He stopped for a moment and looked at each of the men. "Do any of you want to fly once more with an instructor before you attempt a solo? Anyone?"

No one responded. Jack didn't think anyone would. But the way the lieutenant spoke certainly injected a level of seriousness that wasn't there a few seconds ago.

"Okay then," Henderson said. "Since the final three are still wearing their flight gear, we'll reverse the order. You three do the solo flights first, then the first three will go last." He looked at Jack and the two guys who would fly with him. "Are any of you confident you remember all the maneuvers, and the order in which you flew them?"

Jack was the only one who raised his hand.

"Okay then, Pilot Officer Turner will lead the flight. You other two gents follow behind him. Leave as much space between you as you were directed to by your instructors. Right, off you go then."

Jack couldn't wait to get back in the cockpit. His mind was usually fairly calm and clear but when he flew it became razor-sharp. He hopped up into the plane, slid the canopy closed and instantly recalled everything he had done before. He went through each task as though the instructor were still behind him telling him what to do.

Soon he was taxiing onto the grassy airfield. He had to wait a few moments for the other two Americans to catch up. But they did and, one by one, they took off. Over the next twenty minutes, Jack pulled off every single maneuver in the proper order and with almost the exact same timing. One of the other men remarked that it felt like they were riding on a rail, repeating everything, even at the same altitudes as before. When they had finished, he led them in the same landing pattern as before. The planes touched down without a hitch and rolled back toward the hangar.

The pilots got out and walked over toward Joe, Seth and Ozzie who were heading their way.

"Piece of cake," Joe said to Jack. "You were like a machine."

Jack looked in Joe's eyes, saw nothing but supreme confidence. They exchanged gear and Joe led the other two back toward the Miles Markers. This time, Joe led the trio in flight, since he had been more confident in his recollection of the flight maneuvers than Seth or Ozzie.

Jack, the other two American pilots and the three British flight instructors stood loosely together by the edge of the airfield and watched the planes take off. It went smoothly and soon they were rising to the correct altitude for the first maneuver. Jack didn't just see what the trio of planes were doing in the air, he could also visualize everything Joe was doing in the cockpit.

Over the next twenty-five minutes, things were a little bumpier than in the first solo flight. At one point, it seemed that Joe must have forgotten something, because he circled around once without explanation. But then he was back on track, and they had only one flight maneuver left to complete.

The forced stall and controlled spin.

Joe pulled his off perfectly. His plane climbed out of it with several thousand feet of altitude left to spare. Seth came in right behind him and gave everyone a scare when he spun for two more seconds then Joe had, but he still pulled out of it with plenty of room.

Ozzie was next. Knowing this was the last maneuver of the exam, as Ozzie's flight climbed to the right altitude, Flight Lieutenant Henderson mentioned to the guys standing there how pleased he was that everything had gone so well. He said that afternoon two squadrons of Hurricanes were due to arrive, and that he—

Henderson stopped talking.

Suddenly, everyone gasped.

Something was wrong. Everyone could see it. It was the way Ozzie's plane was spinning. It didn't look right. He was getting closer and closer to the ground.

"He's not coming out of it, sir," one of the flight instructors said to Henderson.

Henderson sighed. "My God, no."

"OZZIE!" one of the Americans screamed.

And then they all screamed as Ozzie's plane finally pulled out of the spin, just in time to fly, nose-first, straight into the ground.

It exploded in a fireball.

19

TWO HOURS LATER, the five remaining Americans sat around in wooden deck chairs in a grassy area just outside what the Brit pilots had nicknamed "The Hut," something of a small headquarters building near the runway. All the men were still stunned by the sudden turn of events. The Group Captain had canceled all remaining flight activity, at least for the Americans, and he'd ordered the mechanics to give the rest of the Miles Masters a thorough going over, even though no evidence existed to suggest Ozzie's plane had malfunctioned.

Ozzie had said nothing over the radio in those last remaining seconds before the crash. After everyone had run over to the site immediately after, it was obvious the plane had all but disintegrated in the explosion. Jack was certain they'd never piece together any mechanical cause, even if there was one.

"I still can't believe he's gone," Seth said. "Just like that. One slip, and he isn't here anymore."

"You're saying one slip," Joe said, "but we don't know it was Ozzie's fault."

"I'm not blaming him. But the planes seemed fine just before that. Jack, you were watching. Did you see anything that looked wrong? Did the plane seem to be messing up at all?

Cause they seemed just fine to me."

"No, nothing obvious. But I was a little distracted. The Lieutenant was talking to me about those two squadrons of Hurricanes coming this afternoon. He stopped talking, and we both looked up. Ozzie's plane was already spinning by then. You could tell something was wrong, but I didn't see it when it first went into the spin. What makes you so sure it wasn't Ozzie's plane, but something he did?"

"I'm *not* sure," Seth said. "I guess I'm just hoping it was."

"Why?"

"Cause if it was the plane, then I gotta be worrying about something being wrong with my plane. Something I got no control over. Then I gotta start worrying about these Brit mechanics, whether they're any good. If it was Ozzie's fault, then I don't gotta worry so much."

"I don't think any of us will ever know what went wrong on this," Jack said. "But let me ask you something, Seth. You didn't come out of your spin when Joe did. You gave us all a little scare watching you. A few seconds more, and it would've been too late for you. Then you got hold of it and pulled up okay. What was going on there?"

Seth didn't answer right off the bat. Like he was remembering. "That's why I'm wondering, hoping nothing went wrong with the plane. Because I did feel something going on there at the top of my stall, right as the plane came over and started heading down. Like my head started spinning before the plane did. Maybe it was just all the extra speed and power, and we're not used to it. I got disoriented for a few seconds, but I came out of it. Maybe that's what happened to Ozzie, and he could never get it together."

"Any of you guys feel anything like that?" Jack asked. He didn't.

No one else had, either.

"I'm not saying it was any big deal," Seth said.

"You don't have to apologize," Jack said. "The point is, you got it together and pulled out of it. Something happened with Ozzie, and he didn't. None of us have ever flown with each other before. Except Joe and I. All I can say is, before he lost control, Ozzie was doing everything solid. You were too, Seth. There's nothing we can do about it. It's not going to make any sense. My plane felt completely fine."

"More than fine," Joe said. "For a minute, I forgot we weren't flying a Spitfire. I was having the time of my life. I don't think I could ever go back to flying a Jenny."

No one said anything for a few minutes. Jack wasn't sure how he felt. It wasn't like the death itself was so shocking. They had all been confronted with it. Everyone has who flies planes. It was part of the package. If you were close to the guy, you felt the pain of that, losing a friend. If you didn't know him, you were mostly just glad that whatever happened didn't happen to you.

Ozzie dying this way was kind of a mixed bag. Jack didn't really know him that well, and they weren't close. But he still felt bad. The poor guy had come all this way, had all these hopes and dreams, and then smacks the ground his first time out. "Anyone know if he had any family back home? Anyone we need to contact?"

"He and I talked a good bit," Seth said. "He had a brother back in Iowa he wrote to a few times. Probably got a letter from him in his things. I'll check and let his brother know what happened." He sighed. "Poor Ozzie."

THE GROUP CAPTAIN had given the Americans leave for the rest of the day. But before he dismissed them, he confirmed that the rest had satisfactorily passed the exams. This made them eligible to fly the Hurricanes and later, the Spitfires. But then he'd added with some emphasis, that just because they had been cleared to fly these planes didn't mean they could start flying them right away. Especially after what happened with Ozzie. He wanted to be absolutely sure the remaining Americans could fly the Miles Masters as well as they could walk.

So for at least a week, that's what they'd be flying, over and over again.

As they talked about it over lunch at The Black Swan, the guys had all agreed this was no punishment. They were still going to be allowed to fly every day and, even though they had been restricted to fly trainers, these planes were five times better than anything any of them had ever flown back in the US.

At the moment, Jack and Joe were sitting in those wooden deck chairs awaiting the arrival of the first squadron of Hurricanes. They were due to show up any minute. They did their best not to look too far to the right. About two hundred yards in that direction, a handful of workers were cleaning up the debris from Ozzie's crash. Instead, they kept straining their eyes all over the skies, searching for any sign of the Hurricanes.

"Know which direction they're coming from?" Joe asked.

"Think they're coming in from the north," Jack said. "That's where the base is located. Doesn't mean the pilots will fly in from that direction."

"Will be something to actually see them up close, won't it? After only seeing them in pictures."

Jack nodded. Although right now, his mind wasn't totally focused on the arrival of these planes. He was wrestling with whether he should be sitting there with Joe at all. If he had any hopes of ever finding his brother, it would be in London, not here. The captain had only given them leave for the rest of the day. Even if he could get a staff car, he'd have to be back tonight. That meant he'd spend most of his remaining time off driving back and forth. He'd only have two or three hours of search time at best.

Then it dawned on him, it wouldn't work anyway. He'd already concluded his best bet, oddly enough, had come from Joe's hoity-toity idea (that Jack's British side of the family was likely part of the aristocracy). During lunch, he'd worked up the nerve to ask the Flight Lieutenant for some advice. Jack mentioned that he might have some distant relatives living in England but wasn't sure of their last name. He was pretty sure they were part of the British nobility, but he had no idea whether they were dukes or earls, or barons, or whatever. Was there some place that had a list of all these people and what part of England they lived in? He thought maybe if he could see a list of their names, something might ring a bell.

The lieutenant had looked at him as if Jack had to be joking. When he could tell he wasn't, he'd said he might start off in one of the bigger libraries in London. They had all sorts of directories there that Jack could look through, and he was quite sure they had one especially for all members of the aristocracy. Jack thanked him and headed back to his table, hoping the lieutenant would forget that he'd ever asked.

Jack decided a large London library would be where he'd begin his search. But any library would undoubtedly be closed by the time Jack made the trip. That is, if he could even get a car.

"Jack?"

Jack looked over at Joe. "What?"

"Where'd you go? That's the third time I called your name."

"I'm sorry. What is it?"

"What is it? Look." Joe pointed toward the south end of the runway. "The Hurricanes. I think they're here."

20

THE NEXT MORNING, Renée awoke fully rested. The first time that had happened in weeks. When he'd left last night, Elliot said he could tell she was exhausted. He was too. He insisted they both sleep in that morning and let their bodies decide when they were done. It was 9:15. Apparently, her body had decided she needed eleven hours to get caught up.

She remembered the plan for that morning. Elliot wanted to take her shopping for some new clothes. None of the stores were open until ten anyway, so she decided to take a hot bath before getting dressed. They did have a nice bathroom back home. Several, in fact. But none of them had running hot water since she was a little girl. How could she pass up an opportunity like this?

She sat up in the bed and stretched. This must be what it feels like to be a princess, she thought. She'd never been in a finer room. They must have hotel rooms this nice in Paris, but she had never been in one. She glided across the plush carpeting into the bathroom and turned the hot water knob. Not only did the water get hot, but it got hot almost right away.

After adjusting the level of heat with the cold water knob, she closed the drain so it could fill. She stood back a moment to watch. It was like a wonder. She got her underclothes and the outfit that she would wear that day and set them out. The hotel had provided some wonderful smelling soap and shampoo. After setting them on the corner of the tub and tossing a small oval throw rug in front of it, she sat on the edge of the tub waiting for it to fill the rest of the way.

In those quiet moments, her joyful outlook on the day quickly began to erode as she thought about her mother. Here she was, about to enjoy this luxurious bath followed by a pleasant day of shopping for a new wardrobe with a very nice man in total peace and safety, and what would her mother face? Was she even safe? Had the British soldiers all fled the area? Had the Nazis taken over her town? Would Philippe be able to resist all the excitement and danger and remember his promise to take care of their mother? Was he even safe?

Why had she agreed to come here, to leave France? It was her responsibility to take care of their mother. Philippe could not be trusted with such a task, not at his age. Mother was completely dependent on the daily help Renée provided and had been for the last several years. Philippe might remember his duty for a day, maybe two. But what about a week from now? Two weeks? If he forgot, Mother would have no one.

It was a mistake to come here. She was only thinking of herself. Then she remembered. That wasn't true. She didn't even want to come. Her mother had insisted. Renée knew what Mother was afraid of, what the German soldiers would do to her. The thought of that frightened Renée as well.

She looked down at the tub and sighed. Really, there was nothing to be done. Carefully leaning over, she turned the water off. She stood, put her nightgown on a hook and slipped into the soothing hot water. At the very least, she made up her mind to not enjoy this hot bath. She would not soak, would not relax, would not close her eyes and imagine calm, peaceful things.

She would just clean herself up as quickly as possible—the way she bathed at home—and try not to think of the potentially terrible things her mother and brother would face today.

AFTER HER BATH, Renée got dressed and fixed her hair and realized something awful—she had no makeup. She didn't own very much to begin with, but what she had was all in her top vanity drawer back in France. What could she do?

Elliot had just called from the lobby; he would be knocking on her door any moment. It was bad enough that he was going to have to pay for all these new clothes, how could she ask him to pay for new makeup? But how could she walk around every day without makeup? She didn't even have any lipstick. She couldn't even buy that for herself. She hated feeling so helpless.

A knock on the door.

She looked at her face once more in the mirror. She smiled, made a few different expressions. This was silly. He probably wouldn't even care.

A second knock on the door.

She hurried across the carpet, stood straight, fluffed her hair and opened the door. "Good morning, Elliot." He instantly smiled.

"Good morning. I'd ask how you slept, but it seems obvious. You look great."

"Thank you." She stepped aside, and he walked in. "I actually did sleep very well. How about you?"

He gently put his hands on her shoulder and kissed her forehead. "The hours I did sleep were restful. But I wasn't able to sleep in after all. Got a call from my CO, had to go in early this morning for a brief meeting."

"Oh? What about?"

He walked in to the middle of the room, set his hat on the coffee table. "That's just the thing, isn't it?"

"What do you mean?"

"Well, I guess it's one of the things we have to talk about now that you're here in London. My work."

She closed the door and came closer. "I know, you can't talk freely about your work. It was like that back in France."

"Well, it's even more like that now that we're back in England. I can't really discuss my work at all."

"Elliot, you know you can trust me. I would never share anything you tell me with anyone."

"I do trust you, Renée. It's not a question of trust but of law. It's actually against the law for someone who works in a top-secret military position to discuss any aspect of their work with anyone who doesn't hold the same security clearance. I could be arrested and thrown in prison."

"My gosh. I had no idea. You can't even discuss non-secret things? Mundane things?"

He hesitated to respond. "About all I can say is…you know all these young boys and old men you see all over town, the ones dressed as soldiers?"

"Yes. They are volunteers, no? Not real soldiers?"

"Yes, they're volunteers. The government put out a call on the radio for every able bodied man between the age of seventeen and sixty-five to rally to the cause, to help defend the country should the Nazi's invade. It happened before we got here from France. Well, a lot more men responded to the call than we expected."

"You see them everywhere," she said. "Always marching."

"Right, well...I'll be working with some of them. But that's all I can say. Day to day, I can't discuss anything about what I'm doing. I'm very sorry. It has nothing to do with you. I'm only bringing it up now, so we don't have a number of awkward moments over the next few days every time we see each other. It would probably be better for you to just not ask me any questions that have anything to do with what I'm doing when we're apart."

"Okay, I guess I will just have to get used to it."

"It's only until this war is over, Renée. I promise...after, I will get a job that allows me to tell you everything I do at every moment of the day."

She smiled. She could tell he was trying.

"Besides," he continued, "there's nothing that says I can't ask you questions about how your day went." He reached for her hand. "Well, are we ready to go shopping? Is there anything else you need to do?"

"Nothing I need to do, but there is something else I want to say. It's kind of like what you just did, sharing about your work. I need to share something with you up front also. Something I think you need to understand."

"Then maybe we should both sit down for a few moments." He sat on the edge of an upholstered chair.

Renée sat on the side of the couch nearest to him.

"Have I done anything wrong? Anything to upset you?"

"No, it's nothing like that. I've just been doing a little thinking and, now that you're here, I realize these are things I need to be sharing with you. Things that can't wait for a few days or a few weeks."

"Like what?"

"Well for one, me being here in this hotel. It's lovely, the nicest hotel I've ever stayed in. I know you said you picked it because it's close to where you work. But it's just too fancy for me. I don't feel comfortable here. I don't want to have to dress up every time I leave my room just to fit in. When we go shopping, I don't mind buying one nice dress or two, but I don't want all my clothes to be the kind of outfits one must wear in a place like this. I want to dress…more like the way I did in France. Are you okay with that? Will that bother you?"

"No Renée, not at all. I liked the way you looked in France. I was just being dull. I never thought once about you having to dress one way or another because of this hotel."

"Do you understand that means I want to live somewhere else? Like an apartment somewhere nearby. If they're too expensive, I'd be happy to share an apartment with someone."

"We'll start looking for a new place right away. What else did you want to talk about?"

"How I'm going to spend my days. You have your work. I'm sure you're spending extra time with me now because I just arrived. But you'll have to get back to a regular schedule very soon, am I right?"

"You are."

"Which means I'll be stuck here, or in my apartment while you're gone every day with nothing to do. That will drive me crazy. So, I want to get a job. I don't know what I could do just yet, but I would like to start looking. Maybe even today, after we go shopping."

"I have no problem with that, either. In fact, I may even have a few good ideas. And a few good connections."

She liked the sound of that. This was going very well.

"Is there anything else?" he asked.

"No, those were the main things."

He stood, took her by the hand and led her to the front door. Then he paused. "But that reminds me. There's something else I need to say about my work. Something I learned just this morning in my meeting. Over the next several months, I may need to leave London for a day or two at a time. I won't be going very far, mostly in southern England. But the thing is, it will probably be better for you not to ask where I'm going. I'm not allowed to tell you."

21

June 13th, 1940
The Skies Over the English Channel

F LYING AT ALTITUDE, high above the clouds, you would think it was a beautiful sunny day. That's one of the things Jack loved about flying: how beautiful the sky looked when you soared above the clouds. The higher, the better. Right now, they had just cleared ten thousand feet, or Angels 10 as the Brits called it.

"Jack, can you still see the bombers?" It was Joe, flying the Hurricane on Jack's right. "Cause I've lost them."

"I still see them, but they're flying in and out of a cloud bank."

"You Yanks cut out the chatter." It was their squadron leader flying in the lead plane up ahead. "I just radioed the lead bomber. They're going to climb to Angels 15. Follow me up to Angels 17."

They had been flying Hurricanes for two weeks now. Jack and Joe enjoyed flying them so much, they couldn't imagine now how flying a Spitfire could be that much better. This was only their second combat mission. Pretty much the same assignment as yesterday. Escort two squadrons of Blenheim bombers across the English Channel, trying to keep German fighters from shooting them down, while the Blenheims bombed German airfields in northern France.

Yesterday, they had been lucky. The Germans must not have expected them. The British bombers had gotten in and out, dropped all their bombs right on target, before any of the German fighter planes got airborne to retaliate.

In their briefing an hour ago, the Group Captain had said they should never expect to be that lucky again.

After making the altitude adjustment, all the British bombers could now be plainly seen. Jack realized that meant they could be easily seen by German fighters, too.

"Keep a sharp lookout, Gents. We've just crossed the halfway point. We don't think the Germans have radar active in this area, but ME-109's and 110's could be on patrol this far out."

They flew along for the next ten minutes without incident. Jack's mind began to wander. So much had happened in the last two weeks. The promised Hurricane squadrons had arrived in Middle Wallop and the Americans had all been cleared to fly them. So far, no one else in the squadron had died.

Bigger events quickly grabbed everyone's attention. France had completely collapsed, forcing the rest of the British forces to the coast. What happened next was unbelievable. Hundreds of British vessels, even small fishing boats that could hold no more than a dozen men, had rushed across the Channel to take part in an emergency evacuation. Over a seven-day period, 350,000 British troops had been successfully ferried back across the Channel. Instead of being annihilated as many had expected, these soldiers would live to fight another day.

Over the last week, people had become so elated and encouraged by the achievement (the press had dubbed it, "The Miracle of Dunkirk") that Winston Churchill had to remind everyone over the radio: "*We must be very careful not to assign to this deliverance the attributes of a victory. Wars are not won by evacuations.*"

Jack really liked the new Prime Minister, Churchill. He reminded him a little of FDR. Not the way he sounded, certainly not the accent. But he had that same eloquence—maybe even more so than FDR—and he bred that same sense of confidence in people when he spoke.

The mission Jack's squadron was flying today and yesterday had been created by another major event recently announced in the news. France had officially surrendered and requested an armistice with Germany. All their troops in northern France had either laid down their arms or fled south. With the Brits out of France, and now the French army gone as well, the Luftwaffe quickly moved in and began to take over all the airfields close to the northern coast.

This meant that the Nazis were now close enough to England to start launching bombing raids across the Channel. They were within striking distance of London, as well as every coastal town, warehouse and seaport in southern England. Everyone was bracing for the coming invasion.

RAF commanders were convinced that before the swarms of Nazi armies came sailing across the Channel, Luftwaffe fighters and bombers would be sent first, by the thousands, to prepare the way. So, Bomber Command was sending every available RAF squadron to northern France to attack all these newly-acquired airfields. Hoping to catch the Luftwaffe with their pants down.

One of the British pilots flying with Jack's squadron today said during the briefing that the airfield they were targeting today was the very same airfield his old squadron had used three weeks ago.

Suddenly, Jack's headphones filled with static, refocusing his mind on the task at hand.

"Tally-ho, Gents." It was their squadron leader. "Two ME-110's patrolling in the clouds, at two o'clock high. Looks like Angels 15. Don't seem to have noticed our bombers yet, but I'm sure they will any second. Jack, you and your mates up to the task?"

"Roger that, sir." Jack looked up through the cockpit to his right. There they were.

"Right then, you go after them and we'll stay with the bombers. Don't forget, 110's have a tail gunner. Best to come in underneath. Short bursts, gentlemen. Jack, when you're done, check your fuel. Decide whether to rejoin us or head back to base."

"Roger that. Joe? Seth? You're with me."

The three Hurricanes banked to the right and split off from the rest of the squadron. They really hadn't received any training yet on tactics, just some informal instructions in chats with a few experienced British pilots. But Jack knew Joe and Seth would stay close and mirror what he did.

The tip the Brit pilots kept emphasizing was, *"Don't shoot at the enemy. Shoot ahead of him, so that he flies into your bullet stream."*

As they gained altitude, he made a wide arcing turn so that their planes would come in from below and directly behind.

Hopefully, out of view from the pilots and tail gunners. "Guy's, I'll take the lead plane. You two focus on the wingman. Remember, all we got is twenty seconds of ammo. So, short bursts. Two to three seconds max. Don't shoot until I do. Watch your tracers. As soon as we start hitting them, they're going to bank and dive. Stay on the wingman. I'll stay with the leader. We'll meet up after."

"Roger that," Seth said.

"Got you, Big Daddy," Joe said.

Jack hated when he called him that. They continued to climb and close the distance between them and their prey. Apparently, Jack's approach had worked. Neither plane had moved.

He couldn't believe it. He was doing it. He was flying a fighter plane on a combat mission and about to fire his guns into a Nazi plane. There was the swastika on the tail. He waited to fire until he had almost come too close, then he let him have it. His plane shuddered. He had fired the guns several times before in practice but still wasn't used to the sensation.

His aim was dead on. Instantly pieces of the center fuselage began tearing off. Then Joe and Seth began firing at the wing man. As expected, the lead plane instantly banked to the left and dove down. Jack followed. The wing man banked to the right and dove in the other direction.

Jack had definitely hit the lead fighter but apparently didn't cause too much damage. But now that the 110 had dived below his altitude, the rear gunner saw him. Instantly, he began to fire. Due to the tight curve of the dive, the tracers came in behind Jack's Hurricane. But Jack knew this was likely an experienced gunner. He'd make the necessary corrections any second. Without hesitation, Jack fired a short burst to see where his tracers landed. Then he tightened his turn just enough to move his gun sights forward a couple of yards. He fired, instantly killing the gunner who slumped forward then slid partially out of view.

HE HAD JUST killed a man. But he had no choice. And he was about to kill another. Keeping his angle and aim intact, he was about to fire straight into the cockpit. But he stopped. Without a rear gunner, he was no longer in any real danger. The 110 pilot must have known the rear of his plane was unprotected. He kept weaving it back and forth and up and down, as if trying to throw off Jack's aim.

Jack wondered why he wasn't taking more evasive action. Like this, he was a sitting duck. Then he realized, his controls must be damaged. Jack decided to give the man a fighting chance and aimed for the left engine. A three-second burst later, it was on fire. The German pilot straightened out and kept flying forward. Jack realized he was heading toward France.

"No, no, no." Jack wasn't going to let this guy fly his plane back to base, so it could be repaired and flown again. He gave a short burst into the right engine. It didn't catch fire, but it started to smoke. The pilot got the idea. Jack watched him bail out. Just as his parachute opened, the 110 began to spin wildly out of control, headed for the ocean.

"Get him off me! Seth, get him off." Jack heard Joe's frantic cry over the radio.

"I'm trying, Joe. I dove down too far. But I'm climbing up now. I see you."

"My plane's shot up. It's not working right. He gets me again, I'm going into the drink."

"I'm coming, Joe," Seth said. "Hold on."

"I see you, Joe," Jack said. "I'm at the same altitude, but the 110 is too far away for a good shot. Close the gap for me."

"How Jack?"

"Dive down then pull up into a loop."

"If I do that, he'll follow me. My plane'll stall. I'll be a sitting duck."

"Just do it. Trust me. Now."

Joe obeyed, and sure enough the 110 followed him into the dive then up into the loop. This caused both planes to slow way down, allowing Jack to close the gap. More importantly, it took the 110's rear gunner out of commission. He could no longer fire on Jack. Two seconds later, Jack released a three-second burst straight into the cockpit of the ME-110, which was now facing straight up. Both the German pilot and rear gunner were killed instantly.

The plane stopped climbing. It stalled, hung there in space for a second then fell backwards into a spin.

Joe screamed into the radio, "You did it, Jack!"

Jack looked up at Joe's plane just as his nose came over the top and began heading back toward earth. Joe quickly got it under control. Jack took a look at the compass and banked to the right until they were on a heading that would take them back to Middle Wallop. A few moments later, Joe pulled into his proper slot on Jack's left.

"I'm right behind you guys," Seth said. "If you slow down a little, I can catch up."

"We can do that," Jack said.

"I saw what you did, Jack," Seth said. "Saw the whole thing. It was friggin' amazing."

"Yes, it was," Joe said. "I owe you…bigtime."

22

THE THREE AMERICAN PILOTS reached the airfield at Middle Wallop without further incident, although at a much slower airspeed than on the way out, due to Joe's plane damage. They got quite a scare as they came in for the landing. Joe couldn't tell whether his landing gear had locked in place. Seth had to fly in a circle around Joe to confirm everything looked okay.

Once on the ground, they taxied to their designated spots and turned off their engines. Jack and Seth got out first and made their way toward Joe's Hurricane. For some reason, he hadn't left the cockpit.

"Man, look at that," Seth said. "He really took some hits."

Jack surveyed the damage, amazed Joe had even been able to fly the plane home. He counted twenty-three separate bullet holes. Instantly, his respect for the Hurricane's durability shot up several notches.

"What's he doing in there?" Seth asked.

Jack banged on the side of the plane. "You coming out?"

Joe finally slid the canopy back. "I'm coming. Just needed a moment to get my wits…and to thank the Man Upstairs." He looked down at his two friends. "For a few minutes back there, I was sure I was done for." He looked at Jack. He pointed up. "I thanked him, so now I'm thanking you."

"You're welcome. You'd have done the same if it was me. And I'll probably need you to do the same for me several more times before this is over."

"In some countries," Seth said, "a guy saves your life, you become his slave for life."

Joe started climbing down from the cockpit. "I think I'm already his slave, so we have to come up with something else."

"I'm just glad things worked out," Jack said.

"Don't look now," Seth said, "but we got company."

Jack turned. It was Flight Lieutenant Rodney Hughes, their Intelligence Officer, walking across the field, pen and paper already out, the pipe he always smoked clenched in his teeth.

"Debriefing time," Joe said.

"You Yanks are the first ones back. From the sounds of it, the boys had a pretty rough time of it over the German airfield. Not the cakewalk we found yesterday. They're on their way back now."

"Did we lose anyone?"

"Two bombers and one Hurricane. One of the Polish chaps. Not sure how to pronounce his name."

"We almost lost a second Hurricane," Seth said, "except for some quick thinking on Jack's part."

"Well, that's what I'm here for. Tell me all about it." Over the next ten minutes, they did. Joe did most of the talking. Seth added a few of the finer points Joe missed. When they finished, Hughes said, "Well done Flight Officer Turner. We'll have to confirm things from the gun cameras, but looks like you've racked up your first two confirmed kills." In fighter pilot lingo, each downed plane was considered a kill. He walked over to

Joe's plane and gave it a closer inspection. "You'll need to get with the mechanics on this battle damage. You said it's more than cosmetic, correct?"

"Cosmetic?" Joe said.

"He means superficial," Jack said. "But yes, he's got way more than cosmetic damage here. He had a rough time flying this kite back. Tell them to check the whole thing over, including the landing gear."

"How long will that take, to get her back in shape again?" Joe said.

"Not my expertise," Hughes said. "But we don't have any extra Hurricanes to spare, so my guess is you'll be grounded for at least a couple of days."

"Couple of days," Joe repeated. "You mean like, I'll just be sitting on my butt while the rest of the guys go out on missions?"

"Unless you've learned how to fly like Peter Pan," Seth said.

"That's how it'll be for a while," Hughes said, "until our manufacturing facilities get up to snuff. They've got orders to build hundreds more but, for now, we've none to spare. But the boys will get your bird good as new in no time. Anything else to report?" He looked at all three men, who shook their heads no. "All right then, get yourselves cleaned up. Lunch will be served shortly in the Officer's mess." With that, he closed his notepad and walked back the way he came.

AFTER LUNCH, AND after Jack and Joe had conferred with the flight mechanics, they were able to take a short break back in their room. Jack sat at the desk, Joe stretched out on his bunk.

"I keep seeing, and feeling, that moment when my plane

was straight up in the air, just hanging there about to stall. I winced, expecting those bullets from that ME-110 to start tearing into my back. Then nothing happened. I bank and start coming down and see you go whizzing by below me, and that Nazi fighter spinning out of control, smoke pouring out of it." Joe sat up. "My insides are all mixed up, you know? One extreme to the other. Total terror then total joy. You think we'll ever get used to this?"

"I don't know, Joe." It was funny. Jack understood why Joe was wrestling with things. What he didn't understand was why he wasn't. He never felt like he was in danger even once during that mission, but he had just killed four German airmen and destroyed two German planes. That was pretty big stuff. Why wasn't he all tied up in knots like Joe?

Joe lay down again. "I'll tell you one thing, it's not going to do me any good to be sitting around here the next two days by myself, while you guys go off on missions. I want to get back in the saddle again, you know? The sooner, the better."

Jack was having the opposite reaction. He was envious of Joe. What he wouldn't give for two days leave right now. They had been so busy ever since arriving at the airfield; they'd only been given two days leave total. Jack had wanted to go to London, but could only get permission for a staff car for one of those days. He had made it to London, and he had found a library that kept a thick directory filled with all the names of British aristocracy.

The operative word here was "thick." Between the drive there and back, and the two hours he'd spent driving around London trying to find the library, he'd only had four total hours to search that thick directory. Even if he had two full days, based on the time he'd already put in, he'd maybe get through a third of it.

Of course the problem was, he didn't know his grandfather's last name. It certainly wasn't Turner, because that was his father's name. It would have been his mother's maiden name; a name he'd never heard anyone mention. Jack was told that, in this directory, the living heirs of the current noblemen, regardless of their last name, would be indented and listed after the last name of the nobleman. So far, he hadn't found any secondary heirs named Elliot Turner, which made him wonder…what if his brother hadn't kept, or been allowed to keep, their father's last name? If this had something to do with a scandal, something they were trying to hide, perhaps Elliot's last name was different than his. That was a possibility Jack had to consider.

If that was the case, how would Jack ever find him in the directory, whether he'd gotten two days leave or twenty?

"Jack?"

"Huh? What?"

"Would you?"

"Would I what?"

"See, I knew you weren't listening. Would you do me a favor?"

"I guess. If I can. What is it?"

"Well, I'm thinking you and me can switch places over the next couple of days. The only reason I'm grounded is they need to fix my plane. Your plane's just fine. Not a scratch on it. How about, I fly your plane and you get grounded for two days. You've been wanting to get back to London. Well, here's your chance."

This was actually a great idea. "We can't just do something like that on our own."

"Then we'll go get permission. Let's do it now. We got nothing going on the next few hours. Let's go talk to the Group Captain. I can't see why he'd turn us down. Somebody's got to sit out the next few days. I don't want to be stuck here on my butt, and you've got that project you're working on. You can tell him you've got some personal business to attend to. You've got to be on his good side right now after shooting down those two Nazi planes. It's worth a try at least, don't you think?"

Jack stood up. "It's definitely worth a try. Let's go."

23

AFTER STAYING A few more days at The Savoy, Renée had persuaded Elliot to help her find a less-expensive place to live. For her safety, and so they could spend more of their time actually being together (rather than on buses, trolleys and cabs), he'd suggested she live fairly close to where he worked on Baker Street. She was fine with that, but it meant she'd still be living in an upscale part of town.

This was the Mayfair District, an area she could not afford without his help. The Ritz was a five-minute walk. Claridge's store less than ten. The shops at Savile Row were three blocks away. Buckingham Palace was less than a mile.

But tucked away in the midst of all this finery was the Brown's Hotel on Albemarle Street. That's where she had been living the last three weeks. It wasn't as fancy as The Savoy but fancy enough for Elliot. And not too fancy for Renée. She still had two rooms, though smaller than her full-size suite at The Savoy, and she had a more modest bathroom.

He still had to pay for most of her rent, but from the money she made from her new job, she could pay part of it. She also paid for her groceries, except the times Elliot took her out on a date, which hadn't been very often the last ten days. In fact, she'd only seen him once.

Right now, she was about to finish her fifteen-minute walk to work. Selfridge's block-long department store was right up the street. She had gotten the job in the perfume department just over a week ago, all by herself. For a reason she didn't understand at first, Elliot didn't want her to work there. He had arranged for her to become a clerk in a military office, transcribing shorthand on a typewriter. Basically, sitting at a desk all day in a large room with no windows surrounded by a dozen other young women all banging away at the keys, and all wearing these dingy brown uniforms.

While it was true, the building was only a few blocks away from where he worked on Baker Street. It was also true that doing something like that all day for five or six days a week would drive her absolutely insane. How could he complain about her working at Selfridge's? It, too, was very near where he worked. Really, almost halfway between her hotel and his office.

She had gotten the job quite by accident. One day she had walked into the store hoping to find a certain shade of lipstick. Until she found a job, Elliot had given her a small cash allowance. He had wanted to give her much more, but she'd refused. Because of this, she was pretty sure going into the store, that even if she did find a lipstick she liked, she'd never be able to afford it at a place like this. But she had heard so much about Selfridge's over the years, she was still dying to see what it looked like inside.

She was shocked to find that one entire brand of lipstick had been marked down by fifty percent, which put it just within her reach. As she was chatting with the salesclerk, the woman said, "You have such a lovely French accent. And your English seems quite good."

"Why thank you," Renée replied. But it seemed like an odd thing for the woman to say. A moment later, she cleared up Renée's confusion.

"Would you, by any chance, be looking for a job?"

"A job? Actually, yes, I am."

"Would you have to travel far to get here from where you live?"

"Not far at all. I walked here from the Brown's Hotel."

"The Brown's Hotel?" the woman repeated. "You do understand the position I'm referring to is for a sales clerk."

Renée had understood. The woman must have wondered how someone like her could afford to stay at such a nice place, fearing she'd not earn enough if she had accepted the position. "I understand. That is not a problem for me. The pay, I mean. Is it a full-time position?"

The woman said it was and that she'd be working at the perfume counter. Many of their perfume brands came from France. She'd thought Renée's accent might be an advantage. Whether that was true or not, she was glad the woman had thought so. The woman she'd talked with turned out to be in charge of Cosmetics and Perfume.

Renée crossed Duke Street. She was now walking beside the mammoth department store. Fortunately, the world famous ground floor display windows had not been covered up by sandbags, like so many other stores had done in the downtown area. She still enjoyed looking through them every day as she walked by. But she wondered if the store management wasn't taking a great risk.

The things she heard on the radio or read in the newspapers made it clear: everyone in London expected German bombers to start attacking any day now. Elliot believed this. It was the primary reason he'd given for being so unavailable lately. The Germans were going to attack very soon, and his orders kept changing. Their plans kept getting canceled, because he had to do this thing or that to get ready.

But he'd promised her, tomorrow they would have lunch together at a little restaurant and pub they had gone to several times the first week she'd arrived, right off St. James Square. She was so looking forward to it, and she had the day off.

She walked through the front doors, smiling at all the beauty, brightness and colors that greeted her every time she came here. What a wonderful contrast to the scene she'd have faced if she had taken the typing job Elliot had in mind.

Her only regret, which never completely left her mind, was that her mother was not here to see this. She would have loved it. Renée still had not heard a word about her and Philippe's welfare. Elliot had said the Germans must have certainly taken over their town by now, and indeed all of northern France. But he didn't think they were in any particular danger, as long as they cooperated with the German authorities. The only people in any immediate danger were the Jews.

Renée walked over to the perfume section, went behind the counter and set her things in a little cubbyhole. Her coworker, Rose, whose shift today had begun when the store opened was finishing up with a customer. Renée looked around. Only a few shoppers meandered through the aisles nearby. According to Rose, who had worked there for six months, business was slower than it used to be, for several weeks now. She was sure it had to do with the atmosphere created by the impending invasion.

In one of their earlier conversations, shortly after Elliot had come in to see her for the first time, Rose had noticed his uniform and asked Renée what kind of work he did for the war effort. Renée had done her best to explain what she'd understood, but also said plainly his work was mostly classified, and that they couldn't talk about it. Mainly because Elliot could not talk about it with her.

But that had done little to curb Rose's curiosity. She regularly asked Renée for information about things she had read or heard on the radio, as if Renée could provide her with detailed, inside information.

She looked over at Rose who was giving the customer change. The woman walked away, obviously pleased by whatever she'd put in her bag.

Rose came over. "So how did your dinner date go with your boyfriend last night? Where did you go? What did you 'ave? What did you wear? I want to hear it all."

"Unfortunately, I must disappoint you. Elliot had to cancel again. Wherever he was, something had come up, and he knew he wouldn't get back into London until late."

"Aww, I'm sorry. For you and for me. I was looking forward to hearing something romantic, since I've got nothing 'appening in my own life at the moment. But I think I can say with certainty, you 'ave nothing to worry about with that one."

"What do you mean?"

"Nothing. I just mean I think you can believe him when he says something came up and he has to cancel your date."

Renée wasn't sure what she was getting at. She never had any trouble believing Elliot's explanations.

"I've seen the way he looks at you whenever he's come into the store. He's pretty keen on you. Don't ever see 'im looking at other girls."

That was nice to hear.

"That one's a keeper, he is. If I had a man like that, I'd be a right 'appy girl. And you can bet, I wouldn't let 'im get away. He's nobility, did he tell you that? I 'eard one of the shift supervisors talking about him the last time he was here. His father is the Earl of Bainbridge. It's someplace well north of here. One of those monstrous estate homes on hundreds of acres. I 'aven't seen it myself, but that's what that means, if he's an Earl. So I'd latch onto that one, if I were you, and not let go. The day he puts a ring on your finger, you can walk right out of 'ere and never look back."

24

THE NEXT DAY, Renée had slept in a little since she had the day off. Then she took her time ambling through the morning, getting cleaned up and ready for her lunch date. Thanks to her shopping trip with Elliot a few days after she'd arrived, her wardrobe now contained a handful of outfits she was proud to wear. After several minutes of deliberation, she settled on one.

She hadn't been able to reach Elliot to confirm their lunch date was still on, and she was a little nervous about walking all the way to St. James Square without gaining that assurance. Then she decided, either way, it wasn't such a bad walk. She was a big girl. She had enough money in her purse to pay for her own lunch. And she could bring along a book to read in the restaurant and then after, sit on a bench in the square.

Just when she had resolved to make the trip, she learned that Elliot had sent a message to the front desk clerk. The clerk called her over when she'd gone down to the lobby for a cup of tea. The message simply said that he had tried to call her several times but kept missing her. He wanted her to know that things still looked good for their lunch date today at the Cross and Shield. That was the name of the pub-restaurant where they were supposed to meet.

Still looked good.

He probably had meant this message to sound reassuring. And he probably had no idea that the inclusion of these three words created the opposite effect. Like, a definite maybe. Or saying, I certainly hope so. Based on his track record over the last two weeks, it lowered the chances of them actually seeing each other to fifty-fifty.

Either way, she was determined to enjoy this little excursion. She did a quick check of her face, hair, makeup and dress in the mirror, picked up her sweater, purse, and government-issued gas mask and headed out the front door down the hall to the elevator.

It was a fairly pleasant summer's day. Although mostly overcast, the sun kept trying to make an appearance. The streets and sidewalks were as busy as ever. For the majority of Londoners, it was a typical workday. She was only off because she worked in retail.

Walking leisurely down Albemarle Street, she strolled past a squad of middle-aged men in Home Guard outfits marching the other way. Some carried rifles, some broomsticks. Then she crossed a big intersection at Piccadilly and headed for the other side of the street to see some shop windows. Of course, now that she worked at Selfridge's she rarely saw anything in store windows that surpassed the inventory on display there.

When she reached King St. she turned left. Already the bright green foliage of St. James Square was visible at the end between the buildings.

When she reached the square, she glanced at her watch. Still ten minutes to spare. She decided to walk through and around the square before taking the adjoining road to Pall Mall, where the pub was. It felt rejuvenating just to be in the presence of trees again, if only for a little while. She had taken them for granted back home. Here they were a treat, like ice cream or a pastry.

Walking through the park also gave her a respite from all the reminders of the impending invasion. For once, there were no Home Guard troops doing drills. These days, they seemed to occupy every park, square and field. The trees in St. James, now full of summer leaves, blocked much of the outside world. She was surrounded by green. Blue had always been her favorite color, but feeling the effects of all the trees, grass and foliage…maybe it was time to switch to green.

After spending all her remaining time enjoying the square, Renée hurried out and down the road that connected to Pall Mall. A quick right, and she was at the front door of the Cross and Shield.

It wasn't crowded. Her eyes instantly went to the table in the back on the left that they normally sat in. It was empty. Her heart sank just a little. She didn't really expect Elliot to beat her here, but it would have been a nice surprise.

The waitress came up and asked if she had a seating preference. It's not like she could answer, "our usual table." They'd only been there three times before. She pointed to the table and asked if it would be okay to sit there.

"By all means," the woman said. "As you can see, you can 'ave your pick of the tables in that section. Will you be eating alone today?"

"No, my…friend should be joining me any minute." She described him to the waitress and wondered why she didn't call him boyfriend. Wasn't that what he was at this point?

"We get anyone looks like that," the woman said, "I'll send 'im right back. If he's the wrong one, I'll keep 'im for meself."

Renée laughed.

Renée sat facing the front door and set her things beside her. The woman asked what she'd like to drink and did she want a menu? "Some tea would be nice, and a glass of water. I think I already know what I'd like to order. But I can't remember what it's called. It's some kind of pie. I've had it twice before."

"What's in it? Tell me that, and I'll probably know what it is."

"The main thing is pork with lots of cheddar cheese and a number of chopped up vegetables. I don't know them all, but one is rutabaga. And there's a pickle and it."

"That's our Ploughman's Pork Pie. One of our regulars' favorites."

"Do you have any left?"

"We do."

"I'd like some of that, please. But can you wait till my friend gets here?"

"Sure we can. Know what he'll want?"

"I don't. He's gotten something different every time."

"Very good then. I'll be right back with your tea and water, and I'll keep an eye out for your officer friend and send 'im right back the minute he arrives."

"Thank you."

Renée watched the woman walk off then set her eyes on the front door. "Please, Lord. Let him come this time. Keep the war away for just a little while."

FIFTEEN MINUTES LATER, Renée still sat there all alone. A number of people had come in. In fact, the pub was half full. But no Elliot.

The waitress walked up. "You want to keep waiting, Miss? Perhaps your friend's been detained."

What should she do? "Could we just wait five more minutes? If he's not here by then, I'll just order that Ploughman's Pie."

"Very good, Miss. Be back in five minutes."

Obviously, with that answer, it was clear the waitress had already given up on him.

25

Jack was beginning to see cross-eyed. Maybe he should ask the librarian if she had a magnifying glass. This was now his second day of leave. Just as Joe had guessed, the Group Captain had no objections to them switching places. Joe's plane had been grounded, not Joe. So, he let Jack take off for London. Joe was happy as a clam. Although the captain had also said there was a 50/50 chance the squadron wouldn't fly any more missions until Jack got back. Joe didn't care. He'd still wanted to trade places with Jack. A 50/50 chance was better than no chance at all.

Jack leaned back in his chair at the London Library and looked up at the high ceiling. Between yesterday and this morning, he'd spent well over ten hours in this spot. The main floor of the library, the part you saw as you came through the front door from Saint James Square, was lined with rows of thick wood tables. Only a few people sat at them, spaced as far from each other as possible. Tall bookshelves lined the outer walls, extending all the way to the second floor, divided by a thin walkway around the perimeter.

Jack was sure the library was much bigger than what he'd seen, but he had no interest in exploring its many chambers.

He was there for just one book, and it sat spread out before him on the table. It was big and thick and structured something like the telephone books they had back home. Only to get your name in this directory you had to be somebody. Somebody important. Somebody rich and important, with noble blood running through your veins, whatever that meant. He supposed if his grandfather were in this book and the long-lost brother he had never met, then that same noble blood flowed inside of him.

Joe had said it once after they talked about his family connections. "You know what that means, don't you? You're a blue blood, Jack."

Jack thought about all the hoity-toity hotels he had walked past on his way here. Those seemed more fitting for someone of his stature than the hole-in-the-wall dump he had rented last night. He yawned, stretched, rubbed his temples then his eyes. Time to stop these fantasies and get back to the task at hand; which was trying to find the name *Elliot Turner* somewhere in this book.

He was close to the halfway point and wondered if he'd be finished by the time he had to head back to the airfield. He got up and walked toward the restroom. The loo, as the Brits called it. Mainly to wash his face with cold water, see if that helped revive him. When he returned to his chair he stood for a moment and stared down at the book.

An involuntary sigh. Washing his face didn't help. He needed something stronger. Maybe a stiff cup of coffee, if he could find one. Tea abounded here. Everybody served it. What he wouldn't give for a nice cup of java. He glanced at his watch. Already well past noon. Maybe he should take a break. He looked over at the librarian standing behind the main counter. Maybe she knew a place nearby where he could grab a nice sandwich and coffee.

It was worth a try. He got up to ask her.

"You can't miss it," the librarian said. "It's called the Cross and Sword. Right around the corner, on that road just off the square." She pointed out the front window.

"And they serve coffee there?"

"Coffee or tea. It's also a pub. And they've got good food to boot. I've eaten there myself a number of times."

"Great. Can I leave this here with you?" He set down the big directory. "I plan to get right back to it after lunch."

"That would be fine. I'll just set it here on the shelf. It's not like the book's in great demand. Before you, no one's asked to see it for months."

"Good. Then I'll see you back here in about thirty minutes or so."

Jack headed out the front door. As he did, he said a quick prayer, asking God to help him find his brother's name in that book after lunch. He only had a few more hours before he needed to head back to Middle Wallop.

The fresh air and sunshine instantly began to revive him. It didn't hurt seeing so many big leafy trees for a change. In just a few minutes, he turned one corner then another and saw the sign for the Cross and Sword. So far, Jack hadn't been all that impressed with British cuisine, although he was beginning to feel hungry. Mainly, he looked forward to drinking a hot cup of coffee.

He opened the door and was instantly encouraged by the smell. A combination of something pleasant baking in the oven and fresh ground coffee. It made him smile. He walked up just as a waitress set a couple of drinks down at a nearby table. She noticed him and came over. But she didn't say anything at first. Instead she looked him over quite thoroughly, a strange expression on her face. "Can I help you?" he said.

"Say something else."

"Excuse me? What would you like me to say?"

"That's enough," she said. "You're a Yank, aren't you?"

"You mean an American? Yes, but I am wearing a British uniform."

"But it's blue, not khaki."

"Yes. It's definitely blue. I'm a pilot in the RAF."

"We 'ave American pilots in the RAF?"

"A few. Not many." He wondered what this was all about.

"Then you are definitely not the man I'm looking for."

"I'm sorry to hear that," Jack said. "But can I still eat here? More importantly, can I get a cup of coffee?"

"Sorry young man. Don't mean to trouble you none. Of course, you can. Take a seat anywhere. I'll bring you a fresh cup and a menu. You take cream?"

"Yes, and a little sugar."

"Right. 'ave a seat, and I'll be right there."

He did. Picked a table not far away. That was odd, he thought. It sounded like she was looking for someone. She had mentioned khaki. That's the color army officers wore. He glanced around the room. The pub was about half full, but he did notice he was the only one wearing a military uniform, of any color. Maybe they didn't get too many officers in here.

They may not get many military officers in here, but he couldn't help noticing one particular person sitting alone in the back. A beautiful brunette. She appeared to be reading something at the table and didn't look up. He instantly decided, she was the most attractive woman he had seen here in England since the day he'd gotten off the boat.

He suddenly felt the urge to meet her. Like any young healthy man, Jack was used to noticing attractive girls. But this was different. There seemed to be something special about her. Like this was a young woman he would like to get to know. But Jack wasn't the kind of guy who casually picked up women. He had only dated a handful of girls over the years. He didn't have any tried-and-true pickup lines memorized, or any practiced methods of meeting them.

The waitress, as promised, brought Jack a cup of coffee with cream and sugar, and a menu, and set them down before him. "I think everything on this is worth eating, but we are especially known for our pies."

Jack still wasn't used to the idea that, in England, the word *pies* didn't only refer to dessert food. "Thanks. I'll look this over." He picked up the coffee cup and smelled it. "Smells delicious."

"You Yanks do love your coffee."

She started to walk away. "Excuse me, Ma'am. Could I ask you a question?"

"Certainly. You want to know if we 'ave anything on special?"

"No." How could he say this? "That young lady sitting in the back by herself. I know this might sound strange, but…I'd like to meet her somehow. I mean no disrespect. Has she paid for her lunch yet? Perhaps I could do that."

The waitress smiled. "I'm not surprised you'd like to meet

her. She's quite a looker. And she may be alone at the moment, but I don't think she's alone in general, if you get my meanin'. The reason I asked you all those questions when you walked in was because of 'er. She's been waiting for someone, a British army officer, for over thirty minutes now. It appears he's stood 'er up. I don't know if that means she's available for other suitors or not. I can't tell if his absence 'as made 'er happy or sad. She's a French girl, by the way. And to answer your question, no, she 'asn't paid for her lunch yet. She's ordered the Ploughman's Pie, 'er favorite. It's right there at the top of the menu on the second page. When she's through eating, I could mention that it's already been paid for, and point to you, if you'd like. I can't promise you anything will come of it, but you seem like a nice young man, and you've come all this way to help us fight the Nazis, so I'd be 'appy to try."

Jack sighed. So, she wasn't alone. Why did he think someone who looked like her would be? Anyway, it couldn't hurt to try. "Thank you, I'd appreciate you doing that. Even if nothing comes of it, I'll still be grateful. And I think I'd like to try that Ploughman's Pie, if you don't mind."

"Then I'll bring you out a slice."

26

For the last ten minutes, Renée had been reading a copy of the London Times left on the table beside her. She'd completely given up on Elliot making an appearance and hadn't even looked up at the front door when she heard someone come in.

She wasn't mad. Disappointed, but not mad. How could she be? There was a war on. The Germans might be invading England any minute. She was just reading about this in the paper. The signs were all around, everywhere you looked. England had no wish to follow the same fate as her beloved France. They were doing everything possible to get ready. Elliot played a vital role in that effort.

How could having lunch with her compete with that?

Every article in the first section of the paper talked about some aspect of the impending invasion. She kept looking for articles about what was happening back in France. So far, she hadn't found any. One talked about the formation of a group of French pilots made up of men who'd escaped at Dunkirk.

She found an editorial that explored different reasons why France had collapsed so quickly and were defeated so easily by the Germans, compared to the last time around when they had fought so valiantly. In the first war, they'd kept on fighting until the allies secured the victory. Four long years. But now…? She stopped reading the article halfway through. It was too discouraging.

Mainly, she was looking for clues about what life was like for her mother and Philippe these days. Nothing in the newspaper satisfied her curiosity. She said a quick prayer for their safety, similar to the one she prayed several times a day.

Reaching for her teacup, she realized it was empty. She looked around for the waitress and saw her taking someone's order at a table near the front door. Renée decided to keep watching and try to get her attention the moment she looked up.

What?

She saw something that made no sense. The man the waitress was talking to. *It was Elliot!* What was he doing over there? How long had he been there? Why hadn't he come in and made any attempt to find her? He wouldn't have to search long; she was sitting in the same table they had always sat in.

Then she noticed something else that was odd. He was wearing a blue uniform. She had never seen him dressed like that. Was it some kind of disguise? He said most of what he did was top secret. Then she noticed his hair, it was parted on the wrong side. She was sure of it.

THE WAITRESS WALKED away. Instantly, Jack's eyes drifted toward the beautiful brunette sitting in the back. What? She was looking right at him. He looked down. Normally, if a woman like that looked at him, he would return the gaze, offer his best smile. But the girl wasn't smiling. Not even close. If anything, she was glaring at him.

He dared to look up again. She was still glaring. He looked away. What was going on? Had the waitress said something about him to her, something she didn't like? That couldn't be it. The waitress hadn't gone over to the girl's table yet.

Lifting his head slightly, he didn't look straight at her, just enough to catch her in his peripheral vision. She was still looking at him. He was sure of it. He couldn't let this go on. He had to find out what was bothering her.

One more time. He looked up again. She was still looking at him, but her expression had changed. Now it was more…confusion. He decided confusion was better than glaring, so this time he didn't look away. Holding her gaze, he smiled. She didn't smile back. Not good. Should he look away again? Her look of confusion had become stronger. He continued to smile. Finally, her lips began to move. She was sending him a silent message. What was she saying? He couldn't make it out.

He mouthed back the word, "What?" And shook his head, trying to say he didn't understand.

She mouthed the same expression. He thought she said, "What are you doing over there?" But that was crazy. Why would a beautiful girl he'd never met ask such a thing? He must have gotten it wrong. He was just about to get up and go over to her, when she got up and started walking this way.

ELLIOT WAS BEHAVING so strangely. Clearly, he had seen her. But he made no attempt to come over to her. What kind of game was he playing? Whatever it was, it was entirely unlike him. If there was one thing she could count on with Elliot, it was his steadiness and calm demeanor. The only spontaneous thing he had ever done in their relationship so far was fail to show up. And that, of course, was always something beyond his control.

If he wouldn't go to her, she would go to him.

As she reached his table, his smile grew even wider. "Hi," he said. And he said it like he was happy to see her, but also surprised.

She was annoyed with him but tried not to show it. "What are you doing?"

"What am I doing? Well, I'm not sure what you mean. Getting ready to eat lunch? Drinking a cup of coffee?"

"Coffee?" She didn't recall ever seeing Elliot drink coffee, let alone order it at a restaurant.

"It's pretty good, actually. If you'd like to have a cup. The waitress told me you were French. I can hear it in your accent. The French drink coffee, right? More so than tea? You always hear people talking about French cafés."

What was he talking about? Then she realized, his voice was different. His British accent was gone. What was going on here? "What are you talking about, Elliot? You know I prefer coffee. We talked about this on our first date. And why are you talking like this? Why are you wearing that uniform? And your hair, it's—"

"What did you just call me?"

JACK WAS STUNNED. She was talking like they knew each other. And it sounded like she called him *Elliot*.

"What did I call you?" she repeated. "I called you by your name. Is this some kind of trick you are playing on me? You said I can never ask you about your work, but is this some special assignment? Are you, as they say, incognito? In disguise?"

Jack could not believe what she just said. She was really talking to him like they knew each other well. "Did you call me Elliot? As in, Elliot Turner?"

"Of course, I called you Elliot. But why are you doing this? I don't understand."

This was incredible. But there could be no other explanation. *She thinks I'm Elliot. She thinks I'm my brother.* It was like a miracle. "I'm so sorry, Miss. What is your name?"

"Come now, Elliot. Please stop this. There's no one in here who will know if you just act like yourself."

Jack sighed. A wave of emotion arose inside. Somehow, someway, he was sitting here talking to what appeared to be his long-lost brother's girlfriend, maybe his fiancé. *Thank you, God.* "Would you mind taking a seat, so we could talk?" His eyes started to well up with tears. He quickly blinked them away.

She sat across from him. The annoyed look disappeared. The confused look returned, which was entirely reasonable. She had every right to be confused. "You still haven't told me your name."

27

Renée looked into the man's eyes. Did she just see tears forming? They were gone now, but Elliot would never display such emotions. The realization suddenly hit her. But how was it possible? "You're… you're not Elliot, are you?"

The man shook his head. "No, I'm not."

There were the tears again. He wiped his eyes with the cloth napkin.

"I'm sorry. This is embarrassing. I don't know why I'm getting so emotional. Well, yes I do."

"Who are you then?" she asked. He smiled. A different smile than Elliot's.

"My name is Jack. Jack Turner." He held out his hand.

She shook it. He squeezed her fingers gently, and his hands were warm. "Did you say *Turner*?"

"I did."

"That's Elliot's last name."

"I know. I think that's why I'm getting overly emotional. I'm normally not this way."

"You look exactly like him. Now that I'm closer, I can see a few differences. But from across the room, and even as I walked over here, I was completely certain you were Elliot. I wondered why you were dressed that way, and why your hair was parted on the wrong side. And mostly, why you were sitting so far away from me."

"So you and Elliot are, what? Dating? More than that?"

What were they doing? They had never defined it. "I suppose you could say we are…dating. Although we haven't done much of that in the last few weeks. He was supposed to be here today, to meet me for lunch. That was almost an hour ago. Then I saw you sitting here, and I couldn't understand why you didn't join me."

He pointed to the table she had come from. "Is that where the two of you normally sit?"

"Yes. We haven't been here for a few weeks, but the three other times we always sat over there. So you can see why I was confused."

"Totally."

"You must be related to Elliot. Are you… brothers?"

Jack sighed. "We are. But we've never met."

"I didn't know Elliot had any brothers. In fact, I recall him saying he was raised an only child."

"I'm sure that's true," Jack said. "That's how I was raised, as an only child. I'm almost positive he doesn't even know I exist. I only found out about him two months ago. That's why I came here, to England…to find him. Meeting you, here, this way…well, let's just say…that's why this so emotional for me. I've been looking ever since I arrived. I had no idea where he was or any real leads on how to find him. You know what I've been doing the last two days? Sitting at the London Library around the corner, going through this very thick directory— page after page, line after line—searching through all the names of the British aristocracy."

"Looking for Elliot?"

He nodded. "I knew his name isn't the family name. But I don't know what that name is. I've never met my grandfather before, either. The librarian said they often list the living heirs' names in the book. I've been searching through it for hours. I just came in here to get some coffee to help me wake up, maybe get some lunch. Then I was going to go right back at it, keep searching till I have to head back to my base tonight."

"Where is that?"

"A few hours from here. It's called Middle Wallop. But now look…I've met you. It's unbelievable. My search is over. So, can you tell me a little about him? What's he like?"

This was quite extraordinary. If Elliot hadn't missed their lunch again, he'd have come in here himself and met Jack. What a scene that would have been.

"Well," Jack said, "I can see your hesitating to answer. I understand. I'm a complete stranger. But I assure you, I really am Jack Turner. And Elliot really is my brother." He reached into his pocket. "Here's my ID card. See? And here, here's my passport. See? Jack Turner. And I can prove that we're brothers. Well, in a way I can. I have a photograph. Well, not here. It's back at the base. But I have it, taken when he was three years old. It has his name written on the back and the date. That's what started this whole thing, this picture."

"How do you mean?"

"It's been sitting inside a frame on my father's dresser my entire life. I always thought it was a picture of me. But recently I was moving the dresser, and I knocked it over. The glass in the frame broke and, for the first time, I saw what was written on the back."

Just then, the waitress walked up with Jack's food. "Now, isn't this something." She looked at Jack. "You must really have a way with the ladies, to get 'er to come all the way over 'ere and sit with you." She looked at Renée. "He was asking about you earlier, just after he came in. Wanted to know who you were, 'ow he could meet you." She looked back at Jack. "But I'd say, looks like you didn't need me help. You done all right by yourself." She leaned closer to Renée's ear. "I don't blame you, Dearie, you can't wait around forever when a man stands you up. Besides, I don't know what the other bloke looks like, but this one 'ere, he looks like a movie star. So you two have yourselves a good time. Want me to bring your drink over 'ere?"

Renée wondered if she would ever stop talking. "Thank you, Ma'am. I think I will sit here a while longer, so yes, I'd appreciate it if you retrieved my drink. But I'm all done with my food." She looked at Jack's dish. "That's the same thing I had."

"He knows," the waitress said. "I told you, he'd asked all about you."

"Well, it's delicious. I think you'll really like it." The waitress was just about to walk away. "But Ma'am, I need to clear up something you said. We are not together, this young man and I. Not in the way that you mean. He is my date's brother. We've never met before this and saw each other here completely by accident."

"Really?" the waitress said. "Sounds more like Fate, you ask me."

FATE OR THE HAND of God, Jack thought. He still couldn't believe it. Just like that, and he had found his brother.

The waitress returned, gave Renée her drink and walked away. Renée said, "I do believe you, Jack. Can I call you that, Jack?"

"Please do."

"I do believe you are Elliot's brother. It's quite an amazing thing, and I can't wait to learn more about your story. My hesitation in telling you more about Elliot wasn't a matter of trust. I'm just overwhelmed by all this. And besides that, to be honest, I don't know Elliot all that well myself. We've been seeing each other off and on for a few months, but mostly back in France. Elliot's base was right outside my town. Then several weeks ago, the Germans were sweeping through our area and Elliot offered to fly me here, for my safety. My mother insisted I go. But I don't want to give you the wrong impression, that Elliot and I are any closer than we are. Our relationship is still fairly new. And there is this, Elliot is, how should I say…a private person? You seem quite open, very eager to share your thoughts. Like me. But Elliot is, more reserved. I only say this to say, he hasn't told me a great deal about his family life."

"I see." For some reason, it made Jack happy to hear how she described their relationship. "Is there anything you can tell me? Anything at all?"

She took a sip of her drink. "You're right to have been looking in that book, the one in the library. I do know his family comes from great wealth. His father is an Earl, I think. But sadly, I don't even know his name. He said they have a large estate somewhere north of here, with hundreds of acres. I don't know how far away it is. He also said they had servants. His mother, your mother—I'm sorry, perhaps you don't know this…"

"She's dead," Jack said. "My father told me, but he had no details."

"Unfortunately, I can't increase your understanding much on this. I only know, she died when Elliot was quite young, and he was raised by a nanny. You said your father did tell you your mother died. Why did he keep Elliot's existence a secret from you? Why didn't he tell you more about your grandfather? Certainly, he would know the family name."

"I'm sure he knows quite a bit more than he was willing to say. But for some reason, he's not allowed to say anymore. Whatever it is, he's kept the secret my whole life. I could tell, after I discovered Elliot's picture, he wanted to tell me the whole thing. But he said he was sworn to secrecy and couldn't reveal a word of it. That's why I came here. He said if I wanted to find out the answers, I'd have to find them out on my own."

"This is very strange," she said. "I've never heard of anything like this before. I know when you finally get to speak with Elliot, you'll learn a good deal more. But I suspect there will still be many hidden things."

"Why is that?"

"Well think about it, his grandfather kept the secret about you, and that Elliot's father is still alive, hidden from Elliot his entire life. Elliot was told his father was a hero who died in the Great War."

"What?"

"That's what he said. He also said he and his grandfather didn't agree on many things. I can tell they're not very close."

"Well thanks, Renée. Even for sharing that much. I've

learned more about my family in the last few minutes than I've known my entire life."

"This is all very sad," she said.

Jack didn't feel any sadness at the moment. He felt something closer to joy. Even a little excited. Then there was the matter of Renée herself. Seeing her up close this way, listening to her talk, even spending these few minutes alone here with her made Jack aware of a peculiar sensation.

Something he had learned was very common among brothers. Jealousy. He almost said to Renée, "My brother's a lucky man," but knew that wouldn't be appropriate.

28

JACK HAD ASKED RENÉE if she had any firm plans for that afternoon. She was genuinely intrigued by this young man and this bizarre situation, so she'd said no, she didn't. Would she be open to spending a little more time talking with him? She said yes, she would. Then she suggested that he remain there at the restaurant and finish his meal, while she located a phone booth and try to reach Elliot.

That's when she found out he had paid for her meal.

She had found a phone booth at the other end of St. James Square and called the number Elliot had given her a few weeks ago. Most of the time, he wasn't there and she had to leave a message with the clerk. This time was no exception. But this time, her message was so much more important than every other time, so she asked the clerk to please communicate how urgent it was that she speak with him as soon as possible.

The problem was, even if he got the message this afternoon, how would they connect? She and Jack wouldn't be at this restaurant much longer. Then she got an idea. They could relocate to the lobby of Brown's Hotel where she was staying and continue their conversation there. They had a wonderful Tea Room. So that's what she'd told the clerk in Elliot's office.

When she arrived back at the Cross and Sword, Jack was just finishing up his lunch.

"Were you able to reach Elliot?"

She came over and stood by the table. "No, but these days he's in and out most of the time. I left an urgent message for him to contact me as soon as he could."

"How does he usually do that?"

"That's the thing, we need to be someplace and stay there for little while if we have any chance of connecting with him. I thought about my hotel. How much longer do you need before we can leave?"

"As soon as I pay the check." He stood.

"Thank you for paying mine, by the way. You didn't need to do that."

"I wanted to."

She stood, as well. "My hotel is only a short walk from here. It has a nice lobby area with comfortable furniture. I thought we could wait there. At least as long as you are able."

"I've borrowed a staff car from the base." Jack walked over to the waitress and paid his bill, leaving her a generous tip for them both.

"You two have fun," she said as they walked out.

They stopped at the curb. "Why don't you wait here?" Jack said. "I'll be right back with the car."

Renée watched him as he walked away. From the back, only his height and hair color resembled Elliot. The whole way he walked was different. So was the pace. She thought more about the way he'd talked back inside the restaurant. Besides the obvious difference in their accent, Jack also talked faster. He leaned forward as he spoke and always looked her in the eye.

He also became quite animated when he explained things. By contrast, Elliot was reserved.

By the end of their short conversation, she had no problem seeing Jack as a totally separate person from his brother.

JACK BROUGHT THE CAR around the last curve. There she was, standing right where he left her. As beautiful as can be. He thanked God again for this dramatic turn of events. The search for his brother was really over. He pulled the car right next to her, leaned over and opened the door. "Hop in." She did.

"Do you need to stop at the library first?"

"No. When I don't come back, she'll just put the directory away. She said no one ever comes to look at it." He drove around the square. When he reached the first cross-street, he said, "Which way?"

"Turn right. It's not very far. Just a few minutes."

They drove along and she provided directions. When they turned down the street where the hotel was located, she suggested he drop her off at the front door while he found a place to park. That way she would be inside in case Elliot called.

The Brown's Hotel was not as large as some of the hotels in the West End but, to Jack, it seemed equally elegant. And equally beyond his league. He wondered how Renée could afford it. Surely, Elliot must be helping her. He couldn't see any parking spaces along the street, just an area to drop off guests. He pulled the car up to the curb.

The doorman stepped away from the hotel entrance and opened the car door for her. "Good afternoon, Miss Renée. A lovely afternoon."

"Isn't it?" She stepped onto the sidewalk. "This officer is a friend. He's just going to park the car and join me in the lobby for some tea."

The doorman bent down and looked inside, a surprised expression instantly appeared on his face. "Isn't this...?"

"No, it's not Major Turner. But I know why you are confused. It's his brother. They're twins."

"The resemblance is uncanny."

"I know."

Jack smiled and waved.

"If you drive down to the first intersection, sir, I believe you'll find several parking spaces on the next road."

"Thanks," Jack said. "I'll be right back."

"I'll just be waiting inside." Renée turned and stepped into the lobby.

Jack parked the car and started walking along the sidewalk bordering the hotel. Once again, he was impressed with its size and elegance. Many parts of London looked much like any other big American city. Nothing fancy. Crowded streets full of buses and cars. People hurrying to get to wherever they were going, most of them dressed in average, functional clothes.

But not here in the West End. In every way and on every level, it was a cut above. And this was, apparently, the strata of society to which his long-lost brother belonged. These were the kind of places and people he felt totally comfortable being around. From just the few minutes Jack had spent with Renée, he could tell she came from more modest means. Not as far down the ladder as him, but much closer to Jack than this.

There was the doorman up ahead. He smiled at Jack and held the door for him. "Miss Renée is just inside there on the right, Sir."

"Thanks."

"That an American accent, I hear?"

"It is."

He looked like he wanted to say something else but held his peace. Jack could just imagine. *Why are you wearing an RAF uniform?* An even more likely, *Then how can you be Major Turner's twin brother?*

There was Renée, sitting on the edge of a brown leather chair. She instantly stood and smiled. For just a moment, Jack allowed himself the fantasy that she was smiling because of him.

29

"WE CAN SIT inside the Tea Room while we wait," Renée said. "I've already spoken with the man at the front desk. He'll let us know if Elliot calls." She walked through a finely paneled set of doors into a beautifully decorated room. Throughout were little tables covered in linen cloth; two small upholstered chairs were set on either side.

Jack continued to look around as they walked. "In a place like this, I might even learn to like drinking tea."

"Isn't that sad? I've only been here a short while, and I'm already used to it. But you're right, it is very nice. I'm here mainly because of Elliot. He wanted me to live somewhere close to where he works. Before this, I was staying at The Savoy. I felt totally out of place there. Here, I only feel out of place most of the time." They had the room to themselves. She led them across the carpet to a table near the window.

"Where does Elliot work?"

"Somewhere on Baker Street. I can't remember exactly, but it's only a few blocks away."

"You said he's a Major. Do you know what he does?"

"No, I don't. And I'm not even allowed to ask. Whatever it is, it's very important and he can't talk about it at all. The first week I was here we spent much more time together. But lately, I don't see him very much at all. And when we're supposed to get together, like today, something always happens and he's not able to make it. It usually has something to do with getting ready for the invasion."

"I think everyone in England is preparing for that," Jack said. "We certainly are at our airfield. Our CO is talking like it could happen any day."

"I hope everyone is wrong," she said. "I'm praying for a miracle. I saw only a small part of what they did after they invaded my country. It terrifies me to think they might come here."

"Well, I don't think you have anything to worry about. At least for a little while."

"Why do you say that?"

"From everything I'm reading, and the stuff I'm hearing back at the base, the Germans aren't going to just invade. At least not a land invasion. Everyone is saying they won't even start sending any ships across the Channel until they've destroyed the RAF in the air."

"But you're in the RAF, aren't you?"

Jack nodded. "When it starts, it's supposed to start with us. The idea is, a land invasion can't start until they have air superiority. Otherwise, our planes can destroy all their ships before they're halfway across the water. So, I don't think you have to worry about seeing any Germans on the streets of London until you see a major air battle taking place in the skies. That's what's supposed to be next."

"I wish I could say that comforts me," she said. "It does, a little. But now I'll be worrying about you. Aren't you afraid of all these things, even a little?"

Jack liked hearing her say that she'd be worrying about him. "I am, maybe a little."

"Have you ever been in combat before? I mean, in the air?"

"Oh yeah. Several times already. But not with dozens, or even hundreds of planes at the same time. All of them shooting at each other. I can't even imagine what that would be like."

"Have you ever been shot at, by German planes?"

"I have." Should he tell her he'd already shot down two?

The waiter walked up and stood beside the table. He asked what kind of tea they'd like. The Brown's Hotel had seventeen to choose from.

"I have no idea," Jack said to Renée. "Why don't you pick something out for both of us?"

After taking their orders, he directed them to a buffet against a mahogany paneled wall filled with a wide selection of finger sandwiches, scones, cakes and pastries. Then he left.

"I'm not hungry," Renée said.

"Do you mind if I take a look?"

"No, go right ahead. I've tried several of them. They're all delicious."

"Okay, I'll be right back." As Jack sorted through the desert offerings, he noticed Renée had gotten up and walked over to the front desk. She said something and Jack saw the clerk shake his head no. He wondered why in the world his brother would neglect such a woman as this. But then realized, that was just wishful thinking on his part. The hope his brother might be losing interest.

But Jack knew better. He knew the kind of dangerous things underway at every level of the British military. The stakes had never been higher than they were now. The truth was more likely that Elliot desperately wanted to be with Renée and something totally beyond his control kept getting in the way.

He should do the honorable thing and stop hoping Renée might somehow become available.

RENÉE WAS SO disappointed. Still no word from Elliot. She asked the clerk if she could use a telephone, and he said of course. She called Elliot's office again. Again, she was told he had not checked in with their office since the last time she had called. The clerk did say that Elliot had been sent to handle an emergency situation in Brighton, and that he had no idea how much longer he'd be delayed. He guessed he might not be back till well after dark.

When she got back to the table, their tea had been served and Jack had already begun eating his plate of treats.

"These really are delicious. Maybe the tastiest things I've eaten since arriving in England." He set down the scone he had been holding. "Still no word then?"

"No. And the clerk at his office said he wasn't sure he'd even get back into town before dark. I'm so sorry, Jack. You probably can't wait until then, can you?"

"Depends. I can wait an hour or two, but then I'd have to get on the road if I want to get back to the base in time. But look, Renée, I'm not upset about it. Not at all. Before I bumped into you, my prospects of finding Elliot were extremely poor. Instead of sitting here in this beautiful hotel with you like I'm doing now, eating these delicious cakes, my head would be bobbing up and down over a thick, boring directory of aristocratic names. With almost no hope that the effort would make any difference. Now? I've found you, which means I've found him. So, it's just a matter of time. Will it be this evening? Next week? I don't know. But it doesn't really matter. Elliot and I will meet. So, what I'd like to do now, if it's okay with you, is just sit here in this place, enjoy these snacks, drink my tea—which isn't half bad, by the way—and chat with you."

"You want to chat with me?"

He nodded. "I'd like to hear all about your life in France. About your family. How you and Elliot met, how you got here to England. Are you okay doing that? Will it mess up any of your plans?"

Renée smiled. "I'm okay with that. I'm not going anywhere."

"Great," Jack said. "You start telling me your story. By the time you're done, I should be done eating, and I can tell you mine. Though there's not all that much to tell. If Elliot does call between now and when I have to go, all the better. If he doesn't, it will still be time well spent to me."

My, Renée thought, but this man was different than his brother. No. More than that.

He was different than any other man she had ever met.

30

IT WAS JUST after 8PM when Elliot had finally called the front desk. The clerk was just about to put him through to Renée's room when Elliot interrupted him, asking could he just get word to Renée that he was back in town, had gotten her message, and he should be there in less than fifteen minutes.

That was fifteen minutes ago.

Sadly, he would miss Jack. Jack had waited as long as he dared, but he had to start his journey back to Middle Wallop an hour ago. Renée had thoroughly enjoyed the time they'd spent together. She was sure that at least part of that joy was just having several hours of in-depth, uninterrupted conversation with another adult. She and Elliot hadn't spent that much time together in weeks.

But as she thought on it now, she realized…even though several of her dates with Elliot in her first week in England had lasted as long, they were always doing something, like going to the movies or shopping. Their conversations were always short and constantly interrupted by other things.

In just a few short hours with Jack, she already knew so much more about his life than she did about Elliot's. From the little she did know of Elliot's story, his upbringing seemed to be on the opposite end of life's spectrum than Jack's in every conceivable way.

Jack had lived the life of a pauper, Elliot the life of a prince.

Jack was able and willing to talk about most of his childhood experiences, his father's physical handicaps and the special kind of friendship they had enjoyed right up until this terrible family secret had been exposed. It was clear, unlike the contempt Elliot felt for his grandfather, Jack loved his father dearly. This recent revelation had shaken Jack up, but he was convinced his father had only kept these things from him because he'd been forced to do so.

Jack had no idea why all these things had happened, or what had set them in motion, but he was determined to find the answers.

The last thing Jack and Renée had talked about before he left was just how much of his story she should share with Elliot, knowing she would see him way before Jack did. She felt Elliot should hear it all firsthand from Jack, not her. Jack agreed. Then there was this long pause, as if Jack was struggling about what he needed to say next.

The scene replayed in her mind now. As soon as Jack had said it, she wished he had not. But she also knew, considering the reality of their situation, he was right to ask this favor of her, and she had an obligation to fulfill it, though she hoped she never would.

"Renée, I really want to see Elliot. To meet him in person and share all of these things with him myself. And to hear everything he'd want to say to me. That's how I hope this thing goes. But every time I take off in that plane, I have no idea whether I'll get back to the base alive. And I have no idea when I'll get to meet

Elliot myself. So, I'm going to leave word with my friends at Middle Wallop, that if I die on one of these missions they will let you know. And if that day comes, will you share all these things with Elliot for me?"

Remembering it now, and the tender look in Jack's eyes when he'd said these words, brought a tear to her eyes. She walked to the dresser and picked up a tissue. As she wiped her eyes, she prayed, "Please Lord, don't let that happen. Protect Jack. Let him be able to say all these things to Elliot in person."

A knock at the door.

She stood in front of the mirror, made a few adjustments then walked to the door. Peeking through the little hole, she saw it was Elliot. A deep inhale. She opened it. "Hi, Elliot. You look tired."

He walked in, gave her a quick hug then walked past her. "I am. Dead tired. But after getting your message, I knew I had to come right over. Whatever it is, I'm sorry for making you wait so long to deliver it. And sorry again for not making our date at the Cross and Sword. And sorry for not even having the decency to call you and let you know I wouldn't be coming. I suppose Corporal Edwards told you an emergency came up in Brighton. I didn't have a choice. I had to leave immediately to take care of it."

"That's okay. Even before I called your office, I knew it would be something like that. Were you able to… get your situation sorted out?"

"Finally, yes I was. It was beginning to look like I would have to stay there for the night." He walked over and sat in the upholstered chair.

"Would you like a glass of water?"

"Please."

She handed it to him and sat on the sofa closest to where he was. "Did you get anything to eat?"

"Stopped on the drive here, got some fish and chips."

"That's what we ate."

His expression instantly changed. "We? Were you with a friend? Someone from the store?"

"A friend, yes. But not someone from the store." This wasn't the way she intended to introduce this. Too late now. If she read his eyes right, he had just become a little concerned. Maybe even a little jealous. For just a moment, she wondered if he had good reason.

"Anyone I know?"

"Actually Elliot, the person I ate with is also the reason for my urgent message this afternoon. I've been with him since just after lunch until about an hour ago."

"Him?"

She paused, took a deep breath.

"What is it? You seem a little tense."

"That's because of the news I'm about to share with you. It's very big. I'm not sure how it will affect you. And I'm not exactly sure where to begin."

He leaned forward on the chair. "This sounds pretty serious."

"It is."

"Is it someone from home, your home in France?"

"This really isn't about me. It's about you. I guess I should just say it. I've spent the last six or seven hours with your brother, Elliot."

The tension on his face gave way to a smile, like he was

relieved by what she just said. "I don't have a brother, Renée. Don't you remember? I was raised an only child. I don't have any siblings, sister or brother."

"Yes you do, Elliot. His name is Jack, Jack Turner."

He was still smiling. Now he was shaking his head. "Renée, I don't know who you spent the afternoon with, but it wasn't with my brother. I don't have one. And I can assure you, with the utmost certainty, that if I did our family would have never named him Jack."

This wasn't working. How could she make him take this seriously? "Elliot, please understand. You really do have a brother. I wasn't with some kind of imposter, or someone playing pretend. I heard his whole story this afternoon. I believed everything I heard. I could share it with you, but we both felt it would be better for the two of you to meet, and for you to hear what he has to say in person."

He sat back in his chair. "I can see that you are serious about this. I'm not trying to make light of it. But it doesn't make any sense. If I had a brother, don't you think my mother would have said something to me? Where would they have hidden him all these years? And why would he just show up suddenly, this afternoon?"

"I don't know why your mother, or your grandfather, hid this information from you. Jack doesn't know, either."

"Jack—" Elliot said sternly. As if he was angry that she had inserted his name so casually in her explanation.

"Yes, Jack," she said. "That's his name, Elliot. You have a brother named Jack."

"And what makes you so sure he's my brother, Renée?"

"Because Elliot... Jack is your twin. In fact, he looks exactly like you. So much so, that when I saw him walk into the Cross and Sword this afternoon, I assumed it was you coming in late. I had already been there an hour. But then, he didn't sit with me. He didn't even look up at me, and I was sitting at our table. The one we always sit at. I had to get up and go over to him. I noticed he was wearing a different uniform and his hair was parted on the other side, but I just thought you were wearing some kind of disguise. Even when I got right up to his table, I still thought it was you. But the moment he spoke, it was clear he had no idea who I was. And he spoke with an American accent."

"An American accent?" Elliot's face now was utter confusion.

"As we talked, I found out he had come all this way from the US, even joined the RAF, just so he could be in England and find you. Our meeting there today was totally by chance. He had come there from the library on a lunch break. Do you know what he was doing?"

Elliot shook his head no.

"For the last two days, he had been looking through a directory filled with the names of English nobility, hoping to find some trace of you in there. He wasn't even sure the two of you shared the same last name, or what your grandfather's last name was. He had only discovered that you exist a few months ago. His father said he wasn't allowed to share any of the details of what happened. If he wanted to know, Jack would have to come over here and find out the answers for himself."

"Wait… did you say *his father*? Are you saying his father— *my* father is *alive*?"

31

The following morning, Elliot arrived at their office building on Baker Street ten minutes before his CO drove into the back parking lot. Lieutenant Colonel Browning always followed the same routine. Elliot knew he had to meet him there, before he got inside, or else he'd be forced to wait till the end of the day to see him. Elliot couldn't sit on this that long. It was eating him up inside.

Last night, even though his body was completely exhausted, he'd hardly slept a wink. Tossed and turned the whole night. As much as he wanted to doubt the veracity of what Renée had said, he had no doubt that she believed the man she'd spent the better part of the day with was Jack Turner, Elliot's twin brother. And the more Elliot thought about it, the more convinced he became that it might very well be true. Why would this American come all the way over here and spend all his free time trying to find him? Elliot knew how little free time RAF pilots had these days.

True, he could be a con man. But con men usually do their homework. And if he had, he'd have known the Bainbridge Estate, due to a host of unfortunate factors, was living through its final years. There was no great fortune left. Elliot wasn't even sure it would survive the war. And what con man would have his face totally reconstructed to look like his intended target? Especially when there was no financial gain to be had?

No, whatever this was, Elliot did not believe Renée had been the unwitting victim of a con. He had to find out what was going on here. He had to see this man for himself. Before he left last night, he'd asked Renée a number of other questions, but she said she'd rather he get those answers from Jack, than her.

Eight minutes later, like clockwork, Lieutenant Colonel Browning's staff car drove up and pulled into its unofficial parking space. His adjutant got out and opened the door for him. As he did, Elliot was standing right there and offered a full salute.

"Elliot, what are you doing here?" He returned the salute.

Elliot took a few steps back. "I need to see you, Colonel, on a matter of serious importance."

"Seems like most of the things we talk about are of serious importance. Isn't that our job? Couldn't this have waited until I got inside?"

"Not really, sir. I know what your schedule looks like today. I wouldn't get a chance to speak with you until 3:30, when I brief you on the results of my Brighton trip. But this couldn't wait that long."

Browning looked at Elliot's face for a moment. "You don't look so good, Major. Are you feeling well?"

"I'm just tired, sir. Didn't sleep very well last night."

Browning turned and said to his adjutant, "You can go in now, Sergeant. I'll be in shortly."

"Yes, sir."

"Am I correct in assuming this urgent business is more of a

personal nature?"

"Yes, it is. I'd like your permission to take off a day or two."

"Starting when?"

"Starting right now, sir. Something's come up, and I really need to get it squared away as soon as possible."

"Elliot, you know our situation. Everything is teetering on a ledge. The Germans could invade at any moment. I can't spare you for two days. What if everything breaks loose while you're gone? All the operations you're in charge of, who would handle them? There's no one. Everything that needs to be done isn't even written down. It's all in your head."

"I know that, Colonel. But I am current on all my priorities, and the situation you asked me to handle in Brighton yesterday is well in hand. I won't be more than two hours away, and I'll call you every two hours to check in."

"Two hours," Browning said. "This personal business doesn't have anything to do with your grandfather? I don't think I can support—"

"No, Colonel. It has nothing to do with him. I'd be driving two hours in a different direction." Elliot knew why the Colonel had brought this up. Before the war, like many in the aristocracy, his grandfather had been a Hitler supporter. Many felt Hitler and the fascists were a far better alternative to the Communists, who had already demonstrated their hatred for the higher classes. His grandfather and many of his friends had shown their support publicly, although most had backed down once Hitler invaded Poland. But not Elliot's grandfather. He became part of a minority in the aristocracy convinced Hitler would easily conquer England and urged the British government to sue for peace.

"All right, Major. If you must go, then go. But do as you said, call in at least every two hours."

"I will, sir."

"Can you tell me what this is about? Even a little? It's not like you running off like this."

"I'd prefer not to, sir. At least until I have checked everything out. There's a possibility this is all some kind of bizarre misunderstanding. But I won't know for sure, unless I investigate everything myself."

"Okay, then. Guess I'll see you back here in two days. Hope the Germans sit tight until then."

"Thank you, Colonel." He saluted and headed for his car.

Two hours later, Elliot pulled up to the guardhouse in front of Middle Wallop airfield.

The guard stepped up to the car, looked inside and saluted. "Pilot Officer Turner, I don't understand, sir."

"Are you blind, Corporal? You can't tell the difference between a Pilot Officer's insignia and that of a major? I'm not even wearing an RAF uniform."

"No, sir. You're not. And I'm sorry, sir. I do know the difference, but…I don't understand. And your voice…"

"Would you just lift the gate, Corporal?"

"Yes, sir. Right away, sir." He stepped back into the guardhouse. The gate opened.

"I assume that's the headquarters building over there," Elliot said.

"It is, sir."

"Is Group Captain Reginald Gibson here today?"

"I believe he is, sir. He should be in the headquarters building."

"Great, thank you." The corporal saluted as Elliot drove past the gate. Well, Elliot thought, that was bizarre. But obviously, more evidence of what Renée had said about how much he and Jack Turner looked alike. And he'd learned that this fellow, Jack, was merely a Pilot Officer, the lowest ranking officer in the RAF. But then again, he would be, if he was one of the few Yankee pilots who had come over here to help them fight the Luftwaffe.

He pulled up to an empty place in front of the headquarters building. Once inside, he stepped up to a reception desk. Behind it, another corporal sat typing away. He noticed Elliot, instantly stopped, turned and saluted. Then like the guard at the gate, a startled expression came over his face. "I am not Pilot Officer Turner. I am Major Elliot Turner. Is Group Captain Gibson available? I need to speak with him. I'll only need a few minutes of his time."

"Uh, yes sir. He's in. Let me see if he can see you now?" He picked up the phone and dialed two numbers. "Excuse me, sir. There's a Major Elliot Turner out here to see you. He said he only needs a few minutes of your time. I think you'll want to see him, sir. Why? It will become obvious, sir, as soon as you meet. Shall I send him in?" He hung up and looked at Elliot. "Group Captain Gibson will see you, sir. Just go in that door." He pointed toward a door on the other side of his desk.

Elliot stepped inside. Captain Gibson was already looking up. Two things immediately happened. Elliot saluted and the captain's face registered instant shock and confusion.

Captain Gibson returned the salute. "Major Turner?"

"That's me, sir." In the pecking order of the RAF, Captain

Gibson held the equivalent rank of a full Colonel. Two levels above Elliot.

"At ease, Major. Please, have a seat."

"I'm sorry to come here unannounced, sir. But I believe there is a Pilot Officer stationed here named Jack Turner. If so, I wish to see him."

"PO Turner is definitely here. He's one of our best fighter pilots, to be exact. But, you do know he's an American?"

"I've been told."

"And clearly, he's a relative of yours."

"I've been told that, too."

"Then you've never met? Is he some kind of distant cousin? Although, I find that hard to believe. The resemblance between you is astonishing. You look more like…"

"Like brothers?"

"Yes, but even more than that."

"Supposedly, we are twins, sir."

"Twins? Did you say *supposedly*? What does that mean?"

"It's as you say, Captain, Officer Turner and I have never met. Apparently, he's been trying to find me and yesterday, he left word with a mutual friend that he would like to meet. If you could spare him for a few hours, I would like to meet this man in person, and sort this matter out."

"I find this quite amazing, Major. But yes, definitely, the two of you should meet. He's only been here a short while, but I have developed a good deal of respect for Pilot Officer Turner. He has a bright future in the RAF. We have no missions scheduled for today and, unless Goering decides to launch his aerial invasion this afternoon, I suppose I could spare Turner for a few hours. If you'll take a seat out in the reception area, I'll send for him directly."

"Thank you, sir. It's much appreciated." He saluted and stepped back through the doorway. Before the door closed, he heard Gibson say aloud, "Astonishing, simply astonishing."

32

JACK SAT IN his room, trying to get into a book he'd been reading over the last few days. Surprisingly, no patrol missions had been scheduled today. Either the Luftwaffe had taken the day off, or else they'd reduced their attacks on the shipping lanes to a more moderate level. Either way, the services of Jack's squadron were not being called upon. Their CO had suggested the men do whatever they could to enjoy this brief respite. Once the air war began, the concept of "free time" would go out the window.

Jack set the book down. He was too distracted by yesterday's events. The problem was, he wasn't sure which of the two things affected him more. Meeting Renée, which all but guaranteed he would soon meet his long-lost twin brother, or just... meeting Renée. Why did she have to be so beautiful? And so easy to be with? And so easy to talk to? Her presence in the situation added all sorts of layers to what was supposed to be a singular pursuit.

He hadn't come all this way to meet the girl of his dreams; he'd come to find Elliot. But on the drive back last night from London to the airfield, and for all his waking hours after that, he had two thoughts about Renée for every one thought about his brother.

The front door opened. Joe peeked his head inside. "Hey buddy, passing on a message. Someone snagged me on my way back from the mess hall. You got a visitor. Headquarters building. The guy who told me was sent from Captain Gibson, so you better get a move on."

Jack stood. "Who's the visitor?"

"Don't know. They didn't say. Anyway, I gotta use the john." Leaving the door open, he walked down the hall.

Jack grabbed his hat and headed out the door. It was a five-minute walk to the headquarters building. Along the way, he watched two flights of Hurricanes take off. Just some routine training for some of the newer pilots. Even still, made him wish he could join them. That part of this trip had no downsides. Jack still loved flying and couldn't believe how many times he'd gotten the chance to scratch that itch since coming to England.

Just as he reached the front door, it opened and one of the Australian pilots he knew came out.

When he saw Jack, he did a double-take and looked back inside the office. Then back at Jack. "Thought you were already in there, mate. Don't look now, but there's someone in their who's your spittin' image."

"What?"

"Head on in, you'll see."

Elliot. Has to be. He hurried in and glanced around the room.

There he was, rising to his feet, staring right at Jack. A flurry of emotions fired off inside. Disbelief. Confusion. Relief. And a simmering anger, not at Elliot but at whatever had kept them apart till now.

"Pilot Officer Turner?" Elliot said.

"Major Turner?" Jack replied and instantly saluted.

Elliot returned the salute then quickly added, "Let's do away with the formalities, shall we?" He stepped toward Jack with his hand extended.

Jack eagerly shook it. He thought he saw moisture welling up in Elliot's eyes. There was an impulse to hug him, which he quickly killed. But this was his brother. Tears quickly filled Jack's eyes. He wiped them on his sleeve. "I can't believe it's you. You're really here."

THERE COULD BE no doubt. One look at the man standing in front of him and Elliot knew—Renée had not been mistaken.

It was like looking in the mirror.

"I met with Renée last night," Elliot said. "I'm sure you've guessed that. It's why I'm here. What she said seemed impossible to believe."

"Then it's true," Jack said. "You've had no idea I even existed?"

"Not until last night. And until you just walked in here, I still couldn't be certain it was true."

"Do you want to see any papers? My ID? Or passport?"

"That won't be necessary, Jack. Is that what I should call you?"

"Sure. It's what our Dad's always called me, growing up."

Our dad. Elliot sighed.

"Oh, that's right," Jack said. "You didn't know about him before last night, either."

"No, I didn't." Elliot sighed again. "There's so much to talk about. But this isn't the place. Is there a pub somewhere close?"

"Maybe ten minutes away."

"I have a car outside."

"There's a good chance I can go," Jack said. "But I'm not officially on leave. I'd have to clear it first with Group Cap—"

"I've already cleared it with him. He's okayed our visit. Is there anything else you need to do?"

"No. Lead the way." Jack stepped aside and Elliot walked past him toward the front door. "Just turn right at the main road," he said as they walked outside, "and I'll give you the rest of the directions on the way."

JACK SAT IN a corner table at The Black Swan, sipping an almost-hot cup of coffee. Across the table, sat Elliot's pale ale. He'd left a few minutes ago to use the loo. Jack offered up a quick prayer of thanks for this unbelievable moment. How could he not? He'd just met his brother. They were about to have their first real conversation. He had at least a thousand questions. He didn't know where to begin. So much of his thoughts and energy had been spent getting to this moment, he never really prepared for what to do when the opportunity finally arrived.

Elliot came back, slid into his seat and sipped his beer. "Starting to wonder if I shouldn't have ordered something stronger. Don't you drink beer?"

"Sometimes. This time of day I'm more interested in coffee."

"You Yanks and your coffee."

"You Brits and your tea."

Elliot smiled. "Even that, you're an American. I have so many questions. I don't know where to begin."

"I feel the same way. Of course, I'm not in the same state of shock as you. I've known about you for a few months now. Well, about your existence, but hardly any details. But I do remember how I felt that first day when I found out, and that you were over here in England. I knew right then, I had to come."

"How did you find out? What were you told all this time?"

Jack took another sip of his coffee. "I wasn't told anything. There was never even a thought that I might have a sibling. My mom had died before I was old enough to remember her. That's what I was told. I always assumed it was just my dad and me, and that he never remarried. But that kind of made sense, considering his condition."

"His condition?" Elliot said.

"He's crippled. He's been in a wheelchair ever since the Great War. This part of the story, I'm almost positive is true. He was injured in an airplane crash. He was a fighter pilot. I've seen the pictures."

"I was told that, too," Elliot said. "Only I was told he died in the crash. And not just by my grandfather—*our* grandfather—but by my mother, as well." He paused, looked out the window. "That means...she lied to me, too." He sat back. His expression changed to deep sadness. "That's a bit hard to take. I have no trouble believing my grandfather would do such a thing. But not her."

This was so strange, hearing Elliot talk about his mother as someone other than Jack's mother. He meant nothing by it. But it was still strange. This whole thing was so hard to sort out. "Renée said she didn't think you were that close with your grandfather. Well, our grandfather. Guess we should stop correcting each other this way."

"She's right. He and I are not close. For a number of reasons. Maybe in another conversation I'll share some of them with you. But this. Finding out this. It changes everything. My mother may have cooperated with the lie, but I have no doubt who came up with this scheme, and then manipulated everyone involved. I'm sure Grandfather forced her into it. Likely, our father too. My grandfather was a ruthless man. Still is. Although his power over others has deteriorated a great deal in recent years."

Jack set his coffee cup down. "That's the scenario I've imagined, when I've tried to think this through. Someone had to set this terrible scheme in motion. It has to be him."

"Oh, believe me," Elliot said. "It's him."

"I'm finding it hard not to hate the man," Jack said.

"I understand," Elliot said. "But right now? I'm not finding it hard at all."

33

THE BARKEEP HAD just left their table, after bringing Elliot another ale and refilling Jack's coffee cup. He could tell from the first sip that it had come from the same pot as before. A little less hot and a little more bitter. For the last fifteen minutes, Jack had provided Elliot with a thumbnail sketch of his life. He didn't have to skip over much. There just wasn't that much to tell.

Elliot seemed particularly upset by the topic they had just started discussing. He was clearly shocked to learn how poor they were and that they always had been, throughout Jack's childhood. Jack pointed out that America had just gone through a great depression, and that everyone he knew was equally poor. Add to that, their father being stuck in a wheelchair.

"That isn't it," Elliot said. "You don't understand." His face had suddenly grown angry.

"What am I not understanding?"

"This is more of Grandfather's doing. His way of controlling…our father. I'm sure of it."

Jack still wasn't clear on what Elliot was saying.

"He could have done so much more for him, for you. So

much more."

"What are you saying?"

"I want to hear it from his own lips," Elliot said, "but I'm pretty sure I've figured out what the scheme was. At least the money part of it."

Jack decided not to respond, to see if Elliot just needed more time to work through what he was trying to say.

"It's the only thing that makes sense."

Jack took another sip of coffee.

"You said our father wanted to tell you more about what happened, but he seemed afraid to?"

"Not exactly what I said, but that's pretty close. I got the impression he wasn't allowed to say more. He said if I wanted to find out any of the details, I'd have to come here to get them myself."

"Don't you see?" Elliot said. "Grandfather was paying him an allowance all this time. A pittance compared to what he could have provided. But he took advantage of our father's condition, that he could no longer work because of his injuries. And I'm sure he made one of the conditions for Father to keep receiving this money was that he accepted the arrangement, and kept his mouth shut all this time."

"He purchased his silence?" Jack said.

"Exactly."

Now that made sense.

Elliot sipped his ale. "Jack, I am so sorry you and Father were treated so poorly. If you could only see the wealth, the provision that could have been put at your disposal all this time. It's a travesty."

The picture was beginning to become clear. After all,

grandfather was an Earl. *Hoity-toity*, as Joe would say. At this point, Jack didn't care so much about the poverty he'd grown up with. He was more aware of how strange it sounded to hear Elliot call their dad "Father." Jack never called him that. It sounded far too proper.

Elliot continued. "Of course, Grandfather's wealth is a fraction of what it used to be. But back in the day, back when our parents were young and clearly in love, the estate was booming. I can just imagine what must've happened."

Now, so could Jack. "Dad was absolutely the wrong kind of guy for our mother to be dating. This daring young fighter pilot from America."

"It would have been a terrific scandal," Elliot said. "Grandfather would never have allowed it. Not in a million years. Not now, but certainly not back then."

"So, they continue to see each other secretly, defying Grandfather's instructions," Jack said. "At some point, they elope. Some time goes by. She gets pregnant, with us."

"And then Father's plane crashes," Elliot adds. "Bringing their fantasy romance to a screeching halt. I take it our father didn't come from a family of means?"

"He had no family," Jack said. "He grew up in an orphanage."

"So, no help there. And even more evidence of why Grandfather would have rejected him. And I'm sure back then whatever help the US government provided veterans with profound disabilities was minimal."

Jack agreed.

"With Father now chained to a wheelchair, and two twin baby boys to care for, the young couple would have been forced to turn to Grandfather for help." Elliot was looking out the window, as if imagining the entire scenario unfolding in his mind. "They would have been at his mercy." He looked back at Jack. "And Grandfather was not a merciful man."

My gosh, Jack thought. He suddenly realized what must have come next. "You think he came up with the idea of splitting us up? One of us going with Dad back to America, and one of us staying here?"

"Very possibly," Elliot said. "Although, I can imagine that wasn't his first offer. My guess is, he would've suggested Father go home to America empty-handed and leave both of us here to be raised on the estate."

Jack instantly knew, his dad would never have agreed to that. "What a horrible mess. I can't imagine being forced to make such a choice."

"No," Elliot said, "but sadly, I can easily see Grandfather forcing them into such a position, to where they had no choice but to do as he demanded."

Neither said anything for a few moments. Jack suddenly felt an overwhelming sense of compassion for his Dad. All the anger and bitterness he'd been keeping inside since learning of the great family secret simply dissolved.

Jack finally broke the silence. "So, what was your childhood like, being brought up on a proper British estate? What's Grandfather's title again?"

"Earl of Bainbridge. It's a beautiful, majestic place. Like so many of the British Manor homes. Bigger than some, smaller than others. I forget how many rooms it has. Of course, it's been on a steady decline for years. He's had to let go of more than half the staff. And because of some of the foolish choices and allegiances Grandfather made in the years leading up to this war, I fear it will not survive long after the war ends."

"What do you mean… foolish allegiances?"

"It's all very complicated, but to put it simply… Grandfather backed the Nazis. He was pro-Hitler. He may still be, I don't know."

"You're kidding?"

"I wish I was. Like I said, it's more complex than what it sounds. A lot of the aristocracy backed Hitler. At least up until he invaded Poland. But of course, they are all paying for it now and will pay for it even more once Hitler is defeated."

Jack found this news alarming and disturbing, although he was glad to hear Elliot speak of Hitler's defeat. "So, what do you think, Elliot? Can Hitler be defeated?"

Elliot took another sip of ale and leaned back in his seat. "He has to be, Jack. For all our sakes. Although, the work I'm doing now, as we prepare for the invasion, is to help prepare a counterattack should his invasion be successful."

"A counterattack. You mean, if England is defeated? Is that a real possibility?"

"It's up to your lot, Jack, to see that it doesn't happen. Whether or not Hitler invades has everything to do with whether the RAF can stop the Luftwaffe in the air. I'm sure you heard what Churchill called it on the radio last week, *The Battle of Britain*. That's where the next big battle will take place. Not on the homeland, but in the air. If you boys don't stop him, the Nazi's *will* invade England."

WHEN JACK GOT back to the base, he went looking for Joe. Finally found him chatting with some mechanics working on his plane. "Joe," he yelled. "Can I grab you for a minute?" He tried to keep his expression as normal as possible.

"Sure. Excuse me, guys. Just do what you're planning. Sounds good to me." Joe ran over to Jack, standing in the hangar doorway. "So, what's up? Who'd your visitor turn out to be?"

"You're never going to believe who I just spent the last couple of hours with."

Joe thought a moment. "Your brother?"

"How'd you know?"

"Easy. You don't have any friends off this base but me."

"I do, too."

"Name one."

Jack couldn't. "Alright you win. But isn't that crazy? That girl I told you about, my brother's girlfriend? She set it up. He drove all the way from London to see me."

"He look a lot like you?"

"Like looking in a mirror almost. But it was so weird. We were raised so differently. It was like talking to a stranger. He's a Major. Sounds like he's working in intelligence. Said he really couldn't talk about what he did."

"Did he know anything about you? Did you find out anything about your England-side of the family?"

Jack was just about to answer, when Joe blurted out another question.

"Wait, tell me first. He was hoity-toity, like I said, right?"

Jack smiled and nodded. "You could definitely say that."

"So what now, are you rich? I mean, if you're brother's for real, then you're hoity-toity too, right?"

"No Joe. I'm not rich. And by the sound of it, the hoity-toity side of the family isn't doing so well these days." Jack spent the next twenty minutes filling Joe in on the details.

34

August 14th, 1940
Middle Wallop Airfield

A<small>LMOST SEVEN WEEKS</small> had passed since Jack had that first meeting with Elliot. The plan from that point—which didn't happen—was for them to meet several more times over the next few months to get to know each other better, and to fill in many of the blanks they both had about each other's story.

During the first two weeks, Elliot had been the problem, which gave Jack the opportunity to experience Renée's dilemma. On both occasions, Jack had gotten leave and drove all the way to London, only to have his brother not show up. Although, his frustration had been significantly reduced both times when he'd contacted Renée, and she had been able to see him.

Jack's affections for her had only grown since that first interaction at the pub near the library. His feelings seemed to increase almost daily just thinking about her, then made giant leaps forward when he'd gotten the chance to see her in person. But that opportunity hadn't presented itself for any of them in the five weeks that followed.

The Battle of Britain had begun.

Throughout the month of July, the German Luftwaffe had begun attacking ships, convoys, channel ports and coastal towns almost daily. Dozens of British civilians had been killed. All passes for RAF pilots and ground crews had been canceled. Jack couldn't have met with Elliot or Renée, even if he'd tried.

Every day, sometimes two or three times a day, the fighter squadrons at Middle Wallop were scrambled to meet the Luftwaffe in the air over the English Channel. They started the month flying their Hurricanes but that changed a few weeks later when their squadron had been outfitted with brand-new Spitfires.

Although a number of foreign pilots in Jack's squadron had been shot down, so far the rest of the American pilots were still alive and well. Jack and Joe had even managed to down four German planes apiece. With the two confirmed kills Jack had gotten in their first air battle, he was now officially an ace, like his father had been. That point had been acknowledged the following day during their morning briefing, but there was no time to celebrate. The guys had just finished bantering about the news when the phone in the hut started ringing. The men took off running for their planes as the telephone orderly screamed out their rendezvous instructions.

The sound of a ringing phone had almost become a dreaded thing to Jack. So many times over the last month he'd sat around in the dispersal hut with the other pilots, totally exhausted, trying to catch an hour or two of rest, only to be abruptly awakened by that phone, followed by the orderly screaming out instructions. Seconds later, they'd be making the same mad dash to their Spitfires. On more than one occasion, Jack wouldn't be fully awake until his plane went bumping down the runway at full speed.

He was holding a different phone in his hand at the moment, one situated in a hallway just outside the officers' mess. This was supposed to be their day off, although no one was allowed to leave the base. It was a few minutes before 5PM. Jack dialed the number, now from memory, of Renée's hotel. He had called the front desk two days earlier and left a message, asking her to be near the phone at this moment, if at all possible. It had been the only way they had been able to talk this past month, and it only worked some of the time, since Renee's work hours changed every week.

He listened as the phone rang on the other end. "Please pick up," he muttered.

"Jack? Is that you?"

He loved the sound of her voice. "It's me. So glad you could make it."

"Me, too. It almost didn't happen. I was scheduled to work. Got a friend whose shift starts later in the day to switch with me."

"How have you been?"

"I've been fine. We keep hearing about all the bombings happening throughout the South, and the air raid sirens keep going off, but so far London's been spared. But how about you? How are you doing? Are you still going out on missions every day?"

"Sometimes two or three times a day. But so far, I'm doing fine. My plane's been hit several times, but I've always managed to get back to base without a hitch."

"Oh, Jack. Your plane's been shot? By German planes?"

She was clearly upset. He shouldn't have mentioned that.

"But I'm okay, really. And Joe's okay, too. Actually, the other American pilots are doing fine, also."

"I've been so worried about you," she said. "I pray for you every day."

"Thanks. Keep it up. Obviously, it's working." He needed to change the subject. "Have you heard from Elliot recently? Or seen him?"

"We've talked on the phone several times but, if anything, he seems even busier than before. Most of the time when we talk, he's not even in London. Of course, I can't ask him what he's doing or where he's at, but you said he's preparing troops in case we're invaded. Does it seem like that still might happen? Can you tell how things are going? Everyone at work is so scared."

"It's still too early to tell, Renée. We're doing everything we can to stop them. Have you heard anything from home? About your mother or brother?" She didn't immediately reply. It sounded like she was crying. "I'm sorry. Did something happen?"

"That's just it. I don't know. I don't know if something's happened, or if nothing has. I still haven't heard a thing. All I get is the same thing I've been getting all along. Bits and pieces from the radio or the newspapers. But always general things. Nothing about them, or even the town I'm from. It's so hard, this not knowing."

"I'm sorry, Renée. I wish I could do something to help. We don't hear very much about what's happening in France around here. The only negative rumors I'm hearing have to do with how the Nazis are treating the Jews, which is pretty awful. I've done some reading on my own about these people. They've got some crazy beliefs about racial purity but, from what I've read, they consider the French and the Brits to be part of the same race as they are. So, I don't think your family should be in any trouble. Other than the horror of having nuts like that being in charge of everything."

"I hope you're right."

"Me, too. Who knows? Maybe if we can stop the Luftwaffe and the Nazis wind up not invading England, things will settle down a little and communications might open up again between England and France. Then you can find out how they're doing for—"

Just then a siren began to wail in Jack's ears.

"Jack, what's that? Is that an air raid siren?"

"Sounds like it." This wasn't normally how the pilots on base were scrambled for a mission. They had been told in the last month the Luftwaffe had changed their tactics and began attacking RAF airfields, but so far Middle Wallop had been spared. "Hold on a minute. Let me go check."

He set the receiver down and ran outside. Everyone was running around in a dozen different directions. He looked toward the airfield. Several pilots he recognized were suited up and running for their planes. He ran back and grabbed the phone. "We must be under attack, Renée. I've got to go."

"Oh, Jack. Please be careful."

"I will. I've really gotta go."

"Will you call me when you get back from your mission? I'll stay here at the hotel until I hear from you."

"Okay." A pause. He almost said the words *I love you* but didn't. "Pray for me," he said and hung up the phone.

Jack tore off toward the hardstand where his squadron's

planes were stationed. Even on their day off, they were required to stay in a readied condition. He was wearing everything he needed to fly except his Mae West vest and parachute. One of his ground crew would have those waiting for him on a wing of the plane.

As he crossed from the pavement to the grass, he caught up with Joe, still running toward his plane. "You know anything?" Jack asked.

"Guess it's our turn," he said. "A bunch of Junkers JU88s are coming straight toward us from the south. Supposed to be guarded by 109's." Not an ounce of fear on Joe's face. "Now, don't you go stealing any of my planes. Today's my day to become an ace."

"Just don't get so focused on that you get your butt shot off," Jack said.

35

Joe and Jack reached their planes just in time to see two other Spitfires speeding down the grass runway. A moment later, they lifted into the air. Jack grabbed his yellow Mae West life vest and parachute off the wing and put them on.

Joe was already in his cockpit. "Come on, slowpoke. We ain't got all day."

"Start her up," Jack said. "I'm right behind you."

"You going to be my wingman today?"

Jack was normally the flight leader. "No time to worry about formalities. Let's just get these birds up in the air, find these bombers before they destroy this base."

As Jack strapped himself in and closed the canopy, Joe's Spitfire was already moving into place at the foot of the runway. Jack got his plane fired up. He followed in Joe's tracks and watched him head down the runway. In less than a minute, they had taken off, raised their gear and flaps and started climbing to altitude.

"This is Blue One, flying at Angels 8 with Blue Three. Anyone else make it into the air?"

"This is Green One," Jack said. "Joe and I made it." He banked slightly and looked down at the airfield. "See a few other guys heading for their planes, but most of the Spitfires are in the hangars getting worked on."

"Right. Well, head on over to Andover, Green One. We're there now. Just spotted a squadron of JU-88s at Angels 6 making a beeline for the base. Don't worry about forming up. Just pick out a bomber and start shooting as soon as you arrive."

"Roger, Blue One. See any 109 escorts?"

"Supposed to be here, Green One. Don't see any. Just the bombers. But keep your eyes peeled. If they're here, they'll come after us as soon as we attack the 88's."

"Roger that." Jack's head was instantly on a swivel, trying to spot any German fighters. The ME-109s had proved to be a formidable foe. The Spitfire was a match on many levels, but the 109's had more powerful guns, like the 20mm cannon. A few hits from that would send a Spitfire down in flames. The one bright spot was the 109's fuel supply. They weren't designed as long-range escorts and used up most of their gas just crossing the Channel. Both Andover and Middle Wallop were well inland. It was possible the German fighters had simply run out of fuel and headed back to base.

It only took a few minutes to reach Andover airfield. Jack could hear the two Spitfire pilots from Blue Flight coordinating their attack over the radio. Suddenly, a big explosion erupted below, followed by another.

"There goes an airplane hangar," Joe said. "Jack, I see two bombers flying straight and level coming in from the west at 2 o'clock. See 'em?"

"I'm with you. Just remember, side attacks on 88's. They got rear gunners."

"Roger that."

"And short bursts. We only got twenty seconds of ammo."

"I know, I know." Joe banked his Spitfire to get a good angle on the bombers.

Jack followed right behind. Thirty seconds later, they were raking the German bombers with their guns. Jack had waited a moment to let Joe pick his target and went after the other one.

As pieces of the bombers began to fly off, they dove away in separate directions. Joe's bomber had already begun to smoke. He followed it, giving it another short burst. Flames appeared. It began to spin.

Jack's bomber had suffered some damage, but it was still flying. It made a wide arcing turn then headed back toward the airfield. He was still trying to drop his bombs. "No, you don't." He brought his Spitfire around so that his nose pointed to its left side, then fired a three-second burst just in front of it. The bomber flew right into it. Some of his bullets must have struck the bombs, because it instantly exploded in a massive fireball. Jack had to quickly break right to avoid the debris.

A quick once around the sky confirmed there were no German fighters. Jack looked for and found Joe's plane about three thousand feet higher heading south. A further look revealed why; he was chasing one of the German bombers that had already dropped its load on the airfield. As he watched, tracers from Joe's Spitfire poured into the bomber. "Go get him, Joe."

The bomber started smoking then began to fall from the sky like a stricken bird. "With that one, I'm caught up with you," Joe said.

"Afraid not, my friend. Just downed another one of my

own. Still one ahead of you."

Joe banked his plane and headed back toward Jack. "See anymore?"

"Not yet." Jack hadn't seen the other two Spitfires in the last few minutes. "Calling Blue One, anymore bogies?"

"This is Blue One. We're back over Middle Wallop. Head back here now. The base is under attack. I repeat, the base is under attack. A flight of JU-88s got past us."

"Roger that. On our way."

Before they even arrived back at Middle Wallop, Jack and Joe saw thick, billowing clouds of black smoke rising into the air.

"Looks like a direct hit on hangar number five," Joe said.

"Hope those guys got to the shelter in time," Jack said. As they got closer, they saw several smaller buildings were on fire. "See any of the bombers?"

"I see one trying to sneak away. Look south, ten o'clock. See the thin trail of smoke following behind him? But you're going have to get him without me. Took some damage back at Andover. Sprung a leak. I'm running on fumes. Gotta get this plane on the ground."

Jack looked over Joe's plane. "Don't see any smoke. Take her down easy, Ace."

"Will do. Go get that 88." Joe broke off the attack and headed back toward the airfield.

Jack checked his fuel gauge. He had plenty, so he revved the throttle up to close the gap on the German bomber. No reason to let this guy get away, only to refuel, rearm and return to bomb them another day.

The bomber was traveling slower than full speed, probably

due to the damage. Jack decided to come in above him, high and to the right, so he could attack with the sun behind him. The glare of the sun would guarantee Jack got the jump on the rear gunner and his twin machine guns.

Five minutes later, he was ready to press the attack. He dove down and waited to fire until he'd closed to within seventy-five yards. Then he let them have it, a full five-second burst; starting from the starboard engine, across the wing and through the cockpit. The starboard engine caught fire then the entire wing broke clean off. The bomber started spinning and falling toward the ground.

He continued to watch, to see if any of the crew escaped before it crashed. Suddenly, tracer fire began to fly over his canopy from behind. What in the world? Large bangs. Cannon shells began hitting his plane. He banked hard to the left. Who was shooting at him? More tracer fire, this time flying just in front of him. He couldn't help it, he was already into the turn. He flew right into it. More loud bangs. The engine started to smoke. The plane became unstable and began to vibrate.

Get out, before it catches fire.

He leveled the plane, threw back the canopy and began to free himself. More bullets, now hitting his left wing. It was too late to alter his course. Only seconds to spare. He was now standing, about to jump. The rush of wind slamming into his upper body was tremendous. As he jumped, his right foot caught on something inside the cockpit. A surge of pain shot up his right leg. His hand banged into something, then he was falling through the sky.

Ignoring the pain, he pulled on the cord. The chute's canopy filled with air then a jolt in his shoulders. He watched as his beloved Spitfire, fully engulfed in flames, spun around and around as it fell to the ground. Before it hit, his eyes were drawn to the sudden site of an ME-109 swoop by. It seemed to have only missed him by a few feet.

The German pilot did a slow victory role then continued flying south at full speed. Where did it come from? He continued watching until another more pressing problem grabbed his attention. The ground was coming up quick. Fortunately, he had jumped over a farmer's field. But he had two problems.

Big problems.

The pain in his right leg was excruciating. He tried to move it, but the pain was too severe. He glanced at his left hand, now holding the suspension lines. It hurt also, though not as badly. But the lines of the parachute were covered in blood. He tried to close his fingers but could not. Looking down, he had only seconds before he hit the ground. He had learned proper landing procedures in training. But he hadn't trained on how to land on one leg.

Here it comes. Closing his eyes, he said a quick prayer. Seconds later, his good leg touched down and instantly collapsed. The rest of him followed. He hit the ground with a thud.

The last thing he remembered before things went black was not being able to breathe.

36

RENÉE WAS BEGINNING to grow frantic. It had been nearly three hours since Jack had called her. The call had been interrupted by an air raid siren going off. Jack had promised to call back as soon as he was safely back on base. Surely, he couldn't still be flying. By now, the skies were completely dark.

About an hour ago, she had noticed a military officer wearing a similar uniform as Jack sitting in the tea room. She'd asked him if he knew how long a typical mission lasted for pilots flying a Spitfire. He said he was an RAF pilot but didn't fly Spitfires. He was pretty sure they could only stay in the air for an hour and a half. Much less for a dogfight. She knew that term from plenty of conversations she'd had with Jack. Since the Battle of Britain began, dogfights were the main kind of missions Jack flew.

She couldn't wait any longer. She had to know if he was okay. There was a telephone available for hotel guests in the lobby, but she decided to go upstairs and use the one in her room, in case she received bad news. Jack had given her the telephone number for the phone near the officers' mess, the one he used when he called her from the base. Just in case she ever needed to reach him in an emergency.

This felt like an emergency.

Once in her room, she sat in the chair nearest the telephone and pulled out the slip of paper. Her hand was shaking. Picking up the receiver, she gave the number to the operator and waited until the phone began to ring on the other end. It rang seven times but, finally, someone picked it up.

"Hello?" It was a man's voice with an accent she didn't recognize.

"Hello. My name is Renée. I'm a friend of Jack Turner. He's a pilot who flies Spitfires at your base. Do you know him?"

"I'm sorry, Ma'am. My English is not too good. I am pilot from Poland. I fly a different plane. But I think I know this Jack."

Suddenly, the conversation was interrupted by a series of loud noises. "Hello?" she said. "Are you still there?"

"Yes, Yes. I'm still here," he said loudly. "We were bombed short time ago. Very much damage. Men cleaning up behind me."

"Yes, bombed," she yelled back, then realized her yelling was unnecessary. "My friend, Jack Turner…we were on this same phone three hours ago when the siren went off. He had to hang up to fly his plane. Do you understand me?"

"Yes, I understand. Some of our pilots take off and fight German planes." The loud noise stopped just as he finished. "Many planes shot down."

"Do you mean our planes or German planes?"

"Many German planes. But first they drop bombs. One of our planes also shot down, not far from here. But who is flying, I don't know."

Her heart sank. *Oh God, please don't let it be Jack.*

"I must go now," the pilot said. "Help to clean damage."

"Please, sir. If you see Jack, would you please ask him to call me at this number?"

"What is the number?"

"He knows it. I'm at my hotel in London." Then a thought. "Sir, do you know Jack's friend, Joe?"

"Joe? Yes, Jack's friend. I know him better than Jack."

"If you see him, would you ask him to call me?"

"Yes. I can do that. Does he know your number?"

"No. Do you have something to write it down with?"

"Give me a moment." She heard some scratching sounds and static. "Okay, I'm ready."

She gave him the information and thanked him several times before hanging up. The words, "*one of our planes also shot down,*" replayed in her mind, over and over. It had to be Jack. Why else wouldn't he have called? She glanced up at the clock. It was almost 8:15. She'd forgotten to eat anything for dinner.

She still wasn't hungry.

THE TELEPHONE RANG. Renée shot up from the bed. She looked at the clock. An hour had gone by. She didn't mean to fall asleep, just to rest her eyes a few minutes and pray. She ran to the phone and picked up the receiver. "Hello?"

"I have a phone call for you from a Mr. Joe Basset."

"Yes, please put him through."

"Hello? Is this Renée?"

"It is, Joe."

"I'm sorry I'm calling so late. I just got a message from this pilot friend of mine. He said you called a while ago asking about Jack."

"Yes, I did. Jack and I were talking several hours ago when that air raid siren went off, and he had to hang up. But he said he'd call me after the danger passed and he was safely back on base. But he never did. And then the other man, the Polish pilot I spoke to when I called, said that one of your planes was shot down, but he didn't know who it was. And now you're calling me, instead of Jack…" She began to cry.

Joe didn't say anything for a moment. "I'm sorry, Renée. Is it okay if I call you that? I know we haven't met yet, but Jack talks about you all the time. So, it feels like I know you."

She regained her composure. It was comforting to hear him say that about Jack, that he talked about her so much. And she realized, Joe didn't sound terribly upset. He and Jack were best friends. If Jack had died, Joe would be filled with grief. "Yes, please. Call me Renée. Can you tell me what's happened to Jack? Is he all right? Was it his plane that was shot down?"

"Well, that's several questions in a row. Let me answer them one at a time. I can tell you a little bit about Jack, but I don't know a lot of details. He's not all right, not exactly. But he's not dead. I can tell you that for sure. His plane did get shot down. Don't know exactly how at this point. But I understand he was able to bail out and parachute to the ground. Landed just a few miles from here in some pasture."

She was so relieved. "Have you seen him? Have you talked with him?"

"No, I haven't. And doesn't look like I'm going to get to do that now."

"Why? What's happened?"

"Well, I'll get to that. Let me finish telling you what I know.

And I know this to be true, because I heard it from our Group Commander a short while ago. When they found Jack in that field, he was alive but unconscious. He was banged up pretty good. Must have landed hard, and that's likely what knocked him out. One of his legs was all busted up. I know from experience, when you're landing with a parachute you need both your legs to be in solid shape. He has some other injuries, but the CO wasn't sure what they were. But he said they didn't see that Jack was bleeding anywhere. And this is important, they also didn't see any burns."

"Joe, you said a moment ago that you wouldn't be able to see Jack. Why is that? Where have they taken him?"

"Well, we have a sick bay here at the base but, due to all the damage we got from this bombing, and how serious Jack's injuries are, they gave him some first aid and put him in an ambulance. I got there as it was driving off. One of the guys said they were taking him to some hospital in London for surgery."

"Surgery?" she said.

"I think it was just for his busted leg, but I can't be sure. But the guy I was talking to said Jack was conscious before they put him in the back of the truck."

As hard as it was to hear all this, she was relieved that God spared her from her worst fears.

"Look," Joe said, "he's my best friend in the world. If I could, I'd take the next week off and drive to London to be with him. But these Nazi planes are coming over the Channel every day now, so they won't give us any time off. But if I hear anything more about how Jack is doing, I'll be sure to call and let you know."

"Thank you so much, Joe. I appreciate that." Then she got an idea. "I just had a thought. You know about his twin brother, Elliot."

"Yes, Ma'am. He told me all about that."

"I may not reach Elliot tonight, but I'm sure he'll want to know about what happened. And when I tell him, I'm nearly positive he'll be able to find out where they've taken Jack. So, if I find out any news, I'll call you too."

"That's a great idea, Renée. And when you do see him, tell him we're all pulling for him back here, and that I'll get up there, wherever he is, just as soon as they give me a day off."

"I will, Joe. Thank you so much for calling me back tonight."

"You are most welcome."

She hung up the phone. "Thank you, God." After another quick look at the clock, she picked up the receiver again and dialed Elliot's hotel.

The front desk clerk answered. She asked if Elliot was in. He recognized her from previous calls and said, "I'm sorry, Madam, but Major Turner is not here tonight. I can take a message for him, but I'm not sure when he'll be returning. As you know, he's in and out quite a lot these days."

"That's okay. No message this time. I'll try his office number tomorrow morning."

37

THE NEXT MORNING, Renée had called Elliot's office as soon as it opened. She'd left a message with an adjutant asking for Elliot to call her at the hotel as soon as possible. It was a family emergency. She was pretty sure Elliot wouldn't have mentioned his relationship with Jack to anyone there. The young man assured her he'd pass the message on right away.

Two hours later, her telephone rang. She picked it up.

"Hello, Renée? What's wrong? Are you okay?"

"I'm fine, Elliot, but something's happened to Jack. I tried calling last night as soon as I heard, but you weren't home."

"I'm on my way back to London now. Should be there within the hour. What's happened to Jack? Is he all right?"

"He's alive, but I found out from his friend Joe that his plane was shot down late yesterday afternoon, just after five." She explained everything Joe had told her, including that Jack had been transported to a hospital in London for surgery.

"If he wasn't burned or shot, I wonder why he needed surgery."

"I don't know. Is there any way you can find out? And maybe what hospital they brought him to?"

"I definitely can. I may even know where they brought him,

but let me make a few phone calls and get back to you. If there's a chance we can see him today, are you able to go?"

"I hope so. They have me on the schedule as a backup. The girl who's supposed to work was sick yesterday. I'll have to call and see. How soon would you be able to pick me up?"

"Probably within the hour, but let's wait and see if he's even allowed to have visitors yet. I'll call you back as soon as I know. Thanks so much for calling me, Renée. So sorry I haven't been able to spend more time with you lately. Maybe after we see Jack, we can grab a bite to eat on our way home."

"That would be nice. Call me back soon."

JUST OVER AN HOUR later, Renée stood on the sidewalk in front of her hotel. She didn't have to work after all, and Elliot had called from his office on Baker Street. He was on his way to pick her up. He'd said Jack's hospital was in southeast London, a thirty to forty minute drive away. It dawned on her that the car drive there would be the most time she had spent with Elliot in a month.

She was also aware, now at the prospect of being with both men together, that her feelings for Jack had grown far stronger than her affection for Elliot. But was it just that? The amount of time they had spent together? Would she feel differently had Elliot been able to give her equal time? She wasn't sure but didn't think so. They may look the same but in at least a dozen ways they were entirely different. She was almost certain that what she felt for Jack had much more to do with those differences.

But what would it be like when all three of them were together? She looked down the street and saw Elliot's car come around the corner. She stepped up to the curb as he pulled up and got in when he opened her door from the inside.

"So good to see you," he said as they drove off. "I hate that I've had to leave you alone so much. I wish I could say things will improve very soon, but it doesn't seem I have any control over that."

"That's okay, Elliot. I understand." She did understand but what was also true was that she didn't feel very alone anymore. "When you called a few minutes ago you said you'd learned some more details about Jack's injuries."

"Yes, I did." He turned left at the end of the street. "The surgery was for a badly broken leg. Broken in two places, they said. That's why they brought him to the Royal Herbert Hospital over in Woolwich. They have the best orthopedic surgeons there in London. He also has a nasty cut on his left hand that required numerous stitches. He's cracked some ribs and has a concussion. But the doctor I spoke with said he expects Jack to make a full recovery. It'll just take a while."

As he said that last part, his expression changed. "You sound relieved," Renée said.

"I am. Right after Jack and I first met, I called his CO to find out more about him, how he was doing. He said Jack was one of the finest pilots on base. Very skilled and nearly fearless. That made me a little nervous. We're losing so many skilled and fearless pilots these days. When I first got your call, I was sure we'd lost him. But injuries like this, they'll keep him on the ground for a good long while. Maybe long enough for this air battle to end."

Renée hadn't thought about that. But if true, she wouldn't have to worry about losing Jack in one of his dogfights anymore. "That makes me feel a little hopeful. Haven't had much of that lately." He turned another corner. They were now on Piccadilly and drove past the Ritz. Then he turned again, right on St. James Street. "I recognize this."

"We're actually going to be driving right past the little pub we've eaten at before. The one on Pall Mall."

"The Cross and Sword," she said. The one where she'd first met Jack.

"Then we'll be driving past Trafalgar Square. Have you been there yet?"

"I don't think so."

"Then we'll be taking a long drive along the Thames. You'll be seeing all kinds of new London sites you've never seen before. Of course, none of it will look as nice as it usually does, what with all these sandbags everywhere and the Home Guard practicing their drills on every spare patch of grass."

"I'm getting used to that."

They drove along for the next thirty-five minutes without too much conversation. Occasionally, Elliot would point out some point of interest or other and share some story about it. But that was pretty much it.

That was one of the very different things about Jack. Their conversations. They never had any long, blank sections where no words were exchanged. Jack would use such moments to ask her questions about her job at the store, her family life, what is what like where she lived in France, or childhood memories. He never minded her asking him about similar themes in his life. And he had a strong sense of humor. Laughter was always a part of any conversation with him that was more than a few minutes long.

She looked over at Elliot, his eyes fixed straight ahead on the road. Was he so reserved because of his personality or his upbringing? Was it just because he was British and part of the aristocratic class? How different would he have been had he and Jack grown up together in America? Or for that matter, how much different would Jack be from the man he had become had he been raised here, in Elliot's circumstances?

STILL HALF ASLEEP, Jack tried to roll on his side but something prevented him. A stab of pain for one thing, but something else besides. He opened his eyes. The room was very bright, the light coming in from the window suggesting it was late morning, if not midday. He could turn his head without pain but it made him dizzy.

There was something on his head. He reached to feel what it was and saw his left hand wrapped in bandages. A spot of blood about the size of a quarter stained his palm. He looked down and saw his right leg in a cast that started at his thigh. It was suspended slightly in traction. Something was leaning up against both of his sides, to keep him from rolling over. Using his unbandaged hand, he reached for one of them. A rolled up towel.

Then he became aware of other noises. Men groaning. Someone reading a book aloud. A chair scraping across a wooden floor. Sounds out in the hall. Then he remembered, the air raid. Going after that second German bomber. Watching it start to burn and spiral downward. Then the tracers, the loud bangs. He'd been hit. The engine smoking. The controls, no longer responding. Throwing back the canopy, then bailing out. The ME 109 flying past him, the victory roll.

He remembered. He'd hurt his leg getting out of the plane and cut his hand somehow. That's right. The ground coming up quick below him. Hitting hard. Then nothing until now. Where was he? Some kind of hospital, obviously. But not at Middle Wallop. On one side of him was a wall. The man on the other side of him was asleep. Who could he ask?

He suddenly felt very tired. Maybe he would just close his eyes and rest a few minutes. A doctor or a nurse had to come by at some point, right? He could ask then.

Moments later, he was asleep.

38

"**H**E'S ASLEEP. MAYBE WE should come back later."

"I think we should wake him. The doctor said we should be able to see him at least for a short visit."

Jack's eyes were still closed. He heard a woman then a man's voice. He slowly opened his eyes and was surprised to see Renée and Elliot standing beside his bed. "I'm awake." Immediately, he was aware of the pain again.

"You gave us quite a scare, brother," Elliot said.

Jack looked at Renée. Tears were in her eyes. "I'm sorry. I just remembered. I never called you back last night."

Renée smiled, wiped her eyes. "No, you didn't."

Elliot looked confused.

"Jack and I were actually on the phone yesterday when our call got interrupted by the air raid siren. I knew he had to leave to fly and fight the bombers. I asked him to call me when he got safely back on the ground, so I wouldn't worry."

"Ah," Elliot said, "and he was shot down, so he never called you back." He looked at Jack. "The doctor filled us in on your injuries."

"Well then, maybe the two of you can fill me in. I know at least something about my hand and my leg. I remember hurting them while I was bailing out. But I guess I hurt my head somehow, and it hurts like mad when I try to roll over."

Elliot spoke. "Your leg is broken in two places. They had to stitch up a pretty good gash on your hand, you cracked several ribs, and you have a concussion."

"But you're alive," Renée said. "That's what matters. And the doctor said all these things will get better in time. But the best part, at least for us, is that you won't be able to fly for a while."

"I won't?" What was he saying? Of course he couldn't fly. "Do you know for how long?"

"At least for a couple months," Elliot said.

"A couple months… the war could be over by then."

"Wouldn't that be wonderful?" Renée said.

"I guess." Then he remembered something. "Joe? Is he all right? How about the airfield? Did it suffer much damage?"

"Joe is fine," Renée said. "He was the one who told me about what happened to you. He said to tell you he was sorry he couldn't come, but all passes are still canceled."

"I called about Middle Wallop," Elliot said. "Only one or two German bombers actually dropped bombs on the base, but they were very effective. Sadly, three mechanics were killed trying to close one of the hangar doors when it suffered a direct hit. The hangar and all the planes inside were destroyed. Some other people were wounded. Another hangar suffered damage, and I think one of the office buildings. But the airfield's already up and running again."

Jack wondered if any of those killed were men he knew. "By the way, where am I?"

"You are at Royal Herbert Hospital in Southeast London.

And you're in very good hands. They have the best orthopedic department in the country."

Just then, a nurse walked in. "Excuse me. Major Turner? You have a telephone call. I've already forgotten his name, but it's a Colonel. He says it's urgent."

"I'll be right there." He looked at Jack and Renée. "I'm sorry. I have to get this." He left the ward following the nurse.

Renée stepped closer to his bed. "Oh, Jack. It was so horrible last night, waiting for your call. After the third hour, I knew something terrible must've happened."

"I really am sorry. I was knocked unconscious when I hit the ground. I actually just woke up for the first time a little while ago."

"It's not your fault. I was just…so afraid you were gone." The tears reappeared. She pulled a handkerchief out of her purse.

Her hands were resting on the bed rail. Without thinking, he reached for them with his good hand, resting his palm on top of her right hand, just to comfort her. She quickly took hold of it and squeezed.

Now, that didn't hurt a bit. He decided not to let go, just to see what would happen. She stopped squeezing after a moment but didn't let go. Now, this was very nice. Although it made him a little nervous to think that Elliot might return at any moment.

"Are you in a lot of pain?"

"Only if I move." He smiled. "Or if I breathe too deeply. I guess it's these ribs."

"Do you remember what happened?"

"Very well. I had just shot down a German bomber. Maybe

the one who had bombed Middle Wallop. He was on his way home. I was watching his plane go down, to see if anyone got out. When all of a sudden, someone starts shooting at me from behind. Before I know it, bullets were hitting my plane and the engine started to smoke. I knew I only had seconds to get out. I guess I was rushing and hit my leg on something as I jumped. I don't even remember what happened to my hand." A picture of the ground coming at him quickly flashed into his mind, along with the fear about what would happen when he hit. He winced and closed his eyes.

"That's okay," she said. "You don't have to talk about it anymore. Is there anything I can get you?"

"Some water would be nice."

"Here's a glass of water with a straw." She picked it up from the little table beside his bed. "Here. There's a sink over there. Let me pour a little out so you won't have to sit up to drink it."

He watched every move she made. And for the moment, he was unaware of feeling any pain. He couldn't believe this beautiful young woman was here at his bedside. And it seemed obvious, she cared for him. Could it be possible that her feelings matched his own? As she lowered the water glass, he leaned his head forward and took a sip. So refreshing. "Have you still been okay, here in London? Has it been bombed yet?"

"Do you want another sip?" He shook his head no. "No, we haven't. The sirens go off every day. But so far, they've left us alone. I heard some of the people talking in the hotel restaurant. They're saying Hitler isn't destroying London, because he wants to keep it as one of his trophies like he's done with Paris. Of course, people who say that have already given up hope."

"Don't you believe them, Renée? None of our guys are giving up hope. I've gotta admit, it's a little frightening sometimes when you see how many fighters and bombers they have. During some of these air battles, it feels like there's hundreds of planes in the air. And most of them have black crosses. But I think we're winning. I don't know what the count is now, and I know we're losing plenty of our planes, but I'm seeing a lot more Nazi planes go down than ours. And the other positive thing is, if our plane is damaged and our pilots have to bail out like me, we're landing in friendly territory. If the Germans bail out, they become POWs for the rest of the war. That's gotta count for something."

"I hope you're right. I certainly haven't given up hope. And I think most of the people in London haven't either." She rested her hands on the bed rail again.

Jack felt a strong temptation to reach for her hand again, but didn't. A moment later, he was very glad he resisted that impulse. Elliot walked back into the ward and came up to his bed.

"So sorry about this," Elliot said. "Something of an emergency. One of the special Home Guard groups I've been training in Brighton was in a building that took a direct hit. I've got to head down there and see where things are at. So sorry to cut our visit short, Jack."

"Do you both have to go?"

"Well, I am Renée's ride here."

"I understand. It's just that…I won't see anyone else for who knows how long."

"Oh, I don't know," he said, "it's not that far of a drive. I'm sure we'll get up here again soon."

Jack doubted that very much. Not that Elliot was being

insincere, but he knew how many times Elliot's wartime duties got in the way of him and Renée spending any time together.

"And even if Elliot is detained," Renée said, "I can find my way here by myself. All the roads we took from my hotel were main roads. I can figure out the buses or trolleys, or maybe even take a cab."

"See old man?" Elliot said. "We won't leave you in the lurch very long. One of us or both of us will be back very soon. You just do as the doctor says, so you're not in here a day longer than you need to be." He reached out his hand and Jack shook it. Then he turned and walked away.

Renée stepped up closer, took his hand, squeezed it gently and whispered, "I will be here as often as I can and stay for as long as I can. And if Joe gets a day off, and he can get to London, I'll bring him with me. So don't worry. You won't be alone half as much as you think."

Jack squeezed her hand back and, reluctantly, let it go. "Thanks so much for coming. And thank my brother, too. He left before I could say it myself."

"I will. Have to go." She waved, smiled and headed for the door.

Jack rested his head back on the pillow. Once again, unaware of being in any pain.

39

Sept 7th, 1940
Royal Herbert Hospital, SE London

For the last three weeks, Jack had been mending nicely at the hospital. Due to the rib injury, he still had to sleep on his back but at least it no longer hurt to breathe, or laugh. He wasn't on crutches just yet, but his leg was no longer in traction and twice a day he could be rolled around in a wheelchair for thirty minutes at a time. The stitches had come out on his hand, and he almost had full use of it now. And the concussion had been reduced to the occasional headache and dizzy spell.

The doctor had said Jack would be getting another x-ray tomorrow and, if it looked good, he'd let Jack start getting around on crutches.

True to her word, Renée had come out to visit him every chance she got, which turned out to be only four times so far. But he'd loved every minute of her visits, and they'd talked several more times on the phone.

Telephone calls were also the only way he'd stayed in touch with his brother, Elliot, who hadn't been given even a single day off since Jack had first come to the hospital. The Battle of Britain was still keeping him totally occupied. His last phone call came yesterday and, for the first time since they'd begun to get reacquainted, Elliot's comments, even his tone of voice worried Jack. Of course, Elliot couldn't speak plainly but using something of a code with Jack, he got the clear impression that unless something significant happened to alter the course of things, the RAF could not hold out much longer.

They'd been doing a passable job fighting the air war with the Luftwaffe, day after day, and had actually shot down more German planes than they had lost. But the Germans had been pounding RAF airfields relentlessly for the last month, and the simple fact was: they could keep this up indefinitely, while the RAF's inventory of planes and pilots would soon run dry.

Something had to happen very soon, or the RAF was finished.

Jack tried to put his worries aside as he awaited his two guests this afternoon. He knew Renée was coming. She had called yesterday saying she would. It was her day off. But she had called around noon today to inform him she wouldn't be there until almost four, because Joe had called that morning. He had gotten an unexpected one-day pass and wanted to visit Jack. She agreed to wait there at the hotel, so they could visit him together.

Jack was certainly happy to see his good friend. Not so happy that it had cut his visit with Renée down to an hour. Visiting hours closed at 5PM. Even without that restraint, she'd have to leave then just be able to return to her hotel before the blackout began. Every night, every light in London was either turned off or hidden behind a thick black curtain when the sun set.

There was a slight commotion in the hall. Jack looked up

and smiled when he heard Joe's loud voice apologizing to a nurse. Sounded like he had almost knocked over her cart. A moment later, the two of them walked through the doorway. Renée smiled and waved. Joe followed her gaze and saw Jack, propped up in the bed. A wheelchair was parked at the foot of the bed, a concession granted by the head nurse of the ward. Jack had asked if she would let Joe and Renée push him around for his afternoon thirty-minute stroll.

"Look at you," Joe said, extending his hand as he closed the gap.

Jack shook it and held his grip a few extra seconds. It really was good to see his friend.

"You don't look half bad," Joe said. "Way better than I expected."

Renée came close and kissed him gently on the cheek, which is how she typically greeted him on these hospital visits. Jack had wondered if she would do it this time with Joe standing there. He was glad she did. Joe noticed it, too, and made a "way to go, Jack" face behind her back.

"I'm sorry we're coming so late," Renée said. "But I knew how much you wanted to see Joe and, after talking with him earlier, I could tell how much he wanted to see you."

"No, that's okay. I'm just glad you're both here now, regardless of how long you can stay." Jack wondered if she meant anything by the way she'd phrased that second part. He looked at Joe. "Is everything okay? I was surprised they gave you a day's leave, considering how things are going out there. Talked with Elliot yesterday. Sounds like there's been no let up in the air raids. Haven't been any here in London yet, since that oddball one two weeks ago. But from the sounds of it, all the airfields are getting pounded. How are you doing?"

For just a second, the smile left Joe's face. Then a fake one returned. "Elliot's right. We've been getting pounded. Middle Wallop hasn't gotten hit again, but almost everybody else has. Some airfields have been hit two or three times. And we're averaging three sorties a day." He sighed. Looked down toward the floor for a moment. "It's been rough."

"Tell him, Joe," Renée said.

"Tell me what?"

Joe looked at Jack, the smile gone again. "It's just you and me, Pal. We're the only two left."

"What are you talking about?"

"It's why they gave me leave for the day. As of yesterday, I'm the only American pilot left flying out of Middle Wallop. All the rest of the guys who came over with us on the boat are dead. There's just me left, and you. And you can't fly. They were about to assign me this Polish kid as my wing man. He barely speaks English. Can't understand a word he says over the radio. I told the CO I ain't flying with that guy. Well, I didn't actually say it that politely. Kind of lost my composure, you might say."

"You cussed him out?" Jack said.

Joe nodded.

"He could have sacked you."

"He could have but, now that you're gone, I'm the best pilot he's got left in the squadron. Oh, by the way, I racked up three more kills. So, I'm ahead of you now. Officially." He managed a smile at that.

"Congratulations. So, instead of sacking you he gave you a day off?"

Joe nodded. "He even suggested I use the time to come up and visit you, which I was gonna do anyway on my own."

"Seeing me is supposed to be some kind of therapy for you?"

"Suppose so," Joe said.

"I'm sorry I can't be there with you," Jack said. "Really, I am."

"They say how much more time you going to be in that thing?" He pointed at Jack's cast.

"Could be six to eight weeks."

"Longer, or total?"

"Total."

"So, three to five weeks from here?"

"Sounds right," Jack said. "But then they said I might need therapy for a few weeks to get full use of it. They've got to reevaluate me and re-certify me to fly."

"Looks like I need teach this Polish kid how to speak English."

"Is he a good pilot?"

Joe nodded. "Decent."

"Then work with him, Joe. Don't just do it for his sake. Do it for yours, too. I need you to make it through this thing, buddy. I don't want to be the last American standing."

"I hate this war," Renée said. "It's terrible you two are even having to have such a conversation."

"It is," Jack said.

"So, what's that?" Joe said, pointing to the wheelchair.

"That's my ride. How about you help me into that thing and take me for a ride?" He looked at the clock on the wall. "It's just about four. We can take a walk for thirty minutes."

"Where do you want to go?"

"Anywhere on the grounds," Jack said. "It would be nice to go outside. They don't take me out there too often."

"Then that's what we'll do."

Renée stepped out of Joe's way so he could get closer to Jack. Jack slowly swung his legs over the side of the bed. Renée moved the wheelchair in place and held it. A few seconds later, Jack was sitting safely in the chair.

"Ready whenever you are," Jack said.

Just then, everyone stopped what they were doing. Not just the three of them, but everyone in the ward. They all recognized the sound. A deep, low rumbling up in the sky, coming from the south.

Joe walked over to the nearest window and looked in that direction. "Oh, man. This is not good."

"What is it?" Renée said.

Air raid sirens began to wail outside.

Joe hurried back and grabbed Jack's wheelchair, instantly started pushing it toward the door. Renée followed. "German bombers," he said. "Hundreds of them. Headed this way. Whatta you say we skip the walk outside and head for the basement?"

"They wouldn't bomb a hospital, would they?" Renée said as they walked.

"They're Nazis," Joe said.

40

THE NEXT TWO HOURS were the most frightening moments in Renee's life. Worse than the scariest moments back in France. Along with Jack, Joe and most of the patients and staff of that ward, they huddled together in the dark cellar as one explosion after another tore the city of London apart.

At first, it sounded like the bombs were dropping several miles away, far to the west of the hospital. She'd wondered whether her hotel had been hit or any of the other famous buildings nearby. Or Baker Street, where Elliot worked. Jack had said the explosions were much closer. "Sounds like they're hitting the East End."

Then suddenly, thirty minutes ago, a string of explosions hit close by. People screamed. Renée was among them. The whole building shook and shuddered, like it might come down right on top of them. She sat as close to Jack as she could. Stuck in the chair, he did his best to put his arms around her.

When the nearby explosions stopped, he said, "They were hitting about a half-mile north of here. I think they were going after the docks and wharves along the Thames."

"If so," Joe said, "they are gone."

No one spoke for several minutes.

"Are they done?" Renée asked. "Is it over?"

"I don't know," Jack said. "Maybe."

A minute later, Joe started walking toward the stairs. "I'll check."

"Be careful," she said.

"That was pretty awful," Jack said. "I've never been on the ground before during one of those."

"Me, either. I heard explosions off in the distance back in France, but this was much worse. So much scarier than I imagined from reading the newspapers."

After a few minutes, Joe returned and announced to everyone in the basement, "They're leaving. The bombers. I think it's over."

People slowly began to leave. Most by the stairs, some in the elevator. Joe reached Jack and Renée. "You should see it out there. It's like all of London is on fire. At least everywhere north and west of here."

"Why did this happen?" Renée said. "Is Hitler going to start bombing London now?"

"He might," Jack said. "After that bombing here two weeks ago, which I heard some people say was a mistake, Churchill retaliated on Berlin. Maybe that's where this is going now."

Some room opened in the elevator. The three of them got in. When the door opened into the lobby, Jack asked Joe to wheel him outside. They headed into an open, grassy area and stared at the sky, glowing in three directions. North toward the Thames you could actually see the fire line above the trees and rooftops.

"The Royal Arsenal is over that way," Jack said. "Maybe that's what they were after." He looked at Renée. "Do you know where Elliot is?"

Renée sighed. "I'm not sure. But I know he's not in London. Somewhere south, I think. He seems to work mostly near the coast."

"The coast might be the safest place to be tonight," Joe added.

They watched a few more minutes. It was hard to look away. Renée had never felt so helpless. This town, which she had grown to greatly admire, was burning. Likely, dozens of buildings she'd pass by every time she journeyed here were gone, as well as the people who'd lived and worked in them. Just like that, in a span of two hours.

"What are you guys going to do?" Jack said. "I don't think you can go home tonight. Everything's on fire between here and there."

"Well, I gotta try. My pass is only good until midnight."

"Joe, they're not going to write you up on something like this. They know you went to London, and they'll know what just happened here."

"You're probably right. But I can't just sit around here anyway. Most of the people here can't do a single thing about these bombers. But I can. Two or three times a day. Nothing is on fire south of here. I'll find a cab or bus, get them to take me to the train station. Maybe I can go around the damage, one way or another, and be back to the airfield by the morning. Can't have that Polish kid going after these bombers without me." He smiled and stuck out his hand. Jack shook it. "Well, it's been great seeing you. Both of you." He looked at the situation. "Want me to wheel you back to where you belong? Save Renée the trouble."

"That's probably a good idea."

"I don't mind pushing him," Renée said.

"No problem. It'll just take me a minute."

FOR THE NEXT HOUR after Joe left, Renée and Jack visited by his bedside. But it quickly became obvious, all the added excitement had taken a toll on Jack. He'd actually started to fall asleep in the middle of a work story she had been telling. When she stopped talking, his head snapped straight up. "I'm sorry, keep going," he said.

She'd said it was time for him to get some rest and for her to find someplace to sleep. Jack had come up with a plan. He'd become friends with a couple of the nurses. He called one over was able to get her to sympathize with Renée's plight. The nurse said the building next door was a women's ward, and there were several beds empty on the second floor. In light of the situation, she didn't think it would be a problem for Renée to sleep there. Besides, several of the nurses were facing the same dilemma and would probably join her.

After she'd relocated to the women's ward for a few hours, more German bombers appeared over the London skies and began hitting some of the same places they'd bombed earlier. And once again, everyone headed for the basement. Since she was in the building next door, Renée ran to the basement of Jack's building as soon as the sirens sounded and kept searching until she found him. An orderly had brought Jack downstairs. They huddled together in the basement until almost 4AM when the bombs finally stopped.

When the all-clear came, everyone was exhausted. This time, Renée helped Jack get back to his room. For some reason, the man in the bed next to Jack didn't return that night. They'd passed a linen cart in the hallway. Jack suggested she grab a couple of blankets, throw them on top of the bed and just sleep there. So, that's what she did.

By midmorning the next day, they had a better idea about which sections of the city had received the most damage, and which parts were still closed because of fires. Jack helped her figure out a route back to the Westminster area, where she lived and worked. It appeared, at least for now, the bombers had left the entire area mostly alone.

Before leaving, she made sure Jack had everything he needed, then she leaned over and kissed him on the forehead. One of these days, she decided, she would get a little braver than that and kiss him properly.

(Many years later, whenever Renée looked back on this moment, she'd always think the same thing: had she known of the tumultuous events that followed over the next four weeks, she would have given Jack a proper kiss that day.)

41

October 9th, 1940
Royal Herbert Hospital

J ACK'S CAST HAD been off a week now. Using a single crutch, he had just limped back to his hospital bed and sat in the wooden chair beside it. Lately, he'd been spending more of the day sitting up, or else taking walks, like the one he'd just completed. He was more motivated than ever to get out of this hospital and back in the game.

It was especially frustrating that he hadn't been able to see Renée since September 7th, the evening the London Blitz began. Except for a few bad-weather days, the Germans had bombed London without stop. They had flown daytime raids for another week until their losses became too severe. Then they'd switched tactics and bombed London every night. Among the one-thousand other horrible things about this, it had kept Renée from being able to travel across town to see Jack.

She was afraid to attempt the journey and, even had she been willing, Jack would have never allowed it. Life in London these days was dangerous and unstable. The civilian death toll ran into the thousands and the injured in the tens of thousands.

The bombs seemed to fall wherever they pleased. No rhyme or reason. Whether one lived or died seemed to have everything to do with being in the right place or the wrong place at any given time.

When Jack had learned the Brown's Hotel, like so many other high-end establishments in Westminster, had created a nice shelter in their basement for their guests, he'd advised Renée just to go there every night and stay put until the all-clear was given. So far, her hotel had been spared. Surprisingly Selfridge's, the store where she worked, had also been spared. Several other department stores had taken direct hits.

Jack had not only missed seeing Renée for the last month, Joe had been unable to get free, either. But they had talked on the phone a few days ago, and he seemed in good spirits. Still boasting of the number of planes he'd shot down, convinced now that it would be impossible for Jack to ever catch up. Joe seemed to think that the air war was beginning to tip in their favor. In the last week, he'd been averaging only one or two sorties a day, and they were definitely seeing fewer German planes in the air.

Of course, being at Middle Wallop, Joe wasn't being assigned any missions as far off as London. Maybe he'd have a different opinion if he could see what was happening here.

Jack looked up at the clock. Elliot should be here any minute. Jack had only seen him once in the last month, but they had also talked on the telephone a few times. Like this morning. Elliot had called saying he was driving over to see Jack with "two very urgent matters to discuss." It wouldn't have been like Elliot to give out hints, so Jack hadn't bothered to ask.

But he was definitely intrigued.

From earlier conversations, Jack had learned that Elliot still hadn't talked to their grandfather about him. Elliot said his plan was to confront him in person and, so far, the war was not cooperating with that plan. Maybe this was one of the urgent matters Elliot was on his way over here to discuss with Jack.

Jack had an urgent matter of his own to discuss with his brother.

Renée.

More to the point, he wanted to know the status of Elliot's relationship with her. Jack was totally nuts about her. It seemed to him she felt the same way. But both of them were holding back on letting this romance grow into anything more. He supposed it was out of their respect for Elliot and this idea that he had some prior claim on her affections.

Had Jack seen any evidence to support this, he would've never allowed his heart to go where it had plainly already gone. But all Elliot seemed to produce was polite interest. The last time Jack and Renée had talked, he had asked her plainly what her understanding of their relationship was. "I have no idea," she said. "At first, I thought there was something. I think we were actually dating. But then the war took over. I think he cares for me, but I cannot tell if there is anything more."

Jack had wanted to ask her right then if she wished Elliot *did* feel anything more, but he didn't. The right thing to do was to pick the right time and ask his brother that question first. After all, he didn't come all this way to meet the woman of his dreams and fall in love. He'd come here to find Elliot. And he didn't want anything to destroy their chances of becoming real brothers, who treated each other the way brothers should.

Jack heard footsteps and turned to find his brother walking this way. He was about to greet him cheerfully but saw the serious expression on his face. He was holding an opened envelope in his hand. Jack stood. "Hey Elliot, so good to see you."

"You too, Jack. You're looking much better since I was here last."

"Yes. Definitely feeling better, too. I'm ready to get out of here." They shook hands.

He saw Jack grab the crutch. "You don't need two?"

"No."

"Can you walk?"

"Yes. If you don't mind a slow pace. I'm hoping to change this in for a cane in a day or two if they let me."

"Good. I'd like to talk in private. Maybe we could find a place outside? A bench or something?"

"I know just the place."

Jack led him toward his favorite spot, about a five-minute stroll, as the turtle crawls. Elliot wasn't much for small talk, so Jack decided to see if Elliot could tell him any news about the war. "I was talking with my pilot friend, Joe, recently. He seems to think we might be turning a corner in this thing, at least with the air war. Would you agree?"

Elliot looked around to make sure they were far enough away from listening ears. "Your friend Joe might be right. You can't repeat this, but we're getting some very strong indicators that Hitler may have postponed the invasion, if not called it off altogether."

"Really? That would be wonderful news."

"Wouldn't it? It's strange how things have worked out. Ironic, really."

"How do you mean?"

"You recall about a month ago, just before that first heavy

attack on London, that I said if something didn't happen soon to alter the course of things, the RAF might be finished?"

"How could I forget?" Jack said. "But things do seem better now, don't you think?"

"They are better now. Some would say remarkably so. Here's the ironic thing…when Hitler decided to start bombing London that night in early September, he might have actually handed us the victory. In one sense, it's a horrible thing to say, and I'd never say it aloud in a pub. But by redirecting all his energy away from attacking our airfields, it kept us from going under. We had maybe a week or two left of reserves at that point. If he had stayed on the same path he had been on, we'd have been wiped out, and the invasion would have certainly followed. We would have been powerless to stop him."

"So," Jack said. "These attacks on London are what saved the RAF?"

Elliot nodded. "And now, a much stronger RAF is destroying the Luftwaffe. They're still attacking us in London, but their numbers are down everywhere else. And as I said, we're all but certain the invasion's been called off."

They reached the quiet bench Jack had been aiming for, tucked under a sprawling oak tree. "Go ahead and have a seat, Jack. I think I'll stand."

Jack sat. "You said you had two urgent things to discuss." He pointed at the envelope Elliot was holding. "I'm guessing that's one of them."

Elliot held it in front of him, pulled a letter out from it. Then released an audible sigh. "Yes, maybe we should start with this one." He looked at Jack. "It's a good thing you're sitting down."

42

"So as not to cloud the issue," Elliot said, "I'll get straight to the point." He paused, the emotion straining on his face. "Renée has left England. By now, she's probably back in France."

"What?" Jack was stunned. The words sounded like utter nonsense. "You're serious?" Of course, he was. Elliot didn't kid. "How…why?"

"It's in this letter. She says in here she sent you one, too. Probably more red tape involved for you to get it here, so she asked me to come and tell you myself. Just ask a nurse to hunt your letter down. I'm sure—"

"Elliot, why did she leave? How did she leave? What does the letter say?"

He sighed again. "I've handled this badly. I should have seen it coming. I've been so distracted these past weeks."

"How could you have seen it coming?" Jack didn't even see it coming. It made no sense. Why would she do such a thing?

"Well, I suppose it started three or four days ago. I was in Bristol handling a security situation. Apparently, a man came to my Baker Street office, looking for me. I have no idea how he even knew where to find me. But he'd come there that morning from France. Told my assistant he was a fisherman, a friend of Renée's family. He was looking for her, said he had urgent news about her family."

Jack could already see where this was going.

"I should've spoken to the man myself, found out his news first. But as I said, I was distracted and all I could think about was how desperate she had been wanting to get news about her mother and brother."

"I know," Jack said. "She talks about it all the time."

"So, I told my assistant to go ahead and give the man her address and phone number at the hotel. Clearly, a bad idea."

"I take it the news from home wasn't good."

"Not at all. Where should I start?" Elliot scanned the two-page letter. "Obviously, the Germans are settling in as an occupation force. Starting to install military governors throughout northern France. There is a strong indication that an SS Colonel is arriving soon and may commandeer Renée's family home as his headquarters. You know how frail her mother is."

Jack did.

"From what I understand, when this happens, they usually move in with their staff and completely take over. Also, Philippe was forced to leave."

"Why would this officer force Phillipe out? Isn't it a big house? Who else would take care of Renée's mother?"

"I should rephrase that. The Colonel coming is not why Philippe left. An order was given throughout the region, essentially, giving the Nazi's permission to draft every able-bodied young French man to be sent to work in German munitions factories. Basically, as slave labor. He fled to avoid this and has probably joined the French Resistance."

"Resistance?" Jack said. "Is there such a thing, already?"

"Nothing very organized, but it's beginning to take form. Before I left France, that was part of my job. We anticipated the fall of France and had already begun to recruit key men who might lead a resistance effort. Of course, once we were forced out so abruptly, we lost all contact with them. It would seem this fisherman who came looking for Renée was involved with them. He has been making discreet night runs in his trawler, back and forth between Dover and Calais for over a month. In fact, before he left and before I knew there was any chance of Renée returning with him, I arranged for him to smuggle in a crate of two-way radios, so we can start communicating more effectively with the Resistance in that area."

"Wait, so you're saying…Renée traveled back to France, at night, through Nazi-occupied waters, in a boat loaded with spy equipment?"

Elliot looked down. "I know, I know."

"Elliot, if they had been caught, she'd have been shot. Tortured first, then shot."

"I know. I had no idea she was even thinking of going back with him. I didn't even know what the family news was until I read her letter."

"But you managed to find out this fisherman was part of the Resistance and willing to work as a smuggler."

"I never actually talked to the man myself. I just set things in motion. Like I said, it was badly handled."

Jack had to control his anger. Elliot was clearly sorry about this. Then another thought. "Do you even know if they made is safely back to France? When you started, you said she was probably back in France by now. Do you know that for certain?"

Elliot shook his head. "One assumes."

"Assumes?"

"The man's been traveling back and forth safely for over a month. He knows what he's about."

"Maybe. We can certainly hope." Jack felt sick inside. What if they had gotten caught? She could be dead already.

"I do have a way of finding out," Elliot said. It won't be today. Maybe not even for a week. But the point of sending the radios was to open up a line of communication. Specifically, in that region of France. The fact that this SS Colonel is making her home into his headquarters gives us a clear rationale for making inquiries. I promise you, if I learn anything about her welfare, I will tell you."

That was at least some measure of reassurance. But short of learning that Renée had died in the Blitz, this was the worst kind of news Elliot could have delivered. How was Jack supposed to keep his sanity in the days ahead? He would be sick with worry. He'd already stepped up his prayers for her safety every day, just with the nightly bombings. Now, if she'd even made it home safely, she would be taking care of her mother under the eye of a ruthless SS officer.

"I am, sorry, Jack. I wished I would've handled this so much differently."

"That's all right, Elliot. You didn't do anything deliberate here. We'll just have to pray God keeps her safe. What else can we do?"

"Right."

"You said there were two urgent matters you wanted to

discuss. Please tell me the other one isn't this bad?"

"It's really not bad news at all. Mind if I have a seat?"

Jack scooted over to one side of the bench.

"You remember that I said I hadn't mentioned our reunion to Grandfather yet? That I wanted to wait until I could do so in person?" Jack nodded. "As it turns out, with the news that the German invasion has been called off, and since getting ready for that event has been my primary duty, really since coming back to England, I've been given a long-overdue two-day pass, which starts tomorrow. I was thinking, if you're up for it, we could go and see him together."

This was totally unexpected and tapped into a totally separate but equally deep pool of emotions. Jack didn't know what to feel.

"I could pick you up in the morning tomorrow. We could drive there in a few hours. I think having us there both together when I confront him will be far more effective than me just going there alone."

"Is that what you're mostly expecting, a confrontation?"

"Well, it won't get loud or come to blows but, yes, it's not going to be a pleasant conversation. I am not sure how he will react, to be honest. I'm not sure how he's even doing, physically, for that matter. I haven't been keeping in touch these days."

"Has his health been poor?"

"It hasn't been great. I'm assuming it hasn't improved these past several months. I think I already mentioned that the estate has been in decline for some years. Since the war started, especially since Churchill took over and the country has become so united, men like him who publicly supported Hitler, have been blacklisted economically. Many are already ruined. I wouldn't be at all surprised to find we are in the same condition. Of course, he doesn't confide in me on such matters, but I think it's fair to say, the weight of all this cannot have improved his health."

Jack was a little surprised to see Elliot's wholesale lack of compassion for their grandfather. But who was he to judge? If he'd been here and knew what Elliot knew about the situation, maybe he'd feel the same way. "Are you at all concerned that our visit might put him over the top? What if he has a heart attack or stroke? After all the things you said, then you add me to the picture, standing right there in front—"

"I think he'll be fine," Elliot said. "Physically anyway. If he has a couple of bad days after we're gone, I'd think it well deserved. After what he put us through. Especially you and our father." He stood. "You'll forgive me if I'm not feeling a surge of pity for the man at the moment."

Jack guessed their little chat was over. He stood as well.

"So, are you good for tomorrow? Pick you up, say, around nine?"

"That would be fine."

"And it won't all be sour grapes," Elliot said. "It's a nice drive there, once we get north of London. Be a chance to see places the war hasn't touched yet. And the estate itself and the surrounding area are really quite beautiful. Maybe I'll take you on a tour before we meet with Grandfather. Neither of us might be in the right mood after."

43

ON THE FOLLOWING DAY, the first hour of the drive with Elliot proved quite challenging. It wasn't the company, but the view outside. So many London buildings in ruins. Whole blocks in some areas. Nothing had been spared. Churches, government buildings, monuments, architectural landmarks, storefronts.

"Such a waste," Jack said, when they finally got past all the bomb damage and started driving north into the country.

"Isn't it?" Elliot said. "Hard to fathom how long it can take to build something compared to the minutes it takes to tear it down. And we didn't even drive through the worst of it. Some areas are still impassable because of all the debris. Oh, by the way, did you find the letter from Renée?"

"No. I asked a nurse to look. She hadn't found it before we left, but she said she'd keep looking."

As Elliot had promised, the farther they got from London, the more pleasant the surroundings. So much of England's countryside seemed completely untouched by the modern age. Mile after mile, a patchwork of low rolling hills, in various tones of green or beige, interrupted here and there by a smattering of farms or the occasional village.

They eventually began to exchange childhood stories, getting caught up on each other's misadventures and the regrettable decisions of their youth. Although both men agreed, Jack's stories were far more colorful and more often involved skirting the boundaries of the law. Elliot's worst infractions landed him a visit to the Head Master's office, at Eton College, accompanied by a stern lecture and maybe a caning. Jack was fascinated to hear Elliot describe what it was like to grow up in a boarding school, a world Jack couldn't begin to fathom.

As they drove along, Jack kept looking for an opening to discuss Elliot's relationship with Renée, but one never presented itself. He had decided not to push it after the challenging talk they had yesterday at the hospital.

Late in the afternoon, the northerly route they had been taking curved toward the west. "Not much farther from here," Elliot said.

"I had no idea it was this far north."

"Scotland is only about sixty more miles north of here." They came to a fork in the road. Elliot turned right and went down the hill which quickly curved to the left. "The nearest village is just up ahead. Took a little longer to get here than I planned."

Jack looked at his watch. It was almost 4PM. "Is your grandfather expecting us?"

"Somewhat. I called two days ago right after I got word about my leave. Told our butler I was planning to visit in a few days. Didn't mention you. There's a pub up here on the right. We can quench our thirst there and use the phone. I don't expect a problem, but it also has some decent rooms to rent on the second floor. If need be, we can bunk their and visit the house in the morning."

"Whatever you think is best. I'm easy to please."

They both had a pint in the pub. Some of the regulars instantly recognized Elliot but were shocked when Jack walked in. Elliot seemed to enjoy their reaction and admitted freely when asked, "Yes, we are related. No, your eyes aren't playing tricks on you. Meet Jack, my long lost twin brother. And if you share a few words with him, you'll discover something else. My brother's a Yank."

With that, he took a seat. He leaned over and whispered, "They're going to have some fun with that. Considering who Grandfather is, I'm sure the tongues will be wagging long after we've left." He took another sip of his beer then stood back up. "I'll go make that phone call and be right back."

Jack was worried all the patrons would come over and start asking him questions. None did. But it was pretty clear, judging by the looks and expressions on their faces, he had certainly become the main topic of conversation.

A moment later, Elliot returned. "It's all set. The butler said my room is ready. I asked to have one of the guest rooms available, and he said one was always kept in the ready. I didn't mention you, but my grandfather will at least know I'm coming. So finish up and when you're ready, we'll head over. It's just five minutes from here."

They rode back through the village the way they had come, and turned left onto a private road. Soon they had arrived at a large wrought-iron gate. It was closed with a large chain lock around it. Next to it was a small guardhouse, unoccupied.

Elliot got out of the car. "A sign of our changing fortunes. Notice the overgrown vines and the lack of a gatekeeper. He was here the last time I visited. Thankfully, I have a key."

A few moments later, they were driving down a tree lined path toward a beautiful mansion. Perhaps it had seen better days, but it was still majorly impressive to Jack. It looked to be four stories with multiple gabled roofs and more chimneys than he could count. There was a main center section, and matching wings to the left and right. On the left was a smaller, matching building but the end of it disappeared behind a large row of hedges. They drove around a large, rounded driveway with a statue and fountain at the center.

Elliot pulled right up to the front door. "Welcome home, Jack." And he actually laughed.

Jack couldn't help but laugh, too. "This is crazy."

"I suppose half of this place is now yours. Although I suspect that won't add up to much, if Grandfather's been lax on his taxes. Are you ready?"

Jack sighed. "I guess. You're going to do all the talking, right?"

"I'll certainly start it off. It will be interesting to see how the old man reacts. I've thought about it off and on over the last day or so and I can't begin to guess." He opened the car door and got out.

Jack did the same.

As Elliot reached the oversized wooden front door, it opened as if on cue. The butler stood there and greeted him. "Mr. Elliot, how good to see you." He looked at Jack and froze.

"No, Mr. Krebs. You are not seeing double. This is the guest I mentioned. Although, to be more precise, he is really a member of the family, not a guest. Meet Mr. Jack Turner, my twin brother."

Krebs eyes almost bugged out of his head.

"Although, unless I miss my guess, you already know about him. You've been with this family since before I was born, correct?"

Krebs nodded.

"Then you most certainly have met the young man before. Likely as a baby, would be my guess. You might even remember his father. Or should I say, our father, whom I've still never met."

Krebs seemed to be trying to regain his composure. "Won't you come in?" He stepped to the side and both men entered the house. "Do you have any bags?"

"We both just have overnight satchels Krebs, but we can get them ourselves. Is Grandfather expecting us?"

"He's expecting you... and a guest. You'll find him in the parlor in his favorite chair. Would you like me to announce you?"

"No, thank you. And Krebs, I meant no offense by what I said a moment ago. I know you weren't complicit in what happened all those years ago, and I don't hold you one whit responsible."

"Very good, sir."

"Follow me, Jack." He took a few steps then turned left.

Jack did his best to keep up, but he was mesmerized by the interior of this place. The polished wood floors, the oriental rugs, the massive wall paintings, the double-high etched ceilings, the crystal chandeliers, the ornamental crown molding. Instantly, the various living quarters of his childhood—all of them slums—began replaying in his mind as if on a carousel. Jack looked at Elliot, walking past it all as though it were some kind of warehouse or office hallway.

He didn't even see it. Any of it.

They walked past several doorways to a room at the end of a wide hall, then stepped into another amazing place. A large white marble fireplace centered the far wall, with floor-to-ceiling bookshelves covering the walls to the left and right. At the other end, a tall French window lined with burgundy drapes allowed natural light to pour in. Surrounding the fireplace, and placed along the edges of an oriental rug were a pair of overstuffed upholstered green chairs and a much more refined-looking, and less comfortable sofa.

One of the green chairs faced the fireplace, so Jack couldn't see the front. An aged, distinguished British voice emerged from that space. "Elliot, is that you? You've finally decided to pay us a visit?"

"I have, Grandfather. But I'm sure, Mr. Krebs must have mentioned I've brought home a guest. Someone I'm quite certain you will want to meet. Although, *meet* is not the best choice of words. Perhaps I should have said, *Meet again*."

After a long pause, the old man stood and turned around. His eyes went straight to Jack. He was stunned. He looked at Elliot, who was smiling, then back at Jack. His head slowly shook back and forth, involuntarily refusing the image before him.

"Grandfather, it's Jack. Jack Turner, my twin brother. You remember, Jack?"

44

"J...Jack?"

"I think the resemblance is remarkable," Elliot said. "Don't you? Of course, that should be no surprise. Since we both sprang from the same fertilized egg and both grew in the same woman's womb for nine months. What woman you ask? That would be your daughter, our mother. And as it turns out, we were born only minutes apart on the very same day, and at the very same place."

The same incredulous look on his face, Grandfather said, "How did you—"

"How did we finally find each other, after the grand scheme you engineered to keep that from ever happening? Well, it wasn't my doing. That's for sure. I never knew my brother existed until a short while ago. Jack made this happen. And you should hear to what lengths he's gone and the great sacrifices he made to pursue this reunion." He looked at Jack. "Share with him a little bit of your journey, Jack. You know, the boat ride over, the U-boat threats, joining up with the RAF. Flying all those missions against the Luftwaffe." He glanced at Grandfather. "He's actually a war hero. A flying ace, just like our father was. And that cane Jack's holding? Almost two months ago, after downing two Nazi bombers, he was shot down and almost died." Elliot paused to let Jack speak.

Jack didn't really want to, but he added in a few details to what Elliot had said.

"And I've learned," Elliot continued, "Jack did all this not because he had some strong desire to fight the Germans. It was the only way he could afford to get over here from the States. And he took all these risks without an ounce of interest in sharing our wealth. Indeed, when he began his search he had no idea if he did find me, whether I'd be a prince or pauper."

Jack was feeling pretty awkward about now. He was standing here before the man who had denied him the love and comfort of his mother, the friendship and a thousand missed memories with his brother, and had unjustly condemned him and his father to a lifetime of poverty, Jack thought he would be overcome with hatred. Maybe fighting back feelings to lunge at the man and pummel him with his fists.

But all Jack felt was pity. He was an old, worn-out, pathetic, broken shell of a man with nothing but deadness and sadness in his eyes. Jack was, however, enjoying the way his brother was handling the situation.

"Speaking of reunions," Elliot said, "you should know Grandfather, and it humbles me a good deal when I consider it, that Jack's main goal when he embarked on this adventure was to find me. That's it. That was the goal. He wanted to secure a future far different from our past, one where we two, as brothers…" Elliot began choking up as he said this. "Where we would have the opportunity to possibly become friends and at least have the chance to spend some time together doing the kinds of things brothers often do."

Elliot wiped the tears forming in his eyes. Jack looked at the old man. The stunned look was gone. Another look. Jack didn't know what it was. It didn't seem like regret.

"It might bring you some small relief, Grandfather, to know that Jack didn't come here to satisfy some primal urge for revenge against you. We both know, don't we, that a vicious injustice was visited upon him and our father by you many years ago. And this surprises me...not that you might have done something unjust, but that Jack didn't come here on some vendetta to square the score. I'm sure, if I were him, that might be my first and only motivation. But the truth is, he may harbor some dark feelings toward you, and rightfully so, but I haven't heard him utter a single word against you since our first conversation. Whereas I, when I think of you, feel nothing but contempt."

"Do you imagine that this is something new for me, Elliot? Feeling contempt from you?"

"You've felt it before, have you? Then take that feeling and multiply what I'm feeling now by at least a factor of four. What you have done, Grandfather... the heartlessness, the utter cruelty, the wholesale lack of any consideration for the feeling and well-being of others. And not just others, but your own flesh and blood. How could you have done this? How could you have possibly justified something like this? Even in the moral vacuum of a mind like yours?"

"Elliot." He sighed. "You would not be able to comprehend the situation as it was then if I tried to explain it a dozen different ways. Look, I am tired and feeling rather faint. I have to sit down."

"That's fine. But if you must sit down, please sit down over in the other chair. We are not through talking, and I refuse to talk to the back of a chair."

"Very well." Grandfather walked slowly across the rug and did as Elliot requested. The two of them followed behind and sat on the sofa, slightly apart, facing him.

"Actually sir," Elliot said, "I think I do understand a good bit of what was taking place *back then*, as you say. Jack and I both understand it, to a good degree. I think the story goes something like this..." Elliot went on and talked for several more minutes, explaining what they'd imagined their grandfather's scheme was; even what his motivations might have been. Things similar to the conversation they'd had back at the pub when he and Jack had first met. Their grandfather's complete and utter rejection of their father as a proper husband for his daughter. The scandal of her pregnancy. The outrage over their elopement. The ruined reputation of the family name. The economic consequences and ramifications. The fortuitous crash of their father's airplane, and his crippling injuries. The sudden and convenient dependence on the young couple for Grandfather's help. The conjured-up scheme to force their separation. The offer to purchased their parents' silence and willingness to cooperate with the myriad of lies.

Jack watched Grandfather's eyes as Elliot ran through the litany of deceit. Clearly, it was all true.

When, Elliot had finished, "So, how far off was that? Have I missed anything?"

The old man didn't reply at first. Then he said, "I don't know what you are expecting from me, Elliot. Do you want me to say, you have won? You've figured out all my sins and schemes and have laid my soul bare? Okay, then I'll say it. You have won. I have no answer to any of the things you've said. And clearly, seeing Jack here now, and hearing all he has been through to find you, it is obvious my great plan has failed."

"Grandfather, I don't want you to admit I have won. I want you to admit you were wrong. Horribly wrong. More than that, I want you to see it. To see the wrong in it, from top to the bottom. And everywhere in between. You wronged Jack. And me. You wronged our father. And our mother, your own daughter. Forcing two young people who genuinely loved each other, and who got married in the eyes of God, and who were willing to live together as man and wife…you forced them to live the rest of their lives apart. And for what reason? Because Father was an American? Because he didn't have noble blood running through his veins? Grandfather, he was a decorated war hero. A man you should have been proud to welcome into this home. But for your silly, outdated, antiquated ideology you subjected this entire family to so much suffering, heartache and ruin. And what do you have to show for it? Absolutely nothing."

All three of them sat there for what felt like several minutes to Jack. He thought he saw at least some wetness in the old man's eyes, but a few moments later, it was gone.

Finally, he looked at Jack and said, "How did you learn about us? About…your brother?"

Jack was just about to answer when Elliot spoke up. "You needn't worry. Our father didn't break his forced silence, the silence you extorted from him all these years. It happened quite by accident. Tell him, Jack."

Jack explained about the framed picture on his father's dresser that he'd thought was him all these years. About knocking it over and reading what it said on the back. A few other details about his conversation with his dad.

"Did you hear that, Grandfather?" Elliot said. "Our father was so afraid of losing the pittance of an allowance you sent him each month, that even after Jack had uncovered the secret himself, he said Jack would have to come here to find the answers to all his questions on his own." Elliot stood, took two steps toward his grandfather and said in an even more forceful tone, "I want you to hear this. This extortion arrangement ends now. Do you hear me? You will not penalize him a penny. In fact, starting this month, you instruct your accountant to send him four times the monthly allowance from now on. Even with our setbacks here, I know that's a small sum for you. If you do not do this, I promise you…I will never set foot in this house again until it's to arrange your funeral, and long before that I will give an exclusive interview to the Times, laying out this entire sordid affair. You will finish up your days in utter loneliness and isolation, and whatever remains of your reputation will be in tatters."

45

Elliot had dropped Jack off at the hospital the following day just after 3PM. The balance of their time with the Earl of Bainbridge was odd and strained, to say the least. When Elliot had finished his rant, their grandfather just sat there staring at them for the longest time. He didn't say a word.

Finally, Elliot had said, "Right then, I'll let you return to your favorite chair while I give Jack a tour of the house and estate, seeing as he never got the chance to be here before today. Dinner still at six?" Grandfather had nodded that it was. Elliot and Jack left him a moment later.

Just before the grand tour, Elliot briefly apologized to Jack for subjecting him to that exchange but added he'd felt it was necessary, so Grandfather could feel the full impact of his words. He didn't bring the subject up again for the rest of their time together.

It had been a fascinating tour. When he made the effort, Elliot could be an animated storyteller. He didn't just mention the various points of interest; numerous times he added an interesting note of family history or a pleasant personal memory. On a couple of occasions as they passed a mirror, Jack caught a glimpse of the two of them walking together. Both times, the image startled him. It was so surreal. Here he was, walking with his long-lost twin brother, through the historic family mansion, a place in which Elliot obviously felt right at home and where Jack couldn't have felt more like a stranger.

Still, he enjoyed it very much. By the time his head hit the pillow that night in a palatial guest room, at least Elliot no longer felt like a stranger. Jack's thoughts as he'd drifted off to sleep alternated between worries and prayers for Renee's safety, to pleasant thoughts about the way Elliot had defended Jack and their father that afternoon.

But now, Jack was back in the real world, hobbling with his cane through the hallways of Royal Herbert Hospital toward his room. Along the way, he had searched for and found the nurse who'd promised to hunt down that letter from Renée.

He found her and she said she had found it late yesterday afternoon and placed it on the little table next to his bed. Jack hurried toward the ward. When he reached it, his eyes instantly shot to that table. He made a beeline for Renée's letter, sat in his chair and opened it up.

My Dear Jack,

It pains me that I was unable to share these words with you in person, but circumstances would not allow it. I tried to call several times but could not get through. I did send a similar letter with a longer explanation of what's happened to Elliot, figuring a letter would get to him first. Hopefully, he has already spoken to you and explained these things for me.

I only have a few minutes before the family friend who contacted me comes to pick me up and take me back to France. It is late and quite dark. The clouds that were here all afternoon have turned off both the moon and the stars, so our Channel crossing should be safe. So please don't worry.

As you know, I have been overwhelmed with concern about my mother's welfare, as well as Philippe. My family friend brought the first news that I've heard since I left France months ago. Sadly, the news was all bad. I hope when you hear it, you will agree I had no choice. Philippe had to flee or else he would have been forcibly sent to Germany as slave labor. My mother has no one to care for her now but, worse than that, I cannot bear the thought of her being mistreated by an SS Colonel who, I'm told will soon occupy our home.

I know there is some danger for me returning home but, as you know, I left France to escape danger and, look, London is being bombed every night. Hundreds are killed every week all around me. I would be in more danger if I had stayed put. And you, my Love, will be in far more danger than I every day, the moment you are released to fly missions again.

So please, try not to fear for my safety very much. Since these circumstances are unavoidable, I have to believe the Lord will take care of me as I pray He takes care of you.

I must sign off. My friend is here, knocking on the door. A moment ago, I referred to you as my Love. I hope you will forgive me for being so bold. But I felt I must say it. I must tell you how I feel, Jack. Neither of us knows for *certain what the future holds, whether one or even both of us might perish. I will be praying every day against this but, should the worst come, I could not bear it if I didn't get the chance to say how much I have grown to love you. I think about you at least a hundred times a day. When I am with you, I am the happiest I have ever been. And when we are apart, I am in constant longing to be with you again.*

Well, he's knocking again, so I must go. I hope you feel the same. I've been thinking for some time that you do but have been unable to express it out of respect for your brother. At the right time, I will say what I need to say to him, but this is the right time to say what I've needed and wanted to say to you, for quite some time.

With all my love,
Your Renée

Jack was smiling, on the inside even more. But he was also instantly aware of a growing sadness. To now know for certain that she did love him, and it sounded as if her love was as intense as his own, but then to realize he could not see her, touch her or kiss her. Not now, not tomorrow. Who knew how long these terrible circumstances would keep them apart?

He picked up her letter and reread it again, trying his best to focus mainly on the things she said about loving him but he could not help but wonder...where was she now? What was she doing? Was she safe? He couldn't do a thing to protect her. She was right in saying she was likely in more danger living here in London than being there in France. But it didn't feel true.

It felt awful, and he felt helpless.

46

Dainville, a village near Arras, France
Around 4pm

KEEPING HER EYES straight ahead, Renée walked on the other side of the street past three German soldiers, smoking cigarettes as they sat along the only undamaged section of a short stone wall. It outlined the main road heading into town. She ignored their smiles at first, then their stares. Since arriving back, she only came into town when absolutely necessary and, when she did, she felt constant fear, especially when a German soldier came near.

Now she faced three. One yelled out in passable French, "*Bonjour, jolie. Maintenant, je suis amoureux.*"

She did not answer or look back. There was only one man from whom she longed to hear such words, and he was back in England. She wondered what Jack was doing right now. Was he off his crutches yet? Was he still in the hospital?

She side-stepped around some thick ruts in the road, which she realized were actually tank tracks, hardened in mud. As she crested a slight hill, the schoolhouse she'd attended as a girl came into view. Part of the roof had caved in, the wall beneath it a pile of rocks. Rows of desks and the chalkboard were in plain view. It was heartbreaking to see. Half the buildings in town looked the same or worse. Some of them had been built hundreds of years ago. In a flash, the Germans simply destroyed them. They seemed to treat everything that belonged to others with the same indifference. Like children playing catch with priceless treasures.

To Renée, more painful than the damaged buildings were the friends and neighbors killed by German planes. In her village alone, eleven had died in the first two weeks, including three children. She had known every one of them, the story behind each of their lives. Some of their faces flashed in her mind, snippets of conversations. She quickly shut them out before the pain could take hold.

Turning the corner, she looked down the main avenue. She could still scarcely take in the sight. She'd never get used to it, if she lived a hundred years. Bright red and white Nazi flags hung beneath the windows of every government building. German trucks and military vehicles parked along the curbs. Soldiers in gloomy grey uniforms huddled about, rifles and machine guns strapped to their backs, eyeing the townspeople with arrogance and contempt.

Clearly, it was their town now, to do with as they pleased.

Where was the French Army? She'd asked one of her friends that question the second day she had been back in town. Had they even tried to put up a fight? How could they have abandoned everyone so quickly? The friend simply said: "France, as we know it, is no more."

She thought about her brother, Philippe. She had no idea where he'd gone, didn't even know if he was still alive. She fought back tears as she neared the town bakery. She would not give the Germans the pleasure of her grief. The aroma of fresh bread greeted her as she stepped through the doorway. The smell was a surprise, like a gift. But even this delightful place bore the wounds of war. The big case in front was still intact, but a bullet hole had punctured the glass.

"Ah, Renée, so good to see you," Marcel the baker said. "Are you well today? And your mama?" He seemed nervous. His eyes shifted to her left, then back to her face.

"I am fine, Marcel. Mama is holding up, but she is so much weaker than before." The cover story Renée had used to explain her disappearance and reappearance was that she'd evacuated south when the Germans first came, like millions of others. But now that things had settled down somewhat, she'd come back, mainly because of her mother's health.

She glanced to the left and saw two young German officers, sitting at the lone table by the window drinking coffee and eating pastries. "I didn't know you had…customers." She must choose her words carefully. Many of them seemed to speak or at least understand their language.

"What can I get for you this afternoon?" he asked.

She looked at the case, more than half empty.

"Don't worry about that," he said. "I have a fresh oven full in the back. Would you like one loaf or two?"

"Two if you can spare it."

"For you and your Mama, I will get the two biggest."

Marcel seemed his usual cheerful self, but she could see the strain etched on his face. How hard to live so close to these intruders every moment of the day. Her home lay on the outskirts of town.

"Here you go, my dear." He held out the bread in a paper

bag. "Give my regards to your Mama. Any news of Philippe? I haven't seen him for a while."

"No news." She glanced nervously at the soldiers. One of them was staring at her. He smiled, as if expressing interest. She looked away. "Thank you. They smell wonderful." She paid him. "*Merci beaucoup, Marcel. Au revoir.*" She quickly opened the door, hoping to avoid any advances from the officer.

As she left, she heard chairs scraping across the floor. She'd hoped to visit the butchers before heading home but was too afraid the Germans might follow her. She turned left and started down the main sidewalk toward the edge of town, then headed back up the hill. As she hurried along the road leading home, a truck full of German troops raced by. A few stood, made hand gestures and called out to her in German. She didn't understand the words but understood their meaning. They shouted and laughed until the truck cleared the hill and drove out of sight.

She picked up her pace until she came to a field, then took a shortcut through the field that entered her family's property on the west side. Five minutes more and she could see their home just beyond the hedges. It really was a beautiful place, even though it had seen better days. The exterior had not received any attention in years. What had once been a manicured lawn and garden was now a completely overgrown field of weeds.

She walked along a hardened dirt path then through a side gate. She was just about to walk behind the house toward the kitchen door when she heard male voices coming from the front, by the driveway. German voices. Men laughing. She ducked behind a bush and peeked around the corner, horrified at the sight.

A German officer was getting out of a shiny black convertible, Nazi flags mounted on the front fenders. A second officer stood up and got out behind him. They walked up the brick steps to her front door. She pulled back behind the wall. At first, the man knocked politely. Then he began banging.

She acted quickly. Her mother was upstairs in bed.

Though terrified, she tried to sound calm. "Hello," she yelled. "I'm here. I've just come from town. I will let you in." She hurried around the side of the house and up the front steps. She smiled then quickly looked away as she opened the front door and walked inside.

"This is the Bouchard residence?" the older man said in excellent French.

"Yes, it is. I am Renée. My mother and I live here alone. She is upstairs resting. She is quite unwell."

"I assume someone has told you why we are here. I am Colonel Joachim Fromm. This is my adjutant, Leutnant Hartmann."

"We have been told, Colonel. You wish to use our home for your…headquarters?"

"Correct. If it passes muster, that is. We are here now to look things over. We won't need your assistance, for the moment."

"Fine. If you have any questions, just ask."

The two officers walked through the foyer into the living room, picking up this thing or that, eyeing the family paintings on the wall, flicking the light switches to make sure they worked. She stayed in the foyer near the stairway, watching, trying not to make eye contact.

"I can see your desk right over there, Herr Colonel," the

younger officer said. "In front of the bookshelves." He walked over to the deep burgundy drapes. "The room would be much brighter without these."

He walked past Renée into the dining room on the other side of the foyer. "This room could easily seat twenty to twenty-five people, if we had the right set of table and chairs. This thing will have to go." The adjutant walked up to her. "Fraulein, tell me, why is this house so empty? On the outside, it is quite impressive. But inside…it is almost barren."

Renée looked at the Colonel for a moment then back at the younger man. "With respect sir, we had more furniture years ago. But then, my father passed away. Over time, for different reasons, we had to sell many of the better pieces."

"It's not just what is missing," the officer continued. "But what is here. The rugs, the drapes. They are all so thin and worn. And the floors are so dull and cracked."

"I'm sorry our home doesn't meet your approval, sir. As I said, our family fortunes are not what they were years ago. But I am aware of many other homes not far from here that I'm sure would please you. Some of them still have some of their staff intact. If you'd like I could—"

"Nonsense," the Colonel said, joining them in the foyer. "It's perfect. Rugs and drapes, fine furniture, these we can replace. What I like is how close it is to the center of town. And the house itself has plenty of room. It is exactly what I want. Have some vision, Leutnant."

The younger officer clicked his heals together and gave the Heil Hitler salute.

Renée sighed.

"Leutnant Hartmann," the Colonel said, "walk through the

house, room by room, and make a list of what we need. Also tag the things that will have to go."

"But Colonel," Renée spoke up, "my mother is upstairs."

"Which room is she in?" he asked.

"The third room on the right."

"Leave that room alone," he instructed Hartman.

Surprised by his concession, she asked, "And Colonel, there are many things your officer may want to remove that have been in my family for generations. They may not have much monetary value and may not be desirable for your purposes, but—"

"How dare you speak this way to the Colonel," Hartmann said.

Fromm raised his hand and Hartmann fell silent. "Do you have a large room upstairs or some other place we could store them?" he asked.

"We have a large shed out back behind the kitchen. It used to be full, but it is empty now."

"Does it leak?"

"No."

"Fine. Hartmann, have the men put anything we remove into the shed, then lock the shed and give Miss Bouchard the key."

The officer looked stunned but instantly agreed.

"How much time do we have to move out?" Renée asked.

"Oh no," he said. "I don't want you to move out. I want you to stay. In fact, you can serve as my hostess."

Renée was startled. "I don't think I could do that, Herr Colonel. I know nothing about hosting."

"But I can already tell, you will do wonderfully."

"But I don't—"

"Miss Bouchard, I have been asking around. Your family is well-respected in the area. And it's obvious, you have handled our intrusion here today with tact and great poise. Besides, it doesn't seem you have much choice." He said this still smiling. "Where would you go? You have no other family in the region, I understand you have a brother who is gone. And what about your poor mother upstairs? What would you do with her? As you said, she is quite unwell."

Renée knew he was right. She was terrified to know he knew about Philippe. This was all so horrible.

"I've been given the responsibility to oversee the Arras area," Fromm said, "and the surrounding towns and villages. As of this moment, I have chosen your home to serve our Fuhrer's purpose. My intention is to do my best to get along with the local population and work together during this…difficult time. I am offering you, Miss Renée Bouchard, the chance to stay in your home. You and your mother can both stay, in whatever rooms you choose. I will instruct these rooms to be off limits to my staff. As long as I am here, you will never want for food, drink or clothes. On the contrary, as my hostess, you will have the finest of everything."

Renée felt cornered. What else could she do? "We have no staff, Colonel. You are aware of this? And the house needs so much work."

"This is not a problem," he said. "I have the funds to fully staff this home. You may go into town tomorrow and offer jobs to anyone we will need. Cooks, maids, laundry, handymen…as my hostess, you will be in complete charge of this."

Renée looked down toward the floor.

"Come, Miss Bouchard. Let us not begin as adversaries. We will be here together for a long time. Who knows, perhaps in time, we may even become friends." He held out his hand. "Do you accept the position of hostess?"

Renée shook his hand, "I suppose I will." He held her hand a few seconds too long; she pulled it away gently. She feared in that instant his real intentions may not be to move their relationship from adversaries to friendship, but from hostess to mistress.

She would never allow that to happen.

47

THE TWO GERMAN OFFICERS left. Renée wasn't sure whether they'd be back again this evening or tomorrow. She also wasn't sure what the Colonel's expectations were for the house staff. He spoke as if she were being given a blank check, to do whatever she pleased. But even after giving the matter just a few moments thought, a dozen questions surfaced. Details, specifics. She really didn't feel comfortable making all these decisions without speaking to him first.

One thing Fromm did make clear before leaving, his assistant Hartmann would be there first thing in the morning with a truckload of soldiers to move everything they didn't want into the shed. She instantly disliked him and was at least grateful the Colonel seemed like a more reasonable man, and that he was Hartmann's superior.

She glanced once around the downstairs, wondering if any of the things she was looking at now would still be in the house after tomorrow. Then she went upstairs to check on Mother.

She rapped gently on the door then entered after her mother said to come in. "Do you need anything?"

"I'm fine for now. A little tired, but that seems to always be true at any time of the day now. Have the men left?"

"For now. Did you hear anything about what was said?" Mother shook her head no. "It's as we were expecting. They have taken over the house indefinitely. I'm thinking it won't officially start until tomorrow morning."

Dread appeared on Mother's face. "What will become of us?"

Renée walked closer to the bed, leaned against it and took her mother's hand. "I don't think things will be as bad as we feared. He said, the colonel in charge that is, that we could both live in the house in whatever rooms we choose and that he would instruct his staff not to disturb us."

"Really?"

"They also plan to remove most of our furniture, rugs and drapes and replace them with much finer things. But I was able to persuade him not to throw our things away. He's going to store them in the back shed."

Mother's face brightened a little more. "This officer seems much more reasonable than the Germans who have been in this town since they took over. The stories Philippe told me were awful and frightening. I got the impression all Germans are ruthless and cruel. Did you know, they executed six local men the first week they were here? The men hadn't done anything seriously wrong. They'd just committed small infractions, mostly stemming from things they didn't understand. Without a trial, or even being given a chance to defend themselves, they were dragged out into the street and shot."

"I don't think you have a wrong impression of the Germans, Mother. The Colonel's assistant certainly seems like a man who would act that way. And Colonel Fromm may be just as bad. But perhaps since he's here to govern, and since we are already a conquered foe, maybe some things will start to improve."

"So, what did you have to do to get all those concessions from this man? I can't imagine he did all these things with no strings attached."

Renée hesitated before giving her answer. Mother would not approve. "I am to serve as his hostess."

"What? His hostess? What does that mean?"

"I'm not exactly sure. But he seems to want me to be in charge of all his domestic affairs. He's given me permission to hire anyone in town I trust to work here and help me get the house running again, everything in tip top shape. Maids, cooks, kitchen staff. The whole bit. So, I'm going to need your help, Mother. You remember how to manage a house staff, from back before father died."

"But most days I can hardly get out of bed."

"You won't need to. I'll do the work. I just need your advice. A lot of it." Renée sighed. "I didn't ask for this assignment. The Colonel asked me, but then, in a roundabout way, made it pretty clear that I really didn't have a choice. We have nowhere else to go and no means of paying our way. If I do this, we cannot only stay here, but he said everything we need will be fully provided."

"That sounds... pretty nice to me," Mother said. "But the look on your face, what are you not telling me?"

"Mother, he knew about Philippe, that he was gone."

"What? How does he know? Did he say anything? Does he know where he is?"

"I don't know how he knows. I'm sure the Germans have ways of finding out anything they want. But I don't think he knows where Philippe is. If they did, wouldn't they go get him? Do you know where he is? Do you have any idea?"

"No, I don't. But I'm the one who told him to leave. At first, he didn't want to. You would have been proud of him, Renée. The way he took care of me. But I knew if they sent him away to Germany, we would probably never see him again."

Renée wanted to say, if Philippe joined the resistance and they catch him now, he would be shot. How was that better? But she held her peace. "I just hope he doesn't do anything stupid and wind up getting caught. But let's don't talk about this anymore. Are you up for helping me make a list of things I need to do, and the kind of staff I'll need to make this a functioning manor house once again?"

Mother sat up a little straighter. "I think so. We can make a good start at least."

"Do you know where I can find a pen and some paper?" Turns out, Mother had both in a little drawer on the nightstand beside her bed. "Okay then," Renée said, "where do we begin?"

48

Dainville, near Arras, France
1 Month Later

FINALLY, ALL THE COLONEL'S dinner guests had left. Renée had wondered if the last few would ever leave. But they did and even though they had hinted about being allowed to stay in one of the guestrooms for the night, Colonel Fromm hadn't taken the bait. Instead, he had ordered several junior officers to help the drunken senior officers get to their staff cars and see to it that they were safely tucked into their beds at the main hotel in downtown Arras.

Renée walked slowly through the living room, parlor and formal dining room to survey the damage. The staff she had hired to help her with these special events was now running like a well-oiled machine. But they had been working nonstop for the last two days to make this dinner party a success. At least two more hours of work lay ahead just to put everything back the way it was before the guests arrived.

The Colonel came up the front steps, walked through the door into the foyer. "Once again, Renée, the evening was a great success thanks to you. All my guests were greatly impressed by how everything went, from beginning to the end.

I was just talking with one of the generals. Do you know what he asked me?"

"No, Colonel. I can't imagine."

"When I told him that you were managing not only the entire house staff, but organizing all these dinner parties for me, as well, he asked how could someone as young and beautiful as you also be that competent and intelligent."

Renée was used to this by now. It was the Colonel's way of complementing her indirectly. She was well aware of his interest in her. She'd catch him staring at her numerous times during the day when he thought she wasn't looking. And he regularly hinted at how much he would like their relationship to "grow and mature" into something more satisfying for them both.

When he did this, she would always find a way to change the subject or come up with a task that needed her immediate attention. She could tell it frustrated him but, thankfully so far, nothing more had come of it. It seemed he was intent on winning her affections through charm and patience, wholly unaware that such a pursuit was completely futile.

Her heart still, and only, belonged to Jack. She wondered even now what he was doing at this very moment.

"Renée?"

"I'm sorry, Colonel. Is there something else?"

"I suppose not. I'm tired. I'm sure you are."

"I am, sir. And so is the staff. With your permission, can I let them go home now? Most still have a long walk home. As we've done other times, they will be back in the morning to clean everything up and make everything in the house good as new."

"I suppose that would be okay." He walked a few steps up the stairway. "Oh, I almost forgot. That general I just mentioned, he asked if I would schedule a time to have you come to his residence to do an analysis of his house staff. He'd like to see if you can help them make the kind of changes necessary so that things there ran as efficiently as they do here. I told him we could certainly do that."

"Of course, Colonel. If I can be of any help to him, I am willing. Just let me know when you decide."

"Very good. Well, good night then, Renée."

Renée headed back to the kitchen. As soon as she stepped inside, she could tell something was wrong. Everyone seemed tense. She stepped back out into the dining room then through the foyer into the living room, to make sure there was no one else around. Then she returned to the kitchen. "What's going on? What's wrong?"

At first, no one spoke. But everyone's eyes kept shifting toward the back door.

"What is it? What's out there?"

Marie, the oldest woman in the kitchen staff gestured with her finger for Renée to come closer. As she did, Marie walked toward the back door. Renée followed. "What is it, Marie? What's going on?" Marie opened the door. The outdoor light was turned off. Renée reached for the switch.

"No," Marie said. "Please Ma'am, leave it off. You'll see why in a moment." She stepped outside into the darkness with Renée right behind.

There was a sidewalk that ran along the back of the house between the house and the shed. The trash cans were also out here. Behind them, thick woods. "Where are we going? Where are you taking me?"

"You'll see, Ma'am. Just another moment."

They walked in total darkness. Renée could barely make out Marie's silhouette. Marie stepped off the sidewalk toward the trees and stopped.

"Are you still here?" she whispered.

"I am." A man's voice, coming from the trees. He sounded familiar.

"I brought her," Marie said quietly. "I brought your sister."

Philippe? Could it be?

"Renée?"

It was him. The voice was a little deeper, but it was certainly him. "Philippe?" she said quietly. "Where are you?"

"Walk to my voice. Toward the trees."

Marie stepped out of the way as Renée stepped forward. Instantly, two strong hands gripped her forearms and pulled her forward. A moment later, his arms were wrapped around her, squeezing her tight.

"Renée," he said, now crying. "I've missed you so much."

49

RENÉE AND PHILIPPE continued to hold each other for several more seconds. She felt the urge to cry also but restrained it, fearing it would make too much commotion. She looked back at Marie, standing in the shadows, and nodded. "Thanks Marie. But you better go back inside. Please tell the staff the Colonel said, as we've done several times before, they can leave for the night but be back first thing in the morning to clean up. And thank them all for me for doing such a great job."

"I will, Ma'am. Don't stay out here too long." Marie turned and headed back for the kitchen.

Philippe gently grabbed her wrist. "Follow me. I know the path through these woods. We'll just go far enough in, so we can talk without fear." They walked about fifty yards or so and stopped in an area free of branches.

Renée could just make out the back-door light through the trees. "We should be able to talk here, but let's still keep whispering. Guards patrol the house all night long."

"Do they ever come into the woods?"

"No. We should be fine, if we don't make any noise."

"How have you been? How's Mother? I am so sorry I had to—"

"You don't need to apologize. I agree with what you did. Neither of us wanted you to be taken to Germany. But what are you doing now? Where are you staying?"

"We never stay at the same place very long."

"Who is we?" she asked.

"I'm not on my own. A resistance group is forming in this area. Well, it's pretty well formed already. Similar groups are forming all over northern France."

"So you're sleeping, what, outside? What are you doing for food? Are you getting enough to eat?"

"I'm fine, Renée. Really. Look at me. I may have even gained some weight. Only our younger members are hiding all the time. If we are seen, they will arrest us and send us away. Many in our group are living their normal lives, helping us in secret. They're bringing us food and water, blankets and other things. Really, we're fine."

"But Philippe, if you're part of the resistance and you are caught, they won't just arrest you and send you away. You'll be shot."

"That may be true, but what choice do I have? Become their slave? I would rather die than do that. At least with this, I have a chance to do some good. A chance to do my part."

Renée sighed. There really wasn't anything else to say. "Please be careful, Philippe."

"Always. None of us want to get caught, either. So, how was England? How is Elliot?"

"England was fine. Other than missing you and Mother, I was enjoying my time. Until the German planes started attacking. Then it became very bad. London was being bombed every night. Probably still is."

"Did any bombs go off near you?"

"Many times. Buildings and homes all around where I lived and worked were destroyed. Hundreds of people have been killed. I told Jack in my letter that I would actually be safer here than in London."

"Who's Jack? Isn't Elliot with you anymore?"

"Jack is Elliot's twin brother. He's an RAF pilot, and an American."

"An American? How is that possible?"

"It's a long story. I'll tell you all about it another time. But I wound up spending more time with Jack than Elliot. Elliot's duties kept us apart most of the time."

"Speaking of duties," Philippe said, "I am forgetting mine. The real reason I've come here tonight. Well, of course, I wanted to see you and hear about Mother. But there's another reason I'm here. Our group knows all about what's happened here with our house. About the Colonel taking over and using it for his headquarters, as well as all these dinner parties like tonight."

"How long have you been out here watching the house?"

"I came as soon as it was dark enough to move without being seen. The point is, Renée. We know you've been forced to serve this man. I made sure everyone knows you are not a willing collaborator. But as we talked about it, we realized, you being here like this can actually serve to our advantage."

"You're advantage? How?"

"Like tonight, I must've counted four or five high-level German officers leaving the house. I'm sure with you being there every day, you see and hear things, valuable things that will help us know what the Germans are up to."

Renée felt a wave of fear. Now she understood. "Philippe, you're asking me to be a spy?"

"Not officially. You don't have to snoop around or dig up any secrets. No one wants you to put your life in danger. We're just talking about the casual things you hear and see every day. I will come by every so often, like tonight, and give word to Marie that I am in the woods. And whenever you think it is safe, you can come out and fill me in. What harm is there in doing something like that?"

Renée didn't know what to say. She wasn't expecting something like this. "You're right, Philippe. I do hear them speaking about things from time to time, but I can't see how any of the things I hear could benefit your group. You're not an army. How many of you are there?"

"Now? Maybe fifteen or twenty. But more join us every week."

"Even if fifty or a hundred more join you, what is that against the German army? The kinds of things these officers talk about, they are not the kinds of things a group like yours can do anything about. So, what is the point of taking such a risk to learn information that cannot possibly help your cause? They have taken over everything, Philippe. The plans they talk about are about making grand, sweeping changes. Moving entire battalions here or there, all kinds of building projects along the coast."

"I don't know, Renée. Maybe they don't want to know these things for our benefit. Maybe it's for the British, to help them with their plans. I don't know."

"The British? How could it help the British?"

"We have a radio, Renée. Don't you remember? Our leader

said it came across the Channel the night you arrived. He was there to pick it up himself."

Renée had no idea what he was talking about.

"Maybe you didn't see him. But he brought it to us in a crate."

She did remember seeing several crates on the boat.

"Anyway, we have been talking to the British almost every week. They're always asking us about those big things you just mentioned. That's what got us thinking about this idea in the first place, about me coming to you on a regular basis. You and I don't have to judge how valuable the information is. They said just get her to tell you any of the things she hears at the house, and you pass them on to us. I instantly said yes, because it would also give me a chance to see you more often."

Renée felt an internal warning bell go off. "Philippe, I have to go back now. I've already been out here too long."

"Then what do you say? Will you do it? They will be expecting me to come back with an answer."

It frightened her to think of saying yes. But she did wish to see Philippe more often, and if some of the things she heard could benefit the British, wasn't it her duty to try and help? "Okay Philippe, we will try this for little while. Tell them that, that I'm willing to try. But if I ever feel like it's not safe to come out here and meet with you, you must accept that, and be willing to return to your group empty-handed. I will not risk your life or our welfare here at the house. You know what the Germans do to anyone caught doing anything subversive. They shoot people sometimes for almost no reason at all."

"That's fine, Renée. They assured me they didn't want to put your life in danger, so I'm sure they will be fine with that.

But you go on and get back to the house. I will see you soon."

They quickly hugged and parted ways.

As Renée walked back through the woods toward the outdoor light, she suddenly froze and ducked down. A German guard just walked by along the length of the house. She waited till she was sure he'd rounded the corner and quickly made her way to the back door.

Suddenly, her life had become much more complicated and it filled her heart with dread.

50

3 Weeks Later
Black Swan Pub, near Middle Wallop

JACK SAT AT a table in the pub at Monxton, the same table he and Elliot had sat in many times before. Elliot was due to arrive any minute. The situation for both men had changed quite a bit over the past month or so.

Jack's leg had almost completely healed and he'd been returned to his duties at the airfield. He'd been promoted to Flight Lieutenant, the equivalent rank of captain in the US. Joe had been promoted to the same rank. Both were still at Middle Wallop but now flew side by side, commanding a similar number of planes and fighter pilots.

As Elliot had predicted, Hitler's planned invasion of England had been called off. In fact, a few weeks ago the Battle of Britain had unofficially been declared over. The RAF had won, fulfilling Winston Churchill's already-famous words spoken about these brave men back in August: "*Never in the field of human conflict was so much owed by so many to so few.*"

The Nazis were still bombing England, mostly in London. But with only a fraction of the bombers and fighter escorts they had sent between August and October. On some days, Jack's squadron flew only one patrol mission a day. Regular passes had, at least for now, been restored.

Elliot's role had also dramatically changed. He was no longer having to prepare elite Home Guard forces to sabotage the Germans once they'd invaded England. The Germans weren't coming anymore. Exactly what Elliot was doing now instead, Jack didn't know. As before, Elliot wasn't at liberty to say.

The front door of the pub opened. Jack looked up to see his brother walk in. Their eyes met and both men waved. Elliot gave a signal to the bartender on his way to the table, he'd have the usual.

Elliot slid in to the seat. They shook hands. "Good to see you, Flight Lieutenant."

Jack smiled. "You too, Elliot. "Haven't they made you a colonel yet?"

"That would be skipping a few steps, brother. Besides, I don't want to be chained to a desk, so I'm fine if they leave me where I am."

"You said on the phone that you had some news about Renée? How is that possible, or can you not tell me?" Jack hadn't heard a single bit of news about her since she returned home to France. The not-knowing was killing him.

"I can't say too much about the how," Elliot said, "but you already know part of it. Remember the radios I mentioned that we'd smuggled over with the fisherman who brought Renée back to France? One of those radios ended up in the hands of a resistance group forming in the Arras area. I am not over that particular effort, but a close colleague of mine is. I explained Renée's situation and asked him, as a favor, if he ever received any word about her or her family's welfare, could he pass it on to me."

Jack was curious how Elliot might have explained to his friend his interest in Renée. "I'm guessing that has happened?"

"It has. Actually, this news is three days old now, but this was the first chance I had to get away, and I wanted to share it with you in person."

"So, how is she? How are they? Is it bad news or good news?"

"I'm not sure any of it is good news," Elliot said. "Other than the fact that she seems physically safe and well. The SS Colonel did take over the family home, moved in his staff, and is using it for a whole number of things. Basically, he seems to be something of a military governor for the area. And, as a condition for her and her mother being allowed to stay in the home, she had to agree to become his hostess. Essentially, she runs the domestic staff and sets up his dinner parties with the German brass. But that has actually served a good purpose."

Jack couldn't see how that was possible.

"Apparently, she has gained this Colonel's trust. He doesn't confide in her but he and his friends talk freely about some very important things, important to us at least, when she's around. Her brother Philippe serves as something of a liaison between her and this resistance group. Whatever they hear, they pass on to us by radio."

"Elliot, you mean you're using her as a spy? She could be shot if she got caught. One little slip, that's all it would take."

"You're getting angry at the wrong person, Jack. I have no control over any of this. I'm only the messenger. Even if I wanted to stop it, no one would listen to me. This is war, they'd say. She's providing a vital service."

Jack had to get his emotions under control. "Elliot, this is Renée we're talking about. You might not have any control over the situation, but you shared this part of the news as though it was a good thing. Well, it's not. She's in enough danger, from my perspective, just having to share the house with all these Nazi goons. But the danger factor goes way up if she's actively engaged in spying for the resistance."

"I'm sorry," Elliot said. "You're right. She's not just anyone and I shouldn't have talked the way I did. There's another bit of news to share that is rather sad. It's about her mother. She was very weak and unwell, even months ago when I brought Renée back with me to England. Well apparently, the strain of the situation proved too much for her. She passed away, the night before we got this last transmission."

"Poor Renée," Jack said. "That's the main reason she went back to France, to care for her. She must be heartbroken."

"I'm sure she is. If there's any consolation, the report said she passed away peacefully in her sleep. I guess her heart just gave out."

"Is there any more news?" Jack said.

"That's it for now."

"Well, I'm sorry for getting upset with you. And I really do appreciate you coming all this way to fill me in."

"Apology accepted. Next time I'll try not to be such a clod."

Jack laughed.

After taking a sip of ale, Elliot said, "But this does bring up something I've been meaning to talk with you about for a while now. It just never seems to be the right time. Now seems a good a time as any."

"What's that?"

"It's about you and Renée. I think it's time we got something out in the open, sort of clear the air."

Jack knew where Elliot was going.

"It's quite obvious to me and has been for some time that you are in love with her, Jack. And I'm pretty sure Renée feels the same way about you."

Jack looked into his eyes. He didn't see anger or annoyance or anything negative at all. He inhaled deeply. "I suppose you're right. I am in love with her, but you should know it hasn't gone anywhere. Other than a polite peck on the forehead, we've never even kissed."

"I'm not surprised to hear it, and I appreciate the respect you've shown me in trying to keep your distance. Obviously now, this war has put a far greater distance between you. And none of us knows what the future holds. But I want you to know, I'm releasing any claim to Renée's affections. In fact, I should have done so quite a while ago. She's a great girl, and I had some fairly strong feelings for her at first. But what can I say, the war got in the way. It couldn't be helped, but I neglected her terribly after bringing her here. It was just the wrong time for me to even think I could be in a relationship with her, or anyone. The truth is, I'm glad you found each other. She deserves some happiness, and if I had to lose her to someone else, I'm glad that someone was you."

Jack didn't know what to say. Choking back his emotions, he said, "Finding you has meant the world to me, and I'd never want anything to ever come between us. I was pretty worried about having this conversation with you, about Renée I mean. I've replayed what I'd say at least a hundred times in my head. But you've made this so easy. Thanks, Elliot."

51

It was a chilly afternoon, but at least the sun was shining. Mother would have loved that. She hadn't been able to go outside very often the last month or so. The minister was finishing up his remarks at the graveside service but Renée wasn't absorbing what he said. She looked around at the dozen or so people in attendance, all dressed in black, recalling various memories and conversations each one had with her or Mother over the years.

So many people were missing. Either they had died before her, or had fled the area when the Germans came. But someone very important was there, at least as present as he could be. She noticed her brother Philippe standing behind a tree up on the hill. He dared not come any further, but she was at least glad he'd been able to be here, even if from a distance.

As the graveside service ended, Renée turned and looked up at the hill once more. Philippe was gone. She wanted to wave goodbye. But at least she'd get a chance to see him later that night. To cut down on the chances either one of them would get caught setting up their meetings, a decision had been made to rendezvous in the woods behind the house the same time each week. It would give her a chance to see how he was doing with the news and to reassure him that God had granted Mother a quick and painless passing in her sleep. Mother had talked several times, even recently, about how ready she was to depart this life and be with their father. Hopefully, this information would comfort Philippe and ease any suffering he was experiencing about not being there when she died.

It was about 7:45PM. Marie had given Renée the all clear. The patrolling German guards had just left the rear of the house. Renée quickly exited out the back door, down the walkway and slipped into the dark woods, taking the now-familiar path to the spot where she and Philippe always met.

When she got there, she whispered his name but received no reply. She took a few steps in every direction whispering his name again. But still no reply. It was probably nothing, she told herself. Philippe would come. But every other time, he had always been there before her. Something must've happened to temporarily slow him down.

She decided to wait at least a few minutes. Though she couldn't wait long or else she'd be missed back at the house.

Ten minutes went by. Renée was getting tense. She hoped Philippe was okay. Now she'd have to wait a week to find out what happened. But she couldn't wait for him any longer. Carefully, she walked back toward the house. Standing by the edge of the woods, she waited to make sure no German guards were nearby.

Confirming the coast was clear, she hurried down the sidewalk, opened the back door and stepped into the kitchen.

"Going out for a nighttime walk, Renée?"

Renée gasped. It was Colonel Fromm standing in the center

of the kitchen, two armed SS guards standing on either side. "Uh, yes. But not really a walk. I just wanted a bit of fresh air."

"Come now, Renée. Let's don't keep up this charade. We both know why you went outside just now. To see your brother, Philippe. And we both know you didn't see him, did you?"

Renée's heart began to beat a hundred times a minute. Her palms began to sweat.

"He wasn't there, because at this moment he is locked in the West Wing basement, along with two of his resistance friends. My intelligence officer and his associates have been interrogating them almost nonstop since your mother's funeral this afternoon."

Renée's heart sank. That's why Philippe had disappeared.

"I can see you have put it together," the Colonel said. "I was certain he could not stay away from his own mother's funeral. So, my men were there ready to meet him before he could slip away again. Turned out to be quite a catch. We didn't just capture him but what appears to be one of their key leaders."

"Colonel, please, he's just a boy."

"I beg to differ, Renée. He is a spy and a saboteur and, very soon, he and his friends will tell us everything we need to know about their operation. They have already told us several useful bits of information. How do you suppose I knew to be standing here when you came back in from outside?"

Although her heart was racing, she managed a silent prayer, for Philippe and that God would give her courage for whatever she was about to face."

"I'm so very disappointed in you, Renée. I've given you every opportunity to be an integral part of our team here. And I had hoped things between us could have been so much more." He looked at the two guards. "Take her away. Lock her up in the basement with the others."

They grabbed her as he turned and walked away.

52

THE FOLLOWING MORNING just before 11AM, Jack and Joe were meeting with their respective ground crew, reviewing some new engine upgrades scheduled to be installed that afternoon. Technically, both men were on leave. That morning it had been announced that most of the squadron was being transferred to northern Africa to support troops fighting there and in southern Italy. This would take place a week from now, so the pilots were given an extended pass for the time between now and then.

"Jack," someone yelled from the hangar entrance. "Could I speak with you a few minutes?"

Joe's plane was closer to the opening. "Jack, it's your brother."

Elliot? What was he doing here? They had just been together yesterday at the pub. "Excuse me guys," he said to the mechanics and hurried over toward Elliot. As he got closer, he instantly knew the news wasn't good.

"Walk with me," Elliot said. They quickly shook hands and headed for an area of the tarmac free of people.

"What's up? Something wrong?"

"I'm afraid something's very wrong. Renée and her brother

Philippe have been arrested."

"What…how? When?"

"Happened yesterday. I don't have all the details, but the ones I have paint a very dark picture."

"Tell me. What do you know?"

"We received an urgent message last evening from that resistance cell working near the Arras area. They were frantic, to put it mildly. I told you her mother had died a few days ago. Apparently, her funeral took place yesterday afternoon. The SS Colonel guessed correctly that Philippe would want to attend the funeral. He was standing off at some distance away, but they were looking for him and picked him up when he tried to leave."

Jack sighed. This was the worst possible news. He could already imagine the horrible things the Germans had done to Philippe. "So, he told them about his visits with Renée?"

"Possibly. Or one of the other two resistance members they arrested could have given her away. The point is, the Colonel arrested her after she went out into the woods behind their home to meet with Philippe. Of course, he wasn't there."

"Do you know where they have taken her?"

"Our sources have confirmed she, Philippe and the other two men are locked in the basement in the West Wing of her home. We have to move fast if we have any hope of saving her."

"Saving her? Is that even possible? Do you have a plan?"

"I do. It's top secret, and it involves you and, possibly, your friend Joe over there."

"What is it? I'll do it, whatever it is."

Elliot looked around, to make sure they were still far away from any other ears. "I know you know from your pilot training about German interrogation methods. But I'm not sure if they told you, how thorough and how ruthless the Nazis are in situations like this. Everyone who gets captured starts off saying they'll never talk, no matter what. But they always talk. Inflict enough pain over a long enough period of time, and they will talk. Eventually, they'll break. Clearly, someone already has. Either Philippe or one of the other two. How else would the Germans know about Renée meeting her brother in the woods and be standing right there to catch her when she came back in the house?"

Elliot had a point. "But I can't imagine Philippe is the one who broke."

"It doesn't really matter right now who did. The facts are the same. Every hour that goes by, the entire operation there is in danger of being destroyed. The rest of the team have already gone into hiding. As it turns out, one of the two men captured with Philippe is a key leader in that cell. If he breaks, or when he breaks, he will give up every name of every person connected to the operation. He even knows about some of the other groups forming in other areas. We can't let that happen. He has to be stopped as soon as possible."

"What are you suggesting? How do you plan to stop him from saying too much?"

"A bombing mission has already been scheduled. Tonight, Renée's home will be annihilated."

"You're gonna kill them? Kill everyone inside? What about Philippe and Renée?"

"That's where you and Joe come in. They were going to bomb the house as soon as it got dark. I was able to get them to delay it by two hours. That's our window, Jack. Two hours.

After that, her home will be obliterated along with everyone else inside."

"So, Joe and I will fly across the Channel at wave top-level to avoid radar, land somewhere not too far from the property, somehow break in and rescue Renée and Philippe, get them back to the plane, and head back here before the bombers come. That about right?"

Elliot nodded. "I know. Sounds impossible."

Sounds like a suicide mission, Jack thought.

"The only help I can give you is with the landing near Renee's manor home. The resistance team indicated they know of a large field about a mile north of there. It's an old deserted farm with plenty of woods between the field and the house. They said if we give them a time, they will have someone there to mark the field with some lights to help you find it. It won't be anything like a runway, but it—"

"That'll be enough. We'll make it work."

"You're saying we. Are you sure Joe's up for this? I've got to know before I leave."

"Pretty sure, but wait here. Let me go talk to him right now." Jack ran back to the hangar, called out for Joe as soon as he reached the doorway. Joe ran over and Jack led him about fifty yards away. He quickly explained everything Elliot told him.

"Say no more, Jack. Of course I'll go with you. When do we leave?"

"I'm not sure. Let's go see Elliot." They trotted over to Elliot. "Joe's on board. What's the next step?"

"I'd like to take you back with me now, if that's possible. Let me go square things with your CO."

"Not necessary," Joe said. "Jack and I are already on a week's leave. Sounds like we'll be back way before then."

"If things go according to plan," Elliot said, "You'll be back here in England tonight. How about I drive you guys around, so you can gather up your gear?"

"That'll save a few minutes," Jack said. "Where's your car?"

"Just on the other side of the hangar. Follow me."

53

THE LAST TEN HOURS had been a blur for Jack. So many things had transpired in such a short time. He and Joe had had flown their plane across the Channel about twenty minutes ago, flying just above the waves and treetops to avoid radar detection. The ground below them now, every square foot, was Nazi occupied territory.

With the help of British intelligence, they had mapped out a route that would come in just south of Calais and zigzag southward to avoid Nazi airfields and populated areas. The plane they flew in was a stubby little thing called the Stinson Reliant. Joe liked the fact that he and Jack were sitting side-by-side, but that's about all this plane had going for it. After flying Hurricanes and Spitfires it was hard flying at half the speed of their fighters, even at full throttle. The Reliant was small and felt small, but it could hold up to five people, and that was the main thing.

"In about thirty seconds, bank left and head due west." Jack held the map out, aided by a small flashlight which the British called a torch. They had decided Joe would be the pilot and Jack the navigator. "If we're on track, the field we're supposed to land in should be coming up in about ten minutes."

"If not?" Joe said.

"Then we'll have to improvise. But I think we got it."

"I can see the ground surprisingly well for being so dark," Joe said.

"It's that half-moon. But I think we're okay. People looking up won't see us as well against the night sky. Besides, Luftwaffe and German transport planes have been flying all over this area the past few months. So, hearing one plane engine shouldn't rattle anyone's cage. You can probably fly a little higher now, too. Doesn't matter if anybody sees us on radar now."

The plane started to climb slightly. "I'll just get up to a height that'll make it easier to land." After leveling off, Joe said, "It's pretty crazy what we're doing, don't you think?"

"I do, and I really appreciate you doing this with me."

"You're welcome, but did you really think I'd let you go on an adventure like this by yourself?"

They flew on for a minute or two in silence.

"It's going to be strange," Joe said.

"What is?"

"Killing Nazis up close. I know we've been doing that all along in our planes, but we're always so far away. When that commando guy was teaching us this afternoon how to silent-kill guards with a knife, I gotta tell you, I'm not sure I can do that."

"I was thinking the same thing. But these are really evil people, Joe. These same guys have been killing civilians right and left for almost no reason at all."

"I know, but still."

Jack pulled out his Welrod pistol with a suppressor screwed on the end. They'd each been issued one with several clips.

"Just use this. Use the knife as a last resort. It makes a little bit of noise, but with this silencer on the end, I think we should be fine. Besides, we're not hanging around until trouble comes. You heard the guy. Get in and get out." The plan was, Joe would focus on taking out the opposition while Jack focused on rescuing Renée and Philippe.

Twelve minutes later, Jack saw a pair of lights down below, spread about fifty yards apart at the far end of a large field. "That's gotta be our guys. See them, Joe?"

"I see 'em."

"Remember the plan?"

"Fly past them, circle around and land in between them."

"While you do that, I'll get the backpacks ready so we can just hop out as soon as the plane stops." In addition to the pistols they were issued two Sten guns with several clips each.

Although the field was bumpier than they were used to, Joe landed the plane without a hitch. Seconds later, they were out and running toward the edge of the woods. The lights went out. The two Frenchmen greeted them warmly and directed them down a narrow opening through the trees.

A moment later, Jack and Joe were startled when six others emerged from behind trees. The two Frenchmen with them were not alarmed.

"They are with us," one of them said in broken English. "They are here to guard the plane till you return."

"Well, might as well put them to work," Joe said. "Tell them we come bearing gifts. They'll find four crates filled with goodies."

"Goodies?" the Frenchman said.

"Guns, ammo, radios," Jack said.

The man smiled, passed the word on to the others and their faces all lit up.

"I think they like us now," Joe whispered to Jack.

"We better get moving," Jack said to the man. "How far to the house?"

"Not far. Maybe fifteen or twenty minutes through the woods. That is, if we move fast. There will not be a path so stay right behind me. I have practiced this run twice. I will get you there safely."

"You're not going to help us once we get there?"

"Do you need my help?"

"Maybe," Joe said.

"The main reason we need you," Jack said, "is taking care of your two men who were captured. That's if they're still alive. We only have room on the plane to take Renée and Philippe. You need to take responsibility for the others."

"Then that's what we'll do, Monsieur. Come, we must go now."

Jack looked at his watch. "One more thing, we should have plenty of time before they come, but you need to know the house is going to be bombed."

"The big house?"

"Yes, the one you're taking us to. They shouldn't get here for another forty minutes. But tell your men, if they hear planes in the sky, lots of planes, stop whatever they're doing and get as far away from the house as they can."

54

AS PROMISED, JACK, JOE AND THEIR GUIDE arrived just inside the woods behind Renee's manor home. It was much larger than Jack had imagined but about half the size of Elliot's place.

"We will circle around the woods to the right," the Frenchman said. "They are being kept in the west wing basement. There is an entrance in the back. We've seen two guards posted. At that entrance and the other entrance on the side. I've never been inside myself, but I can tell you it is not an open area. One of our members is a childhood friend of Philippe. He says years ago Philippe's father sectioned off the basement into several rooms with a long hallway running through the middle. We have no idea what rooms they are in, or how many more Germans are down there guarding them. I will take you around to the back and wait there till you return. How much time will you need?"

"I don't know," Jack said. "Ten minutes? I don't know."

"Get in, get out," Joe added.

"Very well. Let's go." The three men continued their trek through the woods.

In a few moments, the Frenchman stopped then continued walking again but very slowly. He stopped again and crouched down, so Jack and Joe did the same. He motioned to them with hand signals, pointing through the woods toward the house.

Jack looked and saw an armed guard standing by a dimly lit stairwell that descended down. He understood from the hand signals that the other guard was stationed around the corner on the right. Both men nodded and continued through the woods just until they were safely out of the range of the dim light.

"I'll take this one," Jack whispered. "As soon as he falls, hurry to the corner and get the guard on the side." Joe nodded.

Still crouching, the men walked through the shadows to the back wall. The guard still hadn't seen them. In fact, he was looking the other way. Jack decided to take the shot from here. It was pretty quiet but definitely not silent. The guard instantly dropped. They both hurried to where he lay. Joe continued on to the end of the house where he was suddenly met by the other guard, who'd left his post to check out the noise.

Without hesitation, Joe shot him in the heart. He fell to the ground. He dragged the man across the short grassy area into the woods. Jack realized that might be a good idea and, after removing the man's keys, did the same. They met back at the stairwell.

"So far, so good," Jack said. He walked silently down the stairs, figured out which key unlocked the door then opened it.

Two things happened at the same time. They heard loud shouting and painful screams coming down a long hallway, and observed another German guard standing halfway down the hall. He turned around and saw them, shock on his face. He reached for his weapon and was instantly shot twice in the chest by both Jack and Joe. Their bullets hit the man one inch apart.

Neither of them worried about the slight sound made from the gunshots. It was completely swallowed up by the screams at the end of the hall. Jack quickly took stock of the situation. There were four metal doors on each side of the hallway. The Germans must have put them there, because they looked like jail doors with heavy bolts attached on the outside and a sliding metal window set about five feet from the floor.

"You keep your eye on that open door at the end of the hall," Jack said. "I'll see if I can find Renée and Philippe." Jack hoped the man screaming in agony was not Renée's brother.

RENÉE SAT SCRUNCHED up in the corner on a thin mattress, holding her ears, trying to block out the sounds coming down the hall. No matter how hard she pressed her hands, she still heard some of the horrible things the Nazi butchers were shouting, the thuds being made by fists and sticks, and the terrible screams coming from whoever they were interrogating.

She prayed it wasn't Philippe, but then how could she take any comfort if he'd been spared? The other two men were her countrymen and Philippe's friends. She had heard talk about what the Nazis do to people when they want to extract information, and now she was hearing it for herself.

If they hadn't started torturing Philippe, they would start soon. And how much longer before they turned on her? She remembered the hateful glare in the Colonel's eyes last night. She hadn't seen him all day but had no reason to expect he would show any mercy.

Suddenly, a new sound in the hallway. Someone was sliding the little metal doors over. Were they finally bringing dinner? It didn't matter. She had no appetite.

She looked up. *No, it couldn't be.* "Jack?" It was his face. She was sure of it now.

He raised his finger to his lips. "Don't say a word," he whispered. Joe and I are here. Be ready to leave any second."

Renée leapt to her feet and ran to the door, tears streaming down her face. "Jack, I can't believe it's you." She reached for him through the opening.

He gently grabbed her fingers and kissed them. "I have to go. Are you hurt at all?" She shook her head no. "Be ready to run out of here in a few seconds."

HE WAS SO glad they hadn't hurt her yet, but he didn't have the heart to tell her what they had done to Philippe. He was locked in the room next to hers. Clearly, he had been severely beaten. Bruises all over his face, his lips split. One eye swollen shut. Jack knew he was still alive. He had moved slightly when the little door slid over, but he didn't even look up.

"You ready to do this?" Joe said, his pistol held at the ready.

"Let's end this," Jack said, referring to the horror going on through the open door.

The sound of a whip striking someone's back. A shrieking scream. A man shouted out some vicious-sounding things in French with a German accent. Another crack of the whip. Another scream.

Joe walked through the doorway first, his pistol leveled in front of him. Jack was right behind. "Hey Fritz," Joe yelled.

There were two Germans in the room, an officer seated in the corner like an observer and a massive soldier with rolled up sleeves, holding a whip. The Frenchman was facing the wall tied to a post, his back a bleeding mess. The Germans turned to look at the intruders.

"Englanders!" The officer screamed as he stood.

"No, Americans," Jack yelled and shot the man between the eyes as he reached for his sidearm.

The big German was unarmed except for the whip, which he raised as if to strike Jack and Joe. His face filled with hatred.

"Here you go," Joe said and shot the man twice, hitting his knees.

The man screamed in pain and dropped the weapon as he fell to the ground grabbing his legs.

"How many bullets I got in this thing?" Joe asked Jack.

"Five bullets a clip."

"Okay Fritz, here's two more." Joe shot him in both shoulders. The bullets sent the man flying backwards against the wall. "How's that feel?" Joe walked right up to him. "Hurts, doesn't it? You shouldn't hurt people, Fritz. Don't you know the golden rule? I only wish I had more time so you could feel some more of the pain you dish out on others. But we gotta go." He raised the gun and shot the German between the eyes.

While this was going on, Jack cut the Frenchman loose. He almost fell to the floor, but he was conscious. His face was all beat up, but he kept repeating, *Merci*, over and over as Jack helped him out the door.

55

ONCE IN THE HALLWAY, Jack headed straight for the room where the younger Frenchman was kept. When he opened the door, the young man was standing right there.

"I can speak English, a little. My name is Pierre. I have heard what you were saying. You are here to take us away, no?"

"We are, but we need your help. Your friend over there is very weak. I need you to help him walk, so my friend can have his hands free for his gun."

"I can do this." Immediately, he walked over and took his friend from Joe.

"So you weren't hurt?" Joe asked.

"No, my turn was next," he said.

Jack hurried down to Renee's room and opened her door. She was standing a few steps inside. Before she could come out, he rushed in and embraced her. Then he gently held her head in his hands and kissed her passionately on the lips for several seconds. "That's my reply to your letter," he said.

Her tears gave way to a smile.

"Renée, I have to warn you. Philippe is in bad shape. You need to be ready for this. And I might need your help to get him out of here. We have to move as quickly as we can."

"Okay, I will tell him. And of course I will help any way I can. He speaks a little English. Not as well as I, but I will ask him to use English whenever he can, so you and Joe can understand."

Joe stuck his head in the door. "We've got to go guys."

Jack went next door and opened Philippe's door. He was awake and tried to sit up.

"Oh, Philippe," Renée said as she rushed to his side. "Look what they've done to you."

She helped him sit up the rest of the way. "I didn't tell them anything about you," he said. "It was Pierre."

She told him about Jack and Joe, why they were here and what he needed to do. "Can you walk?"

"I can, I think. With some help."

"I will help you," she said. "We have to move as fast as you can bear it, at least until we get to the plane. Then you can rest."

The three of them walked back out into the hall. Joe led the way with his pistol drawn. Jack was two steps behind him, looking ahead then back at the group. They sidestepped around the dead German guard and made it to the doorway leading outside.

"Let me see if the coast is clear," Joe said. He walked silently up the stairwell. Jack followed. Suddenly, two shots rang out from Joe's pistol. The suppressor worked, but it still sounded too loud for Jack's comfort. Joe looked down at Jack. "Another German guard. Just came around the back from the other end."

"Any more?"

Joe looked around, waited a few more moments. "I think we're okay, but we should get out of here fast."

Jack turned to the others. "We've got to move. We'll go up

the stairs then head straight for the woods. Renée, can you tell them one of their resistance friends is waiting there in the woods. He'll help the two Frenchmen get away once we get to the plane."

Renée whispered Jack's instructions.

"Okay, let's go."

It took about a minute, but the entire group made it safely to the edge of the woods. The French guide came out to help Pierre with their wounded comrade. But suddenly Pierre pulled away from the group and started to run.

"Where's he going?" Jack said. "What's he doing?"

"Coward," Philippe yelled, way too loudly.

The young man ran along the back of the house, jumped over the dead guard Joe had killed ten minutes ago, then kept running.

"Pierre," the Frenchman said as loud as dared. "The fool. He's running toward his home."

Pierre ran even faster. Past the edge of the house then out to the clearing just beyond.

"Halt!" a loud voice shouted in German. "Halt."

Pierre kept running. Everyone else ducked into the woods. Machine gun fire erupted around the corner.

"Alarm! Alarm!" the same German voice shouted.

Jack looked but couldn't yet see the guard. He holstered his pistol and grabbed his Sten gun. Joe did the same. No need for quiet any longer.

More machine gun fire. This time the bullets found their mark. Pierre, still running, shuddered then dropped to the ground.

"Alarm!" the German shouted. "Die Gefangenen sind

entkommen!"

Suddenly, bright lights turned on, illuminating the entire property.

"We've got to go. Now!" the French guide said. "Follow me. Hurry."

They ran back the way they'd come but, this time, deeper into the woods, away from the house. Jack could hear a half-dozen German voices shouting out orders into the sky. They continued to run but Philippe and the other Frenchmen were slowing them down. Jack shouldered his Sten gun. "Here, let me take Philippe," he said to Renée. "Joe, give your gun to our guide friend here and take the Frenchman. We've got to pick up our pace." He looked at the guide. "Lead the way."

They continued their trek, now reaching the edge of the woods behind the main house. They made a turn and headed directly away from the house toward the field, and their plane.

"When we reach the halfway point, my men will be there waiting. I asked them to form a defensive line deep in the woods, in case we were being chased. That way the rest of you will have time to get your plane and take off. And now with the weapons you gave us, we can defend ourselves much better."

"Thank you so much," Jack said. "We are in your debt, my friend."

Renée glanced behind them in the direction of the house. She saw at least a dozen flashlights bouncing off the trees, perhaps a hundred yards away. A loud voice yelled out commands. "It's the Colonel."

"Let him come," the French guide said. "This time we will be ready for him."

They continued moving through the trees as fast as they

could. All the while, the lights behind them closed the distance.

Ten minutes later, the guide yelled out some kind of bird call. "That is to alert my men. They are just up ahead. But you will not see them. When I stop running, you keep on running in the same direction. Less than ten minutes more, you will reach your plane."

"Alright," Jack said. "Remember what I said about the bombers."

A few moments more, their French guide stopped running. "Here," he said to Joe, "I will take my friend from here. You all go on. Let us take care of these Nazi scum." Before Joe released his friend, Renée gave him a big hug and said some things in French. He thanked her, they hugged again and the four of them continue to run toward the plane.

"Jack, let me take a turn carrying Philippe," Joe said.

"No, I got this. Why don't you run on ahead and get the plane going, so we can take off as soon as we catch up?"

"That's a better plan," Joe said. "See you guys in a few minutes." He ran on ahead.

A few minutes later, a massive gunfire exchange erupted in the woods behind them.

56

Renée, Jack and Philippe were almost there. She could hear the plane revving up just ahead and partially see the clearing through the trees. The battle behind them was still raging, though it seemed the amount of gunfire had been cut by half. It saddened her as she realized why. That many men had either just been killed or seriously wounded. She hoped the losses were much greater for the Germans.

"I can see the plane, Renée," Jack said. "We're almost there. How are you doing, Philippe?" No answer. "Philippe?"

"Okay, I'm okay," he said weakly.

Twenty yards further, they broke into the clearing. There was the plane, the propeller kicking up dust and grass. In the moonlight, she could even make out the British markings. It was such a relief to see it.

Halfway across the clearing, a familiar voice shouted from the edge of the woods. "Halt! Renée and Philippe, Amerikaner, halt." Then gunfire. It was the Colonel.

Jack dropped Philippe to the ground. "Get down, Renée." She did. Jack pulled the machine gun off his shoulder and faced the Colonel. A second later, she was startled by the sound of Jack's gun firing toward the woods.

JACK WAS AIMING for the Colonel, but the man dropped to the ground just in time. The two soldiers on either side of him did not and were instantly killed. Jack heard the plane engine quiet down and saw Joe hop out, his Sten gun pointing toward the still-prone Colonel. He fired a quick burst then ran toward them, yelling, "Jack, get them on the plane. Now!"

Suddenly, everyone froze and looked up. A loud rumbling sound was approaching fast from the west.

"The bombers Jack," Joe said. "They're here early." He yelled toward the Colonel. "Hear that, Fritz? That's our boys. Your little headquarters is about to be annihilated."

Jack lifted Philippe, threw him over his shoulder. "Come on, Renée." They ran as fast as they could. Joe fired a long burst at the Colonel to give them cover. Jack helped Renée get in, then jumped in too. "Can you buckle him in?"

"Yes."

The sound of the bombers grew louder. "We've got to get out of here," Jack said. He sat in the copilot seat and glanced at the controls. He heard Joe's gun run out of bullets. From the window, he saw Joe trying to put in another clip.

At the same moment, the Colonel stood and fired his Luger at Joe. Three shots. Joe went down.

"No! Joe!"

Joe wasn't moving. The Colonel looked up toward the bombers then started running toward Jack's plane, his Luger pointed at the cockpit. "Amerikaner, turn off ze plane, now!"

How quickly could Jack get his pistol or his Sten in place?

"Amerikaner, I will not give another warning!" The Colonel passed Joe's lifeless body, his Luger now pointing right at Jack's face.

From the field, Joe sat up. His Sten gun pointed at the Colonel's back.

"Hey Fritz!" Joe yelled.

The Colonel turned.

Joe fired a long burst into the man. His body shuddered and fell back like a tree.

"Joe!" Jack yelled.

"What happened?" Renée said.

He headed for the opening. "Stay put. I'll be right back. Joe's not dead. But the Colonel is. We're getting out of here, sweetheart." He leaned over, kissed her and jumped through the opening.

Jack looked up and saw the leading edge of the bombers approaching.

"I think you better fly us home," Joe said, limping toward Jack. "Got me in the thigh. Remember how to tie a tourniquet?"

"I do. C'mon. Those bombs are going to start falling any second."

Once inside the plane, Jack asked Renée if she could tend to Joe's leg.

"If you show me how."

"I can do that," Joe said. "You get us outta here, Jack. I should be conscious a few more minutes anyway." He looked down at his leg and all the blood spilling on the floor. "Sorry about the mess."

Jack set the plane at full throttle. It lurched forward and began its bumpy ride across the field. No sooner had they lifted off when huge explosions began going off on his left. He looked out the window and saw Renée's family home all lit up and on fire. More explosions, going off all around it. Huge, flaming mushroom clouds rose into the air.

"Is that our house?" Renée asked.

"I'm sorry. I didn't have time to tell you. But yes, it is. When they heard about your brother and those two other men being captured, especially that one guy who was a leader, they couldn't take a chance one of them wouldn't crack and expose the whole network." Jack turned toward her, reached back for her hand. She reached out and held his for a moment. "I'm so sorry."

"I'm not sure we'd have ever come back anyway," she said.

He turned around and faced the front, took one last look out the left window. Bombs were still going off, some now exploding in the woods. He hoped all the resistance guys got out of there okay. "How's Joe doing back there?"

"The bleeding's stopped. He's out, but his pulse feels pretty strong."

"How about your brother?"

"Sound asleep."

He glanced at his watch. At least twenty-five minutes till they cleared the French coast, maybe a few more. He said a quick prayer for a safe journey home then had an idea. "Hey Renée, since the boys are asleep, why don't you come up here and sit next to me? I'm looking at quite a view. With that half-moon up there and a pretty clear sky…shame to waste such a thing."

"Okay." She freed herself from the buckle and went forward toward Jack. But she stopped a moment, wrapped her arms around his neck and kissed him softly on the cheek. "I can't believe you came for us." Tears welled up in her eyes. "You saved us, Jack. You and Joe. How can I ever repay you?"

"I can think of one thing that might even the score. I don't know about for Joe, but it certainly would for me."

She sat in Joe's seat. "What's that?"

"Say you'll marry me."

"What?"

"Marry me. I love you, Renée. Coming here tonight to rescue you and Philippe? I wasn't being a hero. I knew I couldn't live the rest of my life without you. It was either save you or die trying."

"Oh, Jack."

"So, will you? Marry me?"

"But what about—?"

"Elliot? He and I had a good long talk yesterday. He'll be totally okay with this. I'm serious. Please say yes."

"Yes, of course yes." She leaned forward and kissed him.

This time, a very proper kiss.

57

The Present

"HE PROPOSED TO YOU right there," Rachel said, "in the plane? Minutes after he rescued you?"

"He did," Grandma Renée said.

"It's like a fairytale."

"That moment was," Grandma said. "And there were certainly many other moments like that in our life together. But we had our ups and downs, too, like everyone else."

"Still," Rachel said. "Jack wasn't kidding. That is one of the most amazing stories I've ever heard. And now I see where he gets it."

"Gets what?"

"His storytelling ability. That's one of the things Jack's known for. Reviewers say it about his books. Students say it about his lectures. When he tells a story, he makes history come alive. You're just like him. Well, he's just like you."

"Well, thanks for saying it. And thanks for being so patient and being willing to spend so much time with me."

"Are you kidding? I've been having the best time these past two days. I'm so glad Jack insisted I stay here until he gets back."

It was just after 8PM. Sometimes they'd sat on the comfy sofa, sometimes on the porch enjoying the breeze and the view. Except for taking breaks to eat and sleep, this is what Rachel and Jack's grandmother had been doing the past two days.

"You spoke with Jack a little while ago," Grandma said. "Did he say when he's coming back?"

"Tomorrow afternoon."

"That'll be nice. A couple shouldn't be kept apart very long on their honeymoon. Although as I recall, my Jack and I were separated a few days during our honeymoon."

"You were? What happened?"

"Well, after we landed safely back in England, Jack wanted to get married right away. But we had to wait for Joe to get out of the hospital and Philippe to heal up. That took about three weeks. Joe's injuries kept him out of northern Africa for a while, and Elliot was able to get Jack reassigned, so he wasn't sent there, either."

"He was no longer a pilot?"

"No, he still flew planes, just not fighter planes anymore. Elliot worked for SOE, a branch of British intelligence. He was able to get Jack reassigned to work with him, to fly supplies and secret agents across the Channel to help the French Resistance."

"So, he was still flying dangerous missions," Rachel said.

"Yes, and I didn't like it. But it wasn't as dangerous as being a fighter pilot, where every mission people are shooting at you. Jack's missions were always flown at night, like the mission he flew to rescue Philippe and I. The whole goal of those missions was not to be seen. And Jack was very good at that."

"So, he was never shot down again?"

"Thankfully, no. But I'm getting ahead of myself. You asked about how our honeymoon got interrupted. Since Jack was being reassigned, before he started working for the SOE, he was given two weeks leave. That's when we got married."

"Tell me about it," Rachel said. "About the wedding. Was everyone there? Where did you have it?"

"It was a church wedding. Very nice but not a big crowd. Joe was there, but he still couldn't stand very long, so Jack asked Elliot to be his best man. Philippe was there. He and Jack became good friends. And a few of their friends from the airfield came. But that was about all."

"Did Jack and Elliot's grandfather come?"

"No, but things were beginning to mend between them. He sent some nice flowers and enough money for us to go on a honeymoon."

"That was definitely some progress. So where did you go?"

"We took a tour through Scotland, which was lovely. So far away from the war and the bombings, which were still happening in London. But three days before our honeymoon ended, Elliot found us somehow. I don't remember the details, but Jack's piloting skills were desperately needed on some mission to France."

"That must have been hard on you when he left. I mean, our stories hardly compare. My Jack left to do a fundraiser. Yours left to fly a secret mission over Nazi occupied territory. How did you keep your sanity intact through all that?"

"I prayed a lot, worried a lot and cried a good bit, too."

Rachel laughed. "So, what became of Philippe?"

"Well the good news is, all four men survived the war. Jack convinced Philippe to stay in England and go to the University, which Elliot paid for. Jack told him after the war was over, much of France would need to be rebuilt. Which was true. So Philippe studied all about architecture and construction. He graduated shortly after Paris was liberated and returned home. The first thing he did was rebuild a much smaller home on our family property. Then he opened up a construction business and wound up doing very well. He married a local girl named Michelle, and they had three children."

"Did you ever get to see each other?"

"Sometimes, but not as often as I'd have liked. But Jack was sympathetic to the situation. After Pearl Harbor, he switched to the US Air Force and continued serving with them for the rest of his military career. Even though he served with them, he kept taking assignments that kept us in Europe. Like England, France or Germany. That allowed us to visit family more easily than if we had moved back to the States."

"What about Jack's friend, Joe. You said he survived the war. Did they stay friends?"

"For the rest of their lives. They weren't able to be with each other so often, like they'd been when they were young. Joe stayed in the Air Force as a fighter pilot, then went back to the States soon after the war ended. But he stayed in the military, like Jack did, and made it his career. So they kept finding times to connect with each other over the years. Then after both men retired and we moved back to the States, they set up an annual hunting-fishing trip, which they kept up until the year Joe passed. He died two years before my Jack did."

"What about Jack and Elliot's father? What became of him?"

"Oh, I didn't tell you that part of the story. This was very nice. Shortly after the war, Jack and Elliot flew to the US and had a wonderful reunion with him. Because of the extra money Elliot's grandfather had been sending, their father was able to live in a nicer place and get someone to look after him. But they convinced him to fly back to England with them and finish out his days there. He had no family left in the US, so he agreed. Elliot and Jack took good care of him until he died in 1965. But he lived long enough to see all six of his grandchildren be born and was able to spend several holidays with them."

"Six grandchildren," Rachel said. "That must mean Elliot got married and had kids."

"He did. I was so happy when he found Kate. A beautiful and very refined English lady. They were perfectly suited and had two children, a boy and a girl."

"Well, I guess the last piece of the puzzle is Jack and Elliot's grandfather. You said the relationship mended a little. What happened there? Did he ever fully come around? What happened to the estate? Elliot thought he would lose it after the war, to taxes or something."

"Elliot was right. When the dust settled, it became clear the estate would become totally insolvent in less than ten years. Fortunately, their grandfather passed away before that happened. Elliot presided over the estate's demise. It was kind of sad. But so many of the big manor homes fell into the same situation. Hundreds of them, Jack said. Very few were saved like the one in Downton Abbey."

"What happened to the house itself?"

"Eventually, it was demolished. If you go there now, you'll find some beautiful pasture land, but that's all. The truth is, by the time it was destroyed, none of us were surprised. It really hadn't been a part of our lives for years. Our lives were more about the things that mattered. Family and friends, church, work, holidays and anniversaries...making memories together."

Grandma reached over and gently squeezed Rachel's hand. "And see, we're still doing that, aren't we? Making memories together."

58

JACK DROVE HIS rental car the following day on Chambers Road toward the edge of town. He was on his way to the airport in Atlanta to finally get back on track with his honeymoon plans. He had crossed every T and dotted every I. There was absolutely no reason for—and he told the University staff he would not tolerate—another interruption to this trip. They assured him they would leave him alone from now on.

Dr. Mendelson, Jack's boss, had surprised him as soon as he'd arrived back in town. Mendelson decided to give Jack the sizable cash honorarium he had planned to give Dr. Watson. He was the speaker Jack had flown back to replace when Watson canceled because of a car accident. Jack didn't expect the money. He figured he *had* to come back and fill in...it was his job.

But the extra money was nice, and he instantly knew how to spend it. On two things he knew would make Rachel smile. Before he'd checked in at the university, he went home and opened up his laptop. There he'd quickly found on *Amazon* a beautiful, 14 karat gold emerald necklace that would complement the two emerald earrings he'd bought Rachel last Christmas. He ordered it after confirming it would be shipped to Cape Cod by Sunday. Amazon was the only place he knew that shipped on Sundays, and he wanted her to get it the day he came back.

Today was that day.

He wondered when the package would arrive. His only regret was not being there to see her face when she opened it.

It was a few minutes past one o'clock. Rachel and Jack's grandmother had just finished eating lunch out on the porch. Such a pleasant time, and such a beautiful day. Rachel had offered, actually had insisted, that Grandma let her clean up. She was in the kitchen now doing just that, while Grandma enjoyed the breeze and the view a while longer.

Rachel turned off the sink. Was that someone pulling up in the driveway? Jack wasn't due till later this evening. But she definitely heard the low rumbling sound of a vehicle. Drying her hands with a dish towel, she went to check it out. Through a tall window in the dining room she saw Grandma receive and sign for a small package from the mailman. On Sunday?

Grandma read something on the package then looked at the house. She noticed Rachel at the window and waved. "It's for you," she yelled. "Something from Jack."

"From Jack?" What could it be? She hurried outside through the back doors.

Grandma handed the package to her. "Looks like it's from Amazon."

"Amazon?" What in the world? She quickly ripped open the thick envelope. Inside was a long, velvety jewelry box wrapped in bubble paper.

"I bet it's something nice," Grandma said.

Rachel got the paper off and held up the jewelry box. When she opened it, she gasped. She couldn't believe what she saw inside. "I can't believe he got it."

"Oh Rachel, it's beautiful."

"Isn't it? These will be perfect with the two emerald earrings he bought me last Christmas." Then Rachel remembered how much it cost. Where did he get the money? They had already gone over budget on this trip by several hundred dollars.

"There's a card inside," Grandma said. She pulled it out of the envelope and handed it to Rachel. "Could you read it while I put this on?"

Grandma opened the envelope and pulled out the card. "But what if it's…too personal?"

Rachel laughed. "It wont' be," she said. "He might say something romantic, but nothing embarrassing."

"Okay. Here goes." She put on her glasses, attached around her neck by a thin ribbon. "*Rachel, I hope you like this little gift. Think I picked out the one you wanted. Don't worry about the money. It's all paid for. Just enjoy it. Sorry again for interrupting our honeymoon. Call me if you get this before I'm on the plane. I have another surprise to tell you about.*"

"Aww," Rachel said. She faced Grandma. "How's it look?"

"Absolutely stunning," Grandma said.

"I can't wait to see it with the ear rings." They started walking toward the house. Rachel looked at her phone. "He should be on his way to the airport, I think. Mind if I call him now?"

"Go right ahead. I'll go inside, refresh this glass of iced tea. Tell Jack I said Hi."

"I will." She pressed the button and listened as the phone

rang.

"Hey Hon, I was just thinking about you."

"Were you?"

"I was. Can't wait to get back there. Just heading out of town now."

"Guess what just arrived?"

"So, it got there? I was hoping it would. They said it would arrive today, but I wasn't sure, being a Sunday."

"Well, it came. And I absolutely love it. It's beautiful."

"I'm so glad. Can't wait to see it on you. How about we make that happen tonight?"

"What are you thinking?"

"If I don't have any glitches, I figure I should be there by seven. Why don't you and Grandma be all dressed up and ready to go, some place fancy?"

"Okay? I'll ask her. She seems a little tired right now. But I'll go, either way."

"Well, tell her I'm fine if she's not up for going out. We can bring her home something nice. So, did she finish up her story last night?"

"She did. It was so much fun. And you weren't exaggerating. It was like some kind of epic tale."

"Wasn't it? I just wish I'd heard it all when my grandfather was still alive. I would've asked him a thousand more questions."

"Maybe it worked out best this way. Many military guys don't like to talk about their war experiences. And even if he had, he probably wouldn't have shared a fraction of the detail your grandmother included. For one thing, he would've skipped over all the parts where he did heroic things. You've heard these war heroes, they never think they did anything heroic."

"Yeah, you're probably right."

"So, where are you now?" she said.

"Just about two blocks from getting on the highway."

"I can't wait to see you," Rachel said, then remembered something. "Didn't you say you had another surprise to tell me about?"

"Oh yeah, I did. After paying for the necklace, I had just enough money left to extend our honeymoon by two days, to make up for the two days I've been gone. And I've arranged for us to spend them at a waterfront Bed and Breakfast in Gloucester. It's that little fishing town you wanted to see."

"The one we couldn't fit in?"

"That's the one. We're fitting it in."

"That's great, Hon. It'll be so much fun."

"Well, I better get. I just pulled in to a 7-Eleven to grab some coffee before hitting the highway."

"Okay, you drive safe. I hate the traffic in Atlanta."

"I'll be careful. See you soon. Love you, bye."

JACK HUNG UP and pulled into the only open parking space. He was pretty certain he recognized the car on his right. Looking up through the windshield, he saw his good friend, Sergeant Joe Boyd, coming out the front door, holding his own cup of coffee.

Jack got out of the car. "Joe, how are you doing, my friend?"

"Jack? Seems like I'm always bumping into you at convenience stores. I'm doing great, but what are you doing here? And where is Rachel? I thought the two of you were on your honeymoon."

"We were. I mean, we are. We still are. It's a long story. I got called back to the school to put out a fire. Rachel's still up in Cape Cod visiting my grandmother. I was just talking to her. Heading back there now."

Joe walked up to him, gently grabbed his arm and leaned closer. "This isn't good, Jack. Leaving your wife for work on your honeymoon? Take it from me, you don't want to be doing things like this. I let work come between me and Kate, and it almost killed our marriage."

Jack thought about trying to explain, but he couldn't come up with anything that sounded like a good defense. "I hear you, Joe. I just told the folks at school, they interrupt me again on my honeymoon I'm turning in my resignation."

"That's good. You gotta be firm with these people. You give them an inch, they'll grab a mile." He let go of Jack and stepped back. "Say, Jack, I've been meaning to contact you about something. But it can wait till you get back from your honeymoon."

"Something personal?"

"No, it's about a case Hank and I started working on."

"A case?" Jack said.

"Yeah. This one's got a lot of layers, even some history angles in it. We were talking about it yesterday, thought we could bring you in as a consultant. You interested?"

"Yeah, definitely. As long as I can work it around my schedule."

"Good. We'll make it work. You and I work well together. It would be good to get connected again."

"Definitely, Joe. I'll call you as soon as we're back in town."

"Great. And give my love to Rachel. Tell her Kate says hi, too."

"I will."

"And Jack, if you mention this to Rachel, you know, the case…tell her we'll try to keep the dead bodies to a minimum." He kept a straight face for a minute, then broke into a grin.

"See you soon, Joe.

Want to Read More?

Unintended Consequences is actually the 3rd book in the *Jack Turner Suspense Series*. If you've read it first, no harm done. Dan wrote it so that it would work just fine as a stand-alone book. But we think you'd really enjoy reading the first two, *When Night Comes* and *Remembering Dresden.* Those novels focus more on Jack Turner (the grandson of the Jack mostly featured in this book) and Rachel (the couple who appeared at the beginning and end of this book).

Both are set mostly in the present time, although they do connect back to World War II in different ways. Fans absolutely love them. Really, it's the success of those first 2 Jack Turner novels that have allowed Dan to write this 3rd book.

Book # 4 is already being developed (sign up for his newsletter to get the word when it comes out). You can buy the print version or download either one (or both) of the first 2 books in the series now. If buying online, here's the link for *When Night Comes*:

http://amzn.to/1xNat4G

And the link for *Remembering Dresden*:

http://amzn.to/1RO7WvN

Author's Note

If I'm a new author to you and you haven't yet read any of my other novels (besides this one, there are 17 others in print), let me start off by saying thanks for reading *Unintended Consequences*. I hope you thoroughly enjoyed it.

The launching of the *Jack Turner Suspense Series* two years ago opened up something of a new door for my writing. I'm mostly known for writing inspirational novels that include strong emotional and/or spiritual themes (think Nicholas Sparks-type books with better endings). But I always enjoyed reading suspense novels and decided to see if I could write both. The great reader response to *When Night Comes* made that possible.

For those of you who've read and enjoyed my other more inspirational novels, you are familiar with my character-driven storylines, strong romantic threads and, still, lots of page-turning suspense. You'll find all of that in my *Jack Turner Suspense* novels.

To make it easier to tell the difference between the genres, my suspense novels will have a totally different kind of cover than my other books (Classic suspense look). I decided to do things this way rather than to write under a different name.

There is one exception to this cover idea. My first 12 novels were published by a major publishing house who wanted me to only write the Nicholas Sparks-type books. I was able to "slip in" 2 suspense novels that I think every fan of the Jack Turner Series would love (even though the covers look like they're Nicholas-Sparks-type books).

You can get both of these novels on Amazon, or anywhere. They are *The Discovery* and *What Follows After*.

Want to Help the Author?

If you enjoyed reading this book, the best thing you can do to help Dan is very simple—*tell others about it.* Word-of-mouth is the most powerful marketing tool there is. Better than expensive TV commercials or full-page ads in magazines.

Dan would greatly appreciate you rating his book and leaving a brief review at any of the popular online stores, wherever books are sold. Even a sentence or two will help.

Here's the Amazon link for *Unintended Consequences.* Scroll down a little and find the area that says "**Customer Reviews**" (right beside the graphic that shows the number of stars is a Box that says: "**Write a Customer Review**").

http://amzn.to/2pvSvmG

Sign up to Receive Dan's Newsletter

If you'd like to get an email alert whenever Dan has a new book coming out, or when a special deal is being offered on any of Dan's books, click on his website link below and sign up for his newsletter. It's right there on the homepage, right below the Welcome paragraph.

From his homepage, you can also contact Dan or follow him on Facebook, Twitter or Goodreads.

danwalshbooks.com

Acknowledgments

There are a few people I absolutely must thank for helping to get *Unintended Consequences* into print. Starting with my wife, Cindi. Not just for her encouragement and support. Over the years, her editing skills grew to where the editors at my publishing house requested I not send in a manuscript until she's gone through it. Once again on this novel, I promoted Cindi to senior editor. She provided excellent help on edits with the storyline and characters.

I want to also thank my great team of Beta readers, who caught many things Cindi and I missed, even after several passes. Thank you Terry Giordano, Jann W. Martin and Debbie Mahle.

Dan Walsh

About The Author

Dan Walsh was born in Philadelphia in 1957. His family moved down to Daytona Beach, Florida in 1965, when his dad began to work with GE on the Apollo space program. That's where Dan grew up.

He married Cindi, the love of his life in 1976. They have 2 grown children and three grandchildren. Dan served as a pastor for 25 years then began writing fiction full-time in 2010. His bestselling novels have won many awards, including 3 ACFW Carol Awards (finalist 6 times) and 3 Selah Awards. Three of Dan's novels were finalists for RT Reviews Inspirational Book of the Year.

He continues to live in the Daytona Beach area, where he's busy researching and working on his next novel.

6-15